"In Katy Carl's magnificent f
. . . lead characters, more often than not women, confront life-changing choices and sometimes make horrible decisions in their confusing and rapidly changing worlds. *Fragile Objects* is a book that merits reading and rereading."

—**A.M. Juster**, translator, author of *Wonder and Wrath*

"A prophet (or is she?) is ignored at a church fair, a woman uses sin (or does she?) to seek freedom from a fanatical religious upbringing. Katy Carl's strongly written characters move through an enigmatic, fallen world of psychological and social confusion, seeking to act—or at least survive. Imperfect people making decisions based on imperfect information, in most cases without faith (or a few with weary faith). Through these stories, the reader feels "the whole of creation groaning"—crying out for redemption, seeking God."

—**Arthur Powers**, *The Book of Jotham, A Hero for the People,* and *Padre Raimundo's Army*

Praise for Katy Carl's debut novel *As Earth Without Water* (2021)

"Katy Carl's *As Earth Without Water* is a sharp and moving meditation on freedom, choice, and the creative life. 'Art is from the soul,' one of Carl's lost painters insists; this novel certainly reads like it is."

—**Christopher Beha**, Editor of *Harper's*, author of *What Happened to Sophie Wilder* and *The Index of Self-Destructive Acts*

"It is when Carl's . . . characters stop running that they open themselves up to eucatastrophe."

—*The Los Angeles Review of Books*

"Katy Carl gives us a vision of love that refuses to be caught up in consoling fantasy. Amidst the darkness of human sin and self-deception, Carl reveals the true complexity, depth, and promise of human longing. A powerful and stunning debut novel."

—**Jennifer Frey**, host of Sacred & Profane Love podcast

"No one else I know could so subtly and surely reveal the finer registers of emotion—I think of Henry James—in a story of acceptance and conversion. *As Earth Without Water* continues to work on the imagination long after the last page."

—**Glenn Arbery**, author of *Bearings and Distances* and *Boundaries of Eden*

"Readers will want to go back to the beginning to see the quiet, slow growth of this love all over again."

—*America*

Fragile Objects

Wiseblood Books

Published by Wiseblood Books
www.wisebloodbooks.com

P.O. Box 870
Menomonee Falls, WI 53052

Printed in the United States of America

Set in Baskerville Typesetting

Cover Design: Amanda Brown

Paperback ISBN-13: 978-1-951319-11-3

Fragile Objects

short stories

Katy Carl

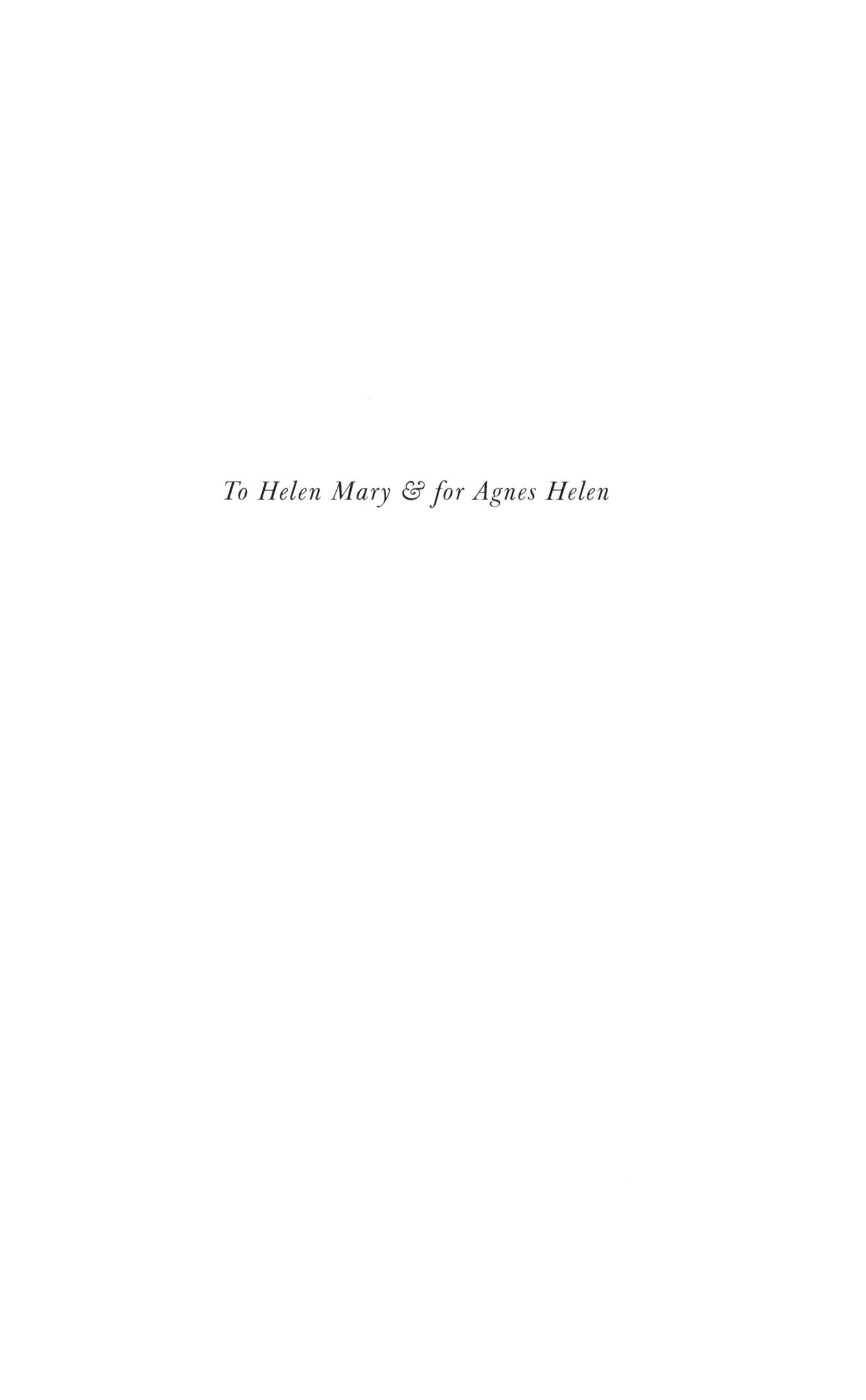

To Helen Mary & for Agnes Helen

"You know how the body seems to shake itself free from an argument, and to apologize for a mood of exaltation; flinging itself down and expressing in the looseness of its attitude a readiness to take up with something new—whatever it may be that comes next to hand."

—Virginia Woolf, "Solid Objects"

CONTENTS

Fragile Objects

When Bub's father picked him up from school in the new silver commuter car with the sunroof, he said they were going to drive over to the boy's grandmother's house in the next county. They would help her out. Maybe they would make her dinner. It should be fun, Dad said. Bub answered only by puckering his face. He threw his backpack onto the soft gray upholstery of the backseat, flung his body limply after it, and buckled up.

Bub and his mother and father lived in the city, but his grandmother, Dad's mother, lived in a small house across the bay, one county over. The long drive out of the city, past the tall robot-shaped government buildings and the one office tower, then through the tunnel and across the water, might have left the boy feeling lost if he had not known this route ever since he was tall enough to sit up and see through the back window of the car.

Mardi Gras had long since ended, but strings of purple and gold beads still clung to the branches of the oaks. The spring had drawn on until it was no longer the lime-and-magenta fireworks show of late February and early March but the humid summer-like sunbath of late April. As they drove across the water along the causeway, a low road that threaded under a long bridge that crossed it yet came to the same destination, Bub heard his father explaining the situation to him.

"These prescriptions make her tired. The loneliness makes her sad. She needs better nutrition, more companionship. Do you understand?"

Bub understood, not what his father said, but what he meant: They had to help. But he didn't answer. The long words meant no more to him than the names of cars or the parts of the long bridge, which he could see both displayed through the car window and reflected in the glare on the inner surface of it. The words, like the images, rolled past him without making any significant contact.

Bub felt a frustration like an eyelash in his eye. The feeling seemed to be located inside the double images on the curved glass of the car window. He could look at the Bayway rising out of the choppy brown water on its pilings but could never hold in his hands the winches and wrenches needed to tighten the bolts, the levers of the amphibious machinery used to set the long supports in place. He could ride only in the backseat of the lacquered silver car, never the front seat, much less put his hands on the wheel.

Not that he much wanted the responsibility of driving. Bub had seen a car crash on the highway once, where a single lane in each direction wove through what used to be plantation land but was now mostly subdivisions and horse farms. That day he and his mother and father had been returning from some megachurch event, some revivalist meeting that had intrigued his mother, in a big-roofed rural arena connected to the fairgrounds of the next state over.

The boy could not have told what they had gained by going to the revival. All he remembered of the event was the pink stage lights, the loud singing, and the humidity, the overheated fog around him created by flabby adult bodies swaying and crying. But he could have told in detail, if Dad had thought to ask him, about the body on the gurney at the roadside afterward, already draped in a white sheet.

Bub's mother had shrieked and twisted around to the back, stretching her hand wildly toward his eyes—he was an only child—"Don't look, don't look!"—but he had seen: the green, green grass, the orange clay, the white sheet, like the Irish flag displayed in school on International Day last year. Then he had been in second grade, still practically a baby. He hadn't even known what death meant before, that it meant you really went away from your body and you never came back into it. That was how much no one wanted to teach him real things.

At the end of the long causeway, the car's engine hummed lower, growling as it pulled up the highway ramp, past the old Civil War fort crowning the hill, through the clear-cut area past the new strip malls and the Zaxby's and Chick-Fil-A, and then into the woods. Dad drove past the newer subdivisions, stopped at the double-bulbed caution signal blinking yellow, and took a turn away from the main road toward the older parts of the little town. Bub noted each landmark: the post office and the public school, four or five different churches, the gas station, the shrimp restaurant. Next, they passed the place with the courtyard fenced in by weathered boards, umbrella tables, banana trees, and year-round Christmas lights, the place that Dad had said was bad. Fishing nets, dirty ones, were strung across the front entry and along the fence. Bub had once asked why these were put here and had been told the nets were for trapping souls. He had not asked any more questions after that. He had not stopped having questions; he had just stopped asking them. Adult talk of souls put a stop to children's questions, either by spreading wishful vagueness or inducing deliberate terror. Bub received this as the way things were and, therefore, as the way they ought to be.

The silver coupe wove its way down another two-lane road through woods before it pulled to a stop in the driveway of Bub's grandmother's place, a barn-red wooden shotgun house with a screened-in porch and a black iron star in a circle hung on the front outer wall. At the very end of the level asphalt drive, in line with the deck and the little jetty that led out over the deep creek behind the house, there sat parked an ancient light-blue Cadillac, its wheel wells traced with rust.

Bub and his father climbed out of the low coupe and entered the porch. The screen door, with its familiar sleeve-snagging rip in the wire mesh, rattled on its hinges when they passed through it. Bub's muscles clenched up as if this tension could hold his clothes away from the teeth of the tear.

Inside the house held an atmosphere of sleep and long hours where waking did not mean much. The cool air smelled of musty vinyl, Ivory soap, potpourri, and cooking grease. Right now, above the smells of cleansing and decay, there was overlaid an odor of sour coffee left on the hot plate to burn.

Grandma had stacked and shelved her belongings all over the main room in soft and delicate profusion. The couches, baby-pink velour, suffocated under multiple zigzag and granny-square afghans in wildly discordant colors: mustard, cranberry, rust, aquamarine.

The coffee tables, glass-topped wood, and the cabinets along the walls held frangible curiosities Bub knew he must never touch: A spun-glass swan, under a willow tree whose branches were also made of thin filaments of glass, rested on a mirror that represented a pool of clear water. The swan's reflection under the willow looked just like another swan swimming beneath, upside down. Two tiny glass cygnets swam after it, mirrored like the mother; Bub had been spanked as a toddler for pocketing one. An apothecary jar of colored marbles likewise made Bub's fingers itch. Bronze baby shoes, as if just dropped from little feet, rested beside plaster hands that seemed to pray. Demitasse cups yearned open next to porcelain roses that fooled you into thinking they bloomed. Sprays of dried cotton bolls bristled from crystal bud vases. Against one wall stood a crazed grandfather clock that struck the quarter hour with a jangle every thirteen minutes.

The clock occupied the spot that, in most houses, would be filled by a television. Here there was an old cabinet set, which Dad had said was from the 1950s and which still used wire rabbit-ears on top and glass tubes inside, but the set had not worked for as long as Bub could remember. The walls were lined with old hardback books, some in jackets, others in woven cloth covers, which he had never seen anyone take down to read.

This place Bub both loved and hated. It meant for him an enclosed world, an olden-times world, above all a female world that would never welcome him or belong to him and toward which he felt at the same time drawn and disgusted. Whenever he remembered that he belonged to the blessed brotherhood of those who ran faster and threw harder and could not ever, ever grow up to be helpless mothers with helpless babies or grandmothers stuck in stuffy old houses, the knowledge made him want to jump and dance.

“Mom?” Bub’s father called. With his thick heavy tread, he stepped over the threshold into the living room. The floorboards shivered; the threads of the glass willow branches rattled. Bub walked after his father, taking pleasure in the lightness of his own step.

In the daffodil-colored kitchen they found Grandma seated at the round table, in a wooden chair. On the waxy table cover in front of her there rested a cup of warm milky coffee. Beside it a little box with seven doors sat, half the doors open. The veiny hands held the warm cup but didn’t lift it to the loose mouth, which, when Grandma looked in Bub’s father’s direction, turned from slack sorrow to a rictus of delight.

“Daniel,” said the old woman.

“Mom,” Dad said. He looked not at her but, as he kissed her cotton-soft and lightly fuzzy forehead, at the pill box on the table.

“What did you do? It’s only Tuesday.”

“Well, yesterday was Tuesday. Today cain’t be Tuesday too,” she said in a tone of voice Bub knew well. It was the same tone his own mother took whenever he wanted to wear beach sandals on a rainy day or a fleece jacket in August.

“You take you a look right here at this calendar,” Grandma went on. From the lazy Susan in the middle of the table she produced a much-folded booklet.

“Mom, this calendar is from last year.” Bub’s father inspected the plastic doors of the box again. “You say you took these yesterday?” he asked, placing his finger on the first box marked T.

"And these today." She nodded and pointed to the W.

Dad checked the M box and found it still full of little tablets. His relief was visible on his face. "Well, we can straighten it all out by Saturday," he said. He gave her a little sidewise hug and then, breathing in, reached down to lift her coffee cup to his face.

"Mom, this milk is off. Don't drink any more of it." He stepped to the sink and poured the contents of the cup down the disposal. Then he went to the fridge to check for the rest of the carton.

Bub sat statue-still through all this business. He had a role in this many-times-replayed scene, and he knew it very well. Until he heard his cue, he sat with his feet tucked under him in a kitchen chair. Bub would be scolded if he swung his legs, if he attempted to rise, if he yawned or made a face, if he bit his nails or lips, if he picked his nose or scratched his skin anywhere it itched, if he touched anything that looked interesting. In a minute he would be asked a question to which he was expected to answer Yes Ma'am and Thank You. Until then he sat studying the clementine paisley pattern of the tablecloth and debating within himself whether to trace the teardrops with a fingertip might invite reproof.

"Godwin," warbled the grandmother. The boy suppressed a wince. Not only at school, but in front of other children at all times, he always gave his name as Bub. The self-adopted nickname meant nothing to him; that was why he liked it.

"Godwin," she repeated, while he was still collecting his thoughts.

"Yes ma'am," Bub said.

"Go in the pantry door there, would you, and bring me the blue tin with the snowflake lid. If we have any cookies today, would you like one?"

"Yes ma'am. Thank you."

There were always cookies. They were usually stale. Bub would be given one, not seven or four or two, no matter how small they were or how hungry he was. About all of this he had learned by long practice not to argue.

Today the tin brought luck: gingerbread windmills studded with almonds. The cookies were hard but not too much so. His father must have brought groceries over the weekend, although Bub was sure he didn't know when, because his parents hadn't fought, and a fight between his parents usually preceded or followed any trip to his grandmother's.

Bub made his windmill last while his father washed dishes, drained the spoiled milk down the disposal, rinsed the carton, scrubbed the sink, peeled carrots, cut open a plastic pouch of meat, and finally shoved meat and carrots off their flat board and into a lidded pot that plugged into the wall. Dad poured water into the pot and shook in salt and pepper before securing the lid on top and then pressing some buttons. Bub's grandmother also watched this process while mouthing a windmill cookie. Finally, Dad microwaved a cup of water and brought it to the table with a weedy-smelling tea bag inside of it. He put the cup on the table where Grandma's coffee had been before, next to the row of damp almond slivers she had first removed from her cookie with her gums and then removed from her mouth with her fingers, laying each ivory nut down one by one on a paper napkin atop the plastic-coated cloth.

"Careful, it's hot," Dad said of the tea. "Let it steep."

The three sat staring at each other across the table for a moment or two. Bub ran scenarios in his mind for what could happen next, based on past visits. The rotary phone on the wall could shrill its firehouse ring, and his mother could be on the other end, demanding audibly to know why the hell her husband wasn't home yet, why he wasn't picking up his cell either. His grandmother could spill her scalding tea, resulting in another trip to urgent care that would end in another talking-to from another tired-looking nurse in scrubs printed with pink and purple flowers. Bub knew his father did not take such women—women like the nurse, or like Bub's own mother—seriously. None of them compared to Grandma favorably: "No experience of life," he would say afterward. "No toughness of character. Never had to pull themselves up in the world. Entitled. Then they dress up in white coats and try to tell you what's what. Wonder how they'd hold up if they had had to make biscuits for another family's children at five every morning from the time they were seven years old, and scrub the floors when the others were all learning to write and to figure, and not be allowed to sleep till the laundry was all clean and folded." Early in her life the grandmother's adoptive family had made a Cinderella of her, a Cinderella before the dress and the ball. None of her connections, from the grandfather who had played the role of prince to the boy at the end of the family line, had ever been allowed to forget this.

Anything could happen now, Bub thought. An airplane could land on the house. An alligator could crawl through the plate-glass sliding door of the back porch. But, probably, it wouldn't. What would probably happen was this. The three of them would move with slow steps to the living room. Dad would help Grandma to a seat on the couch. They would sit and sit. They might talk or not. The grandfather clock would chime, out of tune and time. After the fourth chime they would be allowed to leave. And as they pulled out of the vine-canopied drive Bub would sigh with guilty relief. He would again have spent an hour staring through the never-opened back door at the creek: slow work, no story, but while it went forward, not so bad or so boring. The creek rippled green and brown. Bub could see dragonflies running their switchback plays over it, hear the rhythmic hip-hop songs of frogs. Once he had seen a frog eat a whole dragonfly right near the window on a garden flagstone. That had been worth the hypnosis of the foregoing thirty-eight minutes. The wings had stuck out of the squashy beak so crazily. In the low silver gloom of the cloud-screened sun off the water, each cell had glistened.

Now as Bub had predicted, the three generations moved to the living room, where Bub and Dad—"so good to see my menfolk," Grandma said—sat on the stiff pink cushions. Dad helped Grandma into her own recliner, a forest green overstuffed chair draped with a worn, nubby cream afghan, before coming to sit on the couch with his elbows on his knees. His torso canted forward like the boom of an excavator.

"Time we got you to the dentist soon, Mom, seems like," Dad said after a moment.

"Oh Danny, it ain't worth the trouble. Ain't got many teeth left worth a damn nor many more months left to put up with 'em."

This was, as far as Bub could remember, the exact same line his grandmother had been repeating to his father for years and years, and not only about teeth.

"And the eye doctor?"

"Ain't no point."

"High time I got the oil changed in your car, though," Dad said in a flat voice.

"Oh no you don't," Grandma warbled. "That's how you get my keys. Then I don't ever drive again. I know all the tricks, you see. How I know is I go to church. All those ladies know every back way to get things done. Make happen what they want, stop what they don't. Oh you bet they do. I ain't giving up no keys, not me. You'll have to find some better trick than that."

"Mom, it's no trick. That car sits in the driveway twenty days outta twenty-one. Least we can do's to keep it maintained for ya."

"Oh I know who 'we' are too. That wife put you up to this. You tell her I know she did and you tell me what she says back to that too."

"Mama, there's no trick," Dad repeated quietly.

"Oh I know what there is and what there ain't. I know enough. By now I heard enough too."

"I can get the keys from where you keep them if I want to. But I'd rather have you give them to me."

"Huh. Mighta been born at night but it warn't last night." The windmill sweetness and peace had all gone from her face. Her features had drawn tight shut like the petals of an insulted morning glory.

"Well, if it has to be like that—"

"Oh don't mind me, I'm just a stupid old woman."

A terrible silence fell. Into it the clock jangled.

"I saw Betty the other day down at the store," Dad spoke, into more silence. Betty was the wife of the pastor at the grandmother's church. Grandma did not like Betty but loved to hear of her minor transgressions. Now she refused even this obvious peace offering. Bub pushed the dull edge of his school shoe sole very cautiously down the line of charcoal grout between two dirty white tiles on the floor.

"Winny here got ninety-seven on his last math quiz," Dad tried again. No response.

"Next month we're going up to the fish camp on Wheeler Lake," he then told the silence. "Last time Winny caught a catfish bigger 'n—"

Dad's upheld hands took the shape of a goalpost, between which the full tea mug flew like a football. The liquid fanned out all along the floor, a slick splatter on the tiles. The cup split in two against the drywall behind the couch: Bub read the inscription *#1 Grandma* split into syllables with eerie, wrong perfection.

"Shut up talkin' to me like that," Grandma snapped. "I got more where that come from."

"Your backwoods comes out when you're angry," Dad muttered under his breath.

"What was that?"

"Nothin'. Go get a towel, Win."

Quickly Bub rose and stepped around the spill, toward the front closet where, in an old laundry hamper, large and small cleaning rags were kept.

"And the mop," his father called after him.

While Bub was busy in the front hall, Dad, stumping along in his son's wake, murmured several rapid sentences in a low rumble the boy strained to hear. Bub couldn't, however, make any words out. Finally, realizing that his quiet and stillness must by now seem to mean mischief, Bub loaded up mop and rags in a red bucket that stood close and turned to hand the bundle to his father. He had never seen such a look on the man's face.

"Well, if that's how it is," his father was repeating. "If that's—"

Dad cut his own words short then. He took the mop from his son and began to push the puddle of chamomile around on the tile with the splayed, ropy strings.

Bub stood watching by the front door, very still as if in a deer blind, as if the safest thing to do might be to shrink and calcify, to become one of the knickknacks on the shelves and credenzas. If he called no attention to himself at all, this might stop happening, or turn out never to have really started.

"Win, go get in the car."

Dad turned and tossed him the keys to the silver coupe. They hit Bub in the shin and clattered to the tile, where he crouched with infinitesimal slowness to pick them up.

"Win! Now," his father boomed. A flash of lightning sheared a branch off an oak and sent it crashing into a chain link fence: no, it didn't, the sun remained stubbornly out, and Bub realized the sound had been the scream of the hinges in his grandmother's recliner as she pushed in the footrest and rose to point her accusing finger at his father.

"You! Done hurt me all your life," she cried.

"Hurt me comin' out. Hurt me failin' school. Hurt me makin' eyes and makin' chirrun with that little piece of sumpin'. Hurt me makin' plans about me I ain't never agreed to. Well I ain't never agreed. I ain't never agreed to any of it. They cain't tell me it's in the vows. I said love honor and obey. Obey *him*. Not *you*."

Son and father stood like statues. They calcified, shrank. Yes, the safest thing to be, in that room at any given moment, would have been a piece of porcelain. You would have been put behind glass and protected. Cherished.

"Win. Go."

There was a plea in it now. Bub picked up the keys and went.

Out in the car he stared around the yard and driveway. A box garden held sprouts of spinach and lettuce. When he was smaller, he had helped to plant seeds here. Later in the summer there would be tomato vines, yellow squash, long green zucchini. When had his grandmother found the strength to dig the soil and weed the beds? It couldn't have been her doing. She could barely walk from her table to her chair without help. It must have been his father. His father who was always telling his mother there was no time, no money, for the deck or the flowers or the vegetables in their own backyard. So why—? Because their house was not at the center. It would never be at the center. For his father, this was the center.

The screen door opened. Dad ran out holding a second set of keys in his hands and, with too much force, grabbed the handle of the driver's door and threw it open. The car's small frame trembled. Dad threw the new set of keys into Bub's lap.

"Hold those," Dad said. He started the car and laid his foot on the brake. Then he took out his phone and began texting. His eyes remained focused on the screen while Bub watched the torn screen door shudder open a second time.

"Dad?" said Bub.

"Not now," Dad answered.

"Just . . . it's . . ."

"I said not now."

Once at a sleepover with classmates Bub had secretly watched a horror movie that had a girl monster in it. The story had been that the girl had died, drowned in a well, but because of some ancient curse she couldn't stay in the well but instead was forced to come out and attack people who watched the horror movie and now here she came, robed in white, crouched over, hair covering her face, until you saw—

Bub's grandmother had made her way toward the car at the same incremental speed, in the same hunched and scuttling way, as the girl-monster in the movie. She tapped the glass of the passenger window. Bub's heart raced.

"Dad!" he shrieked.

"Son."

Bub saw his father's rage on one side, his grandmother's on the other, and didn't know which he feared more.

"Roll down the window," Dad told him.

As soon as the glass came open a half inch the old woman's twisted fingers pushed through the crack. Something fell with a plink to land, again, in Bub's lap. Bub picked the object up: two brass keys on a strong silver loop with a green plastic numeral 1 hooked on to it.

"Grandma, your house keys . . ."

"Won't need them no more."

"Mom! Mama—"

"Cain't go nowhere, don't need to lock up after. Ain't leavin' here again so what does it matter. Next y'all gon come up in here, tag all my things. You want this and he wants that. Who's gon take care of it all like I done? Y'all with them empty houses y'all never set foot in more time'n it takes to eat and piss and sleep? Y'all want my wedding china, my chifferobes, my collectibles? What for, for chamber pots? Who's it all gon matter to? You boy? Godwin! You gon take care a my things for me? You gon dust the swans and the willow with a feather? You gon leave the roses bloom all year? Naw. You gon break 'em is what you gon do. With a baseball bat. Soon's I'm cold if not before."

"Mom. This is enough in front of—"

"You don't tell me what's enough. After all I done.

All I hurt."

His father's face seemed to have melted. "Don't talk like that. When I owe you so m—mm—"

"Shut up that cryin'. You don't owe me nothin'."

The grandmother began her slow hitch and shuffle back to the house. Bub's father jolted out of the car and followed her as fast as he could, hoisting his extra weight along. When he touched her elbow to support her, the cane fell from her hand, and she folded to the ground like something made of origami paper.

When Bub's own mother asked him about it much later, Bub would not be able to remember certain parts of what happened next. Not for years would he recall the sound his grandmother's bones made against the asphalt, the sound that came from his father's throat when he heard it. It would not make sense to him, either, the place where the two of them had come to rest at the head of the drive, near the Cadillac, instead of on the front step where they ought to have been. Now Bub only knew that his father had left the car running with him inside it. He knew he must not move or unbuckle his seat belt until an adult came to turn the car off. Yet he also knew that his father and grandmother might really need his help. Bub saw he would have to figure this one out alone.

One time, Bub's mother had taught him how to climb across the console and into the driver's seat to turn off the ignition. Bub tried to follow the steps now, but the key in the ignition wouldn't turn. It only made a skirling locust noise. So Bub looked at the string of letters like his mother had told him and, sure enough, the car had been left in Neutral, not Park.

So Bub grabbed the lever and pushed up with all his might, but not far enough. The lever snapped, not from N to P, but from N to R. From the back axle he felt a lurch. Bub shouted through the closed window for his father's help as he pushed the lever harder than ever and kicked out with his foot while at the same time he tried with both thumbs to press in the button as he pushed: go up up up he willed it, to P, P for park, *P for protect, P for pulverize-me-not. Go go go why won't the thing go? What did I do before?*, Bub wondered even as his kicking foot came in contact with the wrong pedal, not the brake but the accelerator, and the car roared into motion, shooting backward across both empty lanes of the road before thundering to rest against a young tree in a ditch full of red sumac, Virginia creeper, and immature live oaks and pines. On impact there came another roar like the protest of chair springs under the heft of a body too heavy for them. Before the loblolly trunk cracked at the base and shattered the sunroof, showering him with glass, the last thing Bub saw was his father sitting absolutely still, cradling his grandmother in his lap with her body strangely twisted so that both adults' faces turned toward the car under the descending pine tree. Yet the two pairs of glassy eyes seemed not to see the child in danger at all, but only to look inward at their own horror of the future as it hurtled every second toward them.

Pantheon

The white house on the prominent avenue behind the spreading oaks, one of dozens like it throughout the city, shimmered in its floodlights. A shine like this, houses like these, had figured in Rachel's dreams from the onset of memory. To pull up to the columned porch now in Peter's car, to hear the oyster shell drive crunching under the wheels: it hollowed out a space under her ribs into which she felt the chilled air rushing.

Oxygen high, hot flush of adrenaline: not weeks ago, but days, she had been a studious nobody in a back corner of a stucco rowhome, hiding one contraband library book at a time in the waistband of an apron or the pocket of a long, dark skirt. Headscarves, stockings, three services on Sabbaths. Now her dandelion-colored hem grazed her at midthigh, where dark hairs prickled her. If she had paid more attention to the lurid headlines in the grocery checkout, she could have planned ahead to solve this problem. But she had been taught to be afraid of those magazines with their tall neon letters; it had been said their influence could control her, possess her. The force of this fear had not yet faded although it no longer drove her. She needed a path out, yes, but she wanted to grade the path herself.

Rachel thrilled to the word *sinner.* It sizzled over her skin. It was what she was. She had stolen money, more than a hundred dollars, from the community's metal cashbox. She had lied about where she was going. She had planned for a time when everyone else would be in the meeting room; she had cooked up a pretext about preparing something in the kitchen for fellowship. On the way to the bus stop, she had laughed and laughed. She was never going back. She might be a sinner, but she was a free sinner. The oyster shell drive crunched under her feet.

A backbeat shook the wooden floorboards of the porch and jarred her heartbeat into corresponding rhythm. Nothing would trap her again, she thought, as she walked under the cut-glass lintel that glinted iridescent in the floodlights, as she and Peter melted into the clamoring crowd.

Later, decades later, working with her students as a university professor, Rachel would use this moment to illustrate how the dazzling aesthetics of a lifestyle can blind naive people to its dubious ethics. But now, as Peter stepped out of the car and walked around to open her door, now before the invention of the cell phone, now before the common incursion of the Internet, now before she ever held a job or a scholarship or a bank account in her own name, Rachel saw the house with washed eyes. She saw it then as the city of the New Jerusalem, where they shall have no need of lamps or of the sun. And there would be no temple, for the city itself would be their temple.

Peter and Rachel walked up the oyster shell drive and then up four red brick steps between the wide white columns and under a transom of stained glass set in sharp squares and diamonds. As they shouldered through a crowd of swaying fawn-thin girls in shimmering tank tops and dark jeans, the golden glow of the chandelier fell on Peter's wheat-shock of hair.

Rachel decided to make the white house her temple, in the privacy of her mind. No one need know what went on in that privacy: not her stepmother mewling *I just wish my only daughter trusted me more*, not the pastor who was no longer her pastor intoning *A secret kept from me is a secret kept from God and God is not mocked, He will know, He knows even now*. No more. Rachel was free. Free. She could not have known then, she would later have to soothe herself, she could not have known how trapped she still was.

Rachel made up her mind then, too, to marry Peter and to go wherever he could take her, as far away from the life she'd escaped as possible. As though this decision were well known to both of them and yet of no real significance, she smiled up at Peter and then let go of his hand.

Long before her family had enclosed itself behind walls, Rachel remembered seeing houses like this one from the back window of her parents' car. When she was so little that they still lived in the house with the breezeway, so little that they still had not switched churches or moved to the compound, she wondered about life inside these big houses, these shrines to security and prosperity. This was so long ago that the crash had not yet taken her mother, back when they had still owned a car instead of driving the communally-owned vans.

Now she was inside the white house behind the columns, really inside it: she was really herself, she existed, she could verify it. Her feet slid in sandals on the checkerboard tile; her eyes dilated to let in the low light. She could brush her arm against the arm of another person, and the other person would pull back from her and look at her strangely. Apparently you didn't do that, she noted: that was one of the things you really weren't supposed to do. It could sometimes be hard to tell which those were.

Losing track of Peter for a moment, she pressed through the crowded grand hall, where a dance floor had been set up in front of the unlit fireplace. A tall, long-limbed pair of dancers, costumed in Mardi Gras attire—a white man in black, a black woman in white, sequins on their sleeves, flowers in her curls—leaned heavily on each other and oscillated in no visible relationship to the tempo of the music.

Across the chessboard floor, past the debutantes' staircase, under the long gallery, along the wide back corridor lined with old church pews that had been pried out of some chapel and newly lined with red velour cushions, Rachel passed into the huge kitchen as nonchalantly as if she had been at coffee hour after a sermon.

The massive kitchen had been modernized with gleaming tile and with panels of pine weathered to mimic driftwood. A yawning hearth of limewashed brick swallowed one wall. A yawning fraternity pledge sprawled along the baseboard of the other.

Five or six wearers of glasses sat, drinking hard and listening harder, in a breakfast nook to one side. In the corner seat, an animated young man with vertical black curls held forth on the history of streetcars. Their table was empty of everything but their cups, and that was funny. Until now Rachel had thought parties revolved around food: black plastic catering platters, maybe, like those she saw in the cold case at the grocery store; or, in keeping with the fairytale feeling the house gave her, crystal serving dishes like those that might be found in the kinds of books she had been secretly reading. Instead, across the ice-white granite countertops, there lay greasy cardboard flats printed all over with garish red and blue patterns.

A punchbowl without a ladle hunched in a corner of the granite counter. A red plastic cup had been dropped in it for use as a scoop, floating among chunks of fruit. Rachel, accustomed to serving, filled two more red cups full to their brims and made her way back through the crowd to where Peter had started some conversation with another male student. The other student seemed to be boring him; when she walked up, he turned to her with a mild but definitely pleased look.

"Hey, I'd almost given up on you," he said.

Peter smiled and raised an eyebrow as he took a full cup from her, feeling its heft.

"Go easy there," he said.

"I do this all the time," she lied.

He mimicked her shrug. "Okay then," he said, "you know best."

She knew that she knew nothing. Did Peter also realize this? The strap of the messenger bag cut into her shoulder where it met her neck.

"Why don't you put that down?" he said.

Her money itched her skin, a crumpled flap inside her bra. Her awkward bag contained only a library book, the long dark skirt, some scratchy nylons, and the headscarf.

"Where can I leave it?"

"There's a bunch of stuff in the front closet. I think some people are planning to stay the night. You could just throw it there."

Obediently she ran off, her steps paced to the beat of the thumping music, to throw the bag into the closet. She instantly felt much better. When she returned, Peter smiled and placed his hand on the place where she had sewn into the dress an oval cut-out to show the curve of her back. Her skin fizzed with the contrary sensations of chilled air and warm contact on unaccustomed exposures.

In the huge main room, fans whirled under the balustrade. Dancing women frisked and wove in sporadic patterns to the thump of the music. Rachel felt as visible as an onion in a bin of apples, and as appealing. She thought of Kitty at the ball in her pink froth of tulle, Anna in black velvet. Her own yellow minidress with its lumpy seams made her feel like a beacon was trained on her. She thought now with sheepishness of the delight she had felt in finding the pattern and the fabric at the bottom of an old cardboard box in the dormitory closet, the thrill of fear while piecing the dress together—she had claimed to be making placemats, and no one had questioned her. Continually under suspicion for every reason and no reason, she had learned to lie early and often, to lie fluently and well. When she later said she had made a mistake with the placemats, that they had turned out so badly she'd thrown them away, she had been punished for wasting community resources, but no one had even suspected her of not telling the truth.

The fabric, a yellow wool and polyester blend, fuzzed thickly around her body. She could feel a heat rash beginning on her thighs. The wild thought skipped across her mind that she should tear the dress off and run through the room and out the door in the black track shorts and sports bra she had stolen yesterday to wear underneath.

The cold, sweating punch cup in her hand blocked this thought effectively. There was no place she could put it down; she had to keep holding it. Its slick weight anchored her.

All this time they moved through the party; Peter shouted greetings and gestured at people with his drinking hand, while with his other hand he kept hold of Rachel's back. They moved across the chessboard floor and out through French doors into a courtyard behind the house. Around them a low box hedge marked out a wide quadrangle. In the center of the square a copper fountain, long since gone teal with verdigris, bubbled quietly into a ring of red bricks. In one corner, under a dim overhang of Spanish moss, a wrought-iron bench, painted white, listed to one side. The bench looked in the low light like its own ghost.

He led her to the bench, and they sat down unevenly. The hand he had placed on her back made its way to the outside of her hip. His arm tightened around her. Her muscles hummed with delight and terror, not sure how to refuse this contact or to ask for more, not sure even what she ought to do, wanted to do, ought to want.

"You'd better tell me what's really going on," Peter said. "You're not from any magazine staff. Why did you lie?"

Three days ago, Rachel and Peter had met at what

she would later learn was a famous coffee house in the French Quarter, under dozens of lazily spiraling ceiling fans. The coffee house had been her first venture outside of her community's stucco house in the past eight years, except to the library, corner grocery, Walmart, and the abandoned warehouse that had served as her father's church. The warehouse was part of the same compound as the stucco house, where several of the core families lived. When she left, Rachel had felt at first like a groundhog emerging from hibernation. The corners of her vision had been blurry, as if she were filming her own experience through a soft-focus lens.

That day, like tonight, Rachel had been nerved by the boldness of terror. She had coolly lied to everyone she saw. The people she met first—a gentle, old, wealthy, vacationing couple walking slowly together in matched khaki shorts and Margaritaville T-shirts, tube socks and cushioned Reeboks—had sized her up far more quickly than she was able to do the same to them. To them (though she would only understand this later) her outfit had signaled a Hasidic girl on holiday from the East Coast, separated from her family and trying to find them before she or they caved into panic.

Not fully aware of the context in which they were placing her, but happy to exploit their obvious confusion, Rachel had played along with what she could follow from their misunderstanding. She had pretended that her putative parents had told her to meet them at the coffee house, you know, the coffee house? . . . that one place . . . ? The couple had instantly sparked to the name Café du Monde.

This was when Rachel still did many things that no one did. Up to this point her notions of what you could and could not do had been absolute, totalized. She had lived inside the continually shrinking perimeter of *Thou shalt*. Outside its borders lay the margin of *Thou shalt not*, which encompassed things she now knew others did every day, every hour. Once she stepped over that line, it seemed to her that nothing was out of bounds anymore, that she could do anything at all.

So after thanking the vacationers profusely and running off in the sweltering white afternoon, it was a short step for Rachel to march up to the best-looking young man in the place and, heart hammering, ask him where the party was. (In the one glossy magazine Rachel had dared to steal a look at in Walmart, when she was supposed to be shopping for cleaning supplies, she had run across a short story in which people were always asking each other where "the party" was, as though there could only be one party taking place at a time, or only one worth attending.)

He had told her where he was headed that weekend. Then Rachel, facing Peter across the wobbly table, had cobbled together another tarradiddle. This time, she claimed she was a reporter doing a profile on the family that owned the white house where the party was. Yes, the Bonsecour family: could he please get her in; could he introduce her?

In the shade of the open pavilion, Peter had looked at Rachel strangely, but then he nodded, once, with a half-knowing smile on his face. Now on the painted bench, as Rachel's face creased like an infant's, he patted her back awkwardly.

"Oh God, so sorry. I didn't want to upset you, I'm just curious. I would have brought you here tonight anyway. And I might as well come clean, too. I don't know the Bonsecours. They own this house, but they don't live here."

Rachel sniffed, cleared her throat. "They don't?"

"No, they rent it out. My friend Wade's parents rent it."

Even the bifurcated meanings of the word "rent" were enough to slow Rachel down then: she needed a moment to figure out who was doing the renting if they both were renting. No one had ever talked to her, or in front of her, in any significant way about any kind of business or money matter. It wasn't supposed to matter to her, she had been unequivocally told. She was supposed to marry, and her husband was supposed to take care of all of that. And though she did not want this kind of marriage, she could see the appeal of it: you could flourish in obscurity, while you let someone else worry about the messy business of survival.

“They’re out of town,” Peter went on, surmising from Rachel’s silence that she didn’t understand.

So then, were the partygoers all *trespassing*? Anxiety locked her muscles. There flashed in her mind the image of herself in handcuffs and then in the kind of jail cell she had seen in a cartoon as a young child, before all television had been forbidden her. She had been sequestered away, her head filled with invented terrors to try to prevent her from knowing. Now she began to understand, sitting in the garden next to Peter, that the greater danger could dwell in what you did not know.

But Peter read her pause in his own way. “It’s fine. He said I could bring whoever. Don’t worry. Really, you’re okay? I didn’t mean to upset you. It’s much better if you aren’t writing something. That way we can just have fun.”

“Okay.” The syllables fell out of her mouth in a whisper. She made an effort to smile.

Peter raised his arm now and draped it around her bare shoulders. His casual slowness suggested that he, too, did this all the time. But then she had been lying; perhaps he was lying now, too, only with his body. Rachel sat in the grip of a physical emotion she couldn’t name. It paralyzed her even as it filled her with a wish to move, how and toward what she didn’t know. She shivered. She had no words to give to what was happening to her. Those words she acquired later, too late.

Peter didn't notice her distress. He told her all about his research: about ancient Greek and Roman modes and rituals of religious devotion, about the mysteries, the initiations. He told her about the Roman Pantheon, still in use as a Catholic basilica, and then, on a tangent, about the entertainment house by the same name, in London, in the eighteenth century.

Unable to respond, Rachel shaped her mouth to the lip of the cup and drank the purple liquid. It tasted both sweet and astringent. She gulped it down so fast that Peter laughed at her.

"Really, slow down," he said, "unless you need to be good and drunk. Do you?"

Rachel laughed.

"I've tried it with Triple Sec," he went on, "and with Grand Marnier, but never with spiced rum like that." At the distance of memory, Rachel could process this as mere conversation-making, but in the moment, she combed the statement for meaning, like prophecy. "Have you? How do you make it?" he asked.

"Make what?"

"Sangria," Peter said, and that was how Rachel learned that word. With a smirk he added: "You really don't do this all the time, do you?"

Rachel hid the shape her mouth was making by finishing her drink. When it was done, she could smile up at him. Then the thumping from within the house suddenly ended. From the open doors across the courtyard, they heard yelling and groans. Someone had put on a recording of classical harpsichord minuets. There came an even louder cacophony, a wall of complaint, which ended only with the music.

"Okay, okay, but what about this?" shouted a male voice. A whir and a click were followed by the swells of trumpets, saxophones. More grumbling followed, but this time they were grumbles of acquiescence: this was New Orleans. People couldn't exactly get away with naysaying jazz.

Peter's face lit up. "Don't you want to dance?" he asked. He took Rachel by the hand and pulled her up from the seat. She stumbled; while they were sitting on the bench her right leg had fallen asleep. Now it began with dozens of hot stabs to come awake again. With every other step she had to hitch to shift her weight partly off of it.

Peter took her hand again and swung her, first into an underarm spin and then into a loping, round cotillion step she struggled to follow. She lurched right as he went left, left as he went right. Her knee collided with his. The toe of his oxford wedged under her instep in its sandal. Her still-tingling leg buckled. She hit the chessboard floor bottom first. A roar of laughter flew up from all around. The sound echoed off the ceiling like sheets of rain being flung down in a thunderstorm. She tried to get up, but the knee of her sleeping leg gave way. The wall of hilarity flattened her.

Someone flicked the chandelier lights on and off

as if they were browning out. When the flicking ended, the lights remained off. They could only see by the dim glow from the wall sconces along the gallery upstairs.

She saw knees, cleanly shaped, below rumpled khaki shorts, on the dusty checkerboard tiles. Rachel looked away from the tiles and back at the knees, which had not moved.

"You didn't hit your head, did you?" said the owner of the knees, clearly Peter, who else? The question mattered, but Rachel could only hear it as if through a closed door. Its answer might explain the fog in her vision and the ache in her skull. Then again, the thought of an ambulance horrified her: explanations, next of kin, discovery, return to the compound where the elders would claim their rights over her. She shook her head no.

"Good," he said. There was no one looking at them after all. He held out a hand to help her rise. "Let's go upstairs."

Along the upper railing of the hallway and up and down the staircase there sat partygoers lolling with more cold red cups, more greasy cardboard boxes, more of whatever they were smoking that made that pungent smell. They climbed past them up the arching debutante staircase. Each step creaked lightly underfoot as the soft wood curved beneath its carpet to support them. The red velour, once grand but now stained and greyed with age in the center of the tread, caused the soles of her sandals to slip around. They were the only shoes she owned—a pair of old knock-off Birkenstocks whose treads were severely ablated.

She was sweating and trembling by the time they reached the landing, not from exertion but because, having already slipped once, she was afraid of doing so again. The next fall felt inevitable and, Rachel feared, could ruin everything. But what *was* everything? The fog in her head annoyed her.

At the top of the staircase, Peter reached for her hand. This marked the boundary line of physical contact beyond which the elders of the enclave had warned her not to go. To prove she did not agree with them, she tucked herself beneath Peter's arm and pressed her side against his as they walked. She could not help but be aware of the pressure of her hip against his thigh, of the absurd difference in their heights and the texture of their skin, the firmness of the muscle in his, the softness in hers. Even his body temperature seemed a degree or two warmer.

She had been given no language but that of sin for the situation in which she found herself, and so she figured that anything she did from now on was either stained irreparably, or only redeemable retroactively, but either way necessary to live through to the end now that she had begun. She might as well, she reasoned, do what she wanted. But what did she want? She had no language for this either. Her mind fell back on Anna and Vronsky: kisses followed in brisk succession by an infant. Well, and wasn't this a reasonable thing to want? Rachel asked herself. Where on earth else, she asked, did she think she was going from here tonight?

They had walked all along the gallery and then down a smaller, darker hallway where most of the doors were closed. A scattering of couples sat along the walls of this hallway, separated from the rest of the party, some on benches or seats, some on the floor, some on long window seats that stretched between high brocade drapes. The light from the high windows fell on the couples' bodies in long blue shapes.

Peter stepped up to a double door and knocked softly on one side of it.

"Just left, man. No one in there now," said a voice from the floor.

Slowly Peter swung the door inward. The hinge skirled as he replied to the voice, "Thanks." He pulled Rachel by her hand, unresisting, into the room after him.

It was a high-ceilinged bedroom, filled with old, dark wooden furniture, lit only with the dusky scraps of half-shadow thrown from the floodlights in front of the house and filtered through leaves. A smell like stale bread filled the air. Without dropping Rachel's hand Peter leaned over the tall bed, checked over the sheets as though looking for something he'd lost there, and shook his head. He chose a pillow that had been propped against the headboard and set it against the wall. He sat down on the floor with his back against the pillow and patted the carpet next to him. Rachel, uncertainly, sat down beside him, adjusting her hemline.

"Oh, don't worry about that," Peter said. With a smile he slid his index finger along her outer thigh until it stuck under the hem. He pushed the skirt back to where it had been before, only an inch or so, but Rachel frowned.

Peter's smile, too, faded.

He hitched himself a little closer to her. He kissed her neck where the messenger bag strap had marked it. He kissed her jawline, her cheekbone, her temple. He put his hand on her knee but yanked it away at the feel of the hair, with a little laugh that wasn't funny. He covered her lips with his so long that finally, she had to break away with a gasp.

Peter murmured something under his breath. She couldn't understand him at first. Then he showed her how to take little breaths, and when. "Like swimming."

She had never been swimming. She could not find words to tell him this. She began to laugh uncontrollably, to shake with laughter.

"Shh, shh," he said, putting a hand gently to her mouth. "We have to be quiet. Look, I'll lock it."

He turned away from her and crawled over to the door and reached up to the handle, a lever with a thumb-lock that he secured with a click. Then he scooted back and, making a swipe at playfulness, grabbed her in a hug that knocked her down. She began to cry out and he covered her mouth again. "Shh, shh," he repeated.

They went on like this for what felt, to Rachel, like a long time. When she remembered it later, when she was ready to remember it, she realized it must not have been more than five or ten minutes. The paralysis had returned; it seemed to live now in her hipbones and to be anchoring her to the carpet. When Peter pinned her down she couldn't move, couldn't speak. She felt as immobilized as if she were under an anesthetic. The fabric of his cargo shorts chafed against the wool of her dress, roughened against her thigh. He pressed down so hard it hurt her. She began to try to tell him this, but he had grown strangely distant now, as if listening to music only he could hear.

"Shh, shh," he repeated. "Don't worry, it's okay."

He reached for the waistband of her shorts, and she shook her head frantically. He paused.

"No, you're right," he said. "Can't have you getting pregnant." He removed his hand from her clothing, seemed to adjust his own instead. She felt heat on the skin over her ribs, across her dress, but—even she knew that this was not how this worked.

"There. That should be okay." He began to move again.

It wasn't okay. It wasn't. Her ribs hurt. This was not how it worked. Was he having a seizure? Should she say something? He was sweating. He seemed as though he might be about to begin crying until he grunted, slipped, and lay still with his face down in the pillow. She sat up and looked at him.

"Are you all right?" she asked. He didn't respond at first. She sat for a moment worrying about ambulances again, feeling vaguely at fault for whatever had gone wrong here.

At length, Peter nodded without lifting his head.

"Fine, thanks." He spoke half into the pillow. He seemed to be falling asleep.

She held very still and examined the loops and ripples of the ceiling medallion. A broad-armed ceiling fan had been wired through the medallion's apex. Then she stood up, feeling lightheaded. At some point she had stepped out of her sandals. She picked them up off the floor by their straps and walked out. Not until later would she remember her messenger bag; she would never go back for it. Not until later would she notice her bruises. Not until later would she know what to call this.

She walked back down the hall, downstairs, across the chessboard floor, the thumping porch, the bricks of the esplanade in front of the house. The beat grew fainter as she stepped on the damp green grass of the lawn, which was now being irrigated by sprinklers and glistening slickly in the glare from the floodlights. Battalions of blade-like shadows rose up on the path in front of her, cast by the leaves of hostas and hydrangeas. She ignored the bricks' grit against the soles of her feet until they registered a sliding sensation, followed by a piercing one: she looked down to see her own foot outlined against green-edged rectangular prisms of glass, sprayed from a car's broken windshield. Only then did she remember that she was still carrying her sandals in her hands.

She sat on the grass, brushed her soles off, put her sandals back on, and walked down the sidewalk until she came to a bus stop shelter. Here she sat down to wait, not entirely knowing where she intended to go other than as far away as she could get from the white house, from its glamour, its pallid facade.

Company Men

When the bad letter crossed the bishop's desk for the third time, he awoke from the fugue in which he had been admiring the lace-like curls of vapor that rose from his coffee. He rang the desk's brass bell to let Valeria know he was ready for the day's first appointment.

The bishop had known he would have to deal with this for a while now, but he had not been ready to act. He knew what he would have to do, and he saw the too likely result. A bitter salve, this knowledge. The bishop wasn't, no one was, prepared. Nevertheless, it was time.

"Good morning, Your Excellency."

The vicar for priests, Hernandez, passed between his bishop and the blind-slatted window. The younger man's shadow rippled, like a fish's beneath water, through silvery sun that filtered through the fronds of the courtyard's palm trees. Its light fell in stripes across the folds of the older man's jowls.

"Father, did you know we'd had another of these?" the bishop asked.

"They're supposed to come to me, not to you," Hernandez returned. "But most laymen don't know that. It is laymen, isn't it?"

"They say so," the bishop acknowledged. "From St. Margaret's."

"I'm sorry you keep having to absorb their complaints."

"I'm not," the bishop sighed. "If this isn't going away, it's better I should be aware."

Hernandez set the lightest possible touch of his lips to the amethyst in the gold band that burdened the bishop's left ring finger—an homage, Hernandez insisted, to the memory of the Apostles. It was the way he'd been raised. It felt wrong to omit the honor. Looking down, he saw that a glass top with a green edge protected the desk's mahogany gloss. He lifted his smooth face so that the light from the blinds and the palms striated it.

"Any sense of who's really behind them?" Hernandez asked.

"I was hoping you would know." The bishop's tongue meandered through the phrase. The bromeliad's jade-and-blood gradient caught and tangled the early light. The pair might have been discussing a glitch in plans for the yearly golf tournament.

"You can't do much but ask questions, when complaints are unsigned like this," Hernandez replied equably. "Anonymity is the mark of the deranged. Looking to push others to the edge so they'll have company there."

The bishop uttered a hum of indecision. The paper crackled like dry leaves as he unfolded it for Hernandez. "Read that. Does that sound like derangement to you?"

"With respect, do I need to read it? Is it so different from the others?"

"See for yourself. I'm seriously considering reaching out to the police department, having them put a detective on watch."

"You think it could be that bad?"

"If it is, I don't want to find out the hard way."

"Is there an easy way?"

As he read, Hernandez thought not of the matter of the letter, not of the wrongs and the accusations—suggested, but never stated outright. Instead, he thought pityingly of how the bishop's brown cheeks had grown so thick, so heavy. Their loose skin, fragrant with soap, quivered whenever he spoke. Hernandez knew that the bishop was unpleasantly aware of this, that it increasingly held back his once voluble speeches. How disturbing it must be to feel your own face betraying you.

"You aren't possibly thinking that we need to treat this as credible," Hernandez insisted, meeting his bishop's eye confidently. Hernandez had polished, over his years of service, a facial expression that split a flawless difference between deference and a permissible degree of reproach. This was the expression he flicked in the bishop's direction.

The bishop winced. "I'm afraid we don't have the latitude to decide that any longer. It's true that it's mostly rhetoric. But at the core of that rhetoric there are real questions we need to look into."

"But surely there's nothing to fear here. Just more bluster. Laity in some isolated places have been talking like this amongst themselves for decades, since I was a kid. Bombast. Bravado. They need to feel important. Though they aren't. *Because* they aren't."

"Harsh, *hijito*."

"True. No use pulling punches."

Valeria came in then, wearing a red wrap dress, carrying a tray of glazed doughnuts. Well aware that the room-flooding silence—evidence of trust's absence—would continue as long as she stood there, she placed the tray down on the desk with a wry look and left.

The bishop took a doughnut.

"Tell me what you know about St. Margaret's," he asked Hernandez. "You went to seminary with the pastor? Do you think he could have anything to do with this—stirring up anger? Are these men—they do sound like men—making wild claims because they're somehow influenced by him? Have they gone rogue? Or—has *he*?"

Behind his wire rims, the bishop's eyes glowed. Hernandez wondered how much of his old clarity still lurked in that gaze.

"Donner? He was in my cohort. A good man. Solid. Trustworthy. Hardworking—*Dios mio*. With that many parishioners? I wouldn't think he'd have *time* to be rabble-rousing."

"I'm sure I remember him. Wasn't he—something of a firebrand? In your seminary days?"

"Not anymore. A reformed reformer. Something of the old spark still under the ashes, though. He might be able to bring these dogs to heel. Or we may find some simpler solution. I'll go talk to him this week. He'll see sense, I know."

"Good," said the bishop. "And what about the assistant? Mortimer?"

"What about him?"

"What do we know?" the bishop asked.

"Not much. A transplant. He's lived all over. You know these young men," Hernandez sighed. It was one of the topics they bonded over: the foibles of the younger generation. "Awkward, but probably harmless."

"Whoever keeps writing these letters doesn't seem to think so."

"Well, I'll find out."

"See that you do."

The bishop took the letter from Hernandez's hand—using too much force, prying as he might to deprive a child of an unauthorized pocketknife—and drove it face down on to the eight-inch steel spike, partly shielded from view by the bromeliad, on the left side of his desk. Through the back of the thin paper Hernandez saw how the spike had passed neatly between two lines of text. Then the bishop shook his head, carefully removed the paper, and folded it into his coat pocket.

"I'll file this one myself," he said.

*

The next day Hernandez made some phone calls: first to the vicar of priests in Mortimer's old diocese, and then to the new pastor of Mortimer's old parish, and then to the school principal at that parish, and then to Donner at St. Margaret's.

As he drove out to the suburbs to see his old classmate at the end of that week—a visit sandwiched between his own morning Mass and a planned hospital visit—Hernandez mentally ran through the list of blessings for which he owed his bishop gratitude. This did not form any kind of habit with Hernandez although, in strict truth, more than one confessor had asked him to practice it.

Despite the man's generous warmth toward him, Hernandez more and more disliked—even feared—his superior. The fear grew more intense in proportion to the ease with which the two men's thoughts increasingly matched each other. Hernandez did not like to feel himself thinking, as the bishop did, like a businessman. No other vista the lay life presented had more starkly repelled young Oscar Hernandez in childhood. However rationally he could justify the need to plan, to spin, to manage—it was no good shepherd who could ignore his sheep's need for grass in summer or decide on a whim to shear them in winter—something in Hernandez still balked at the calculating tendency.

But in that childhood in the desert, Hernandez had learned only too well that it was the children of the calculating who ultimately prospered in the world. His mother had had to learn to calculate, once they left the shelter, in that gleaming aluminum mobile home an aging couple handed down to her once they had grown too stiff and staid to travel in it any longer. Hernandez had grown up wearing donated shirts and sneakers, shunted from his classmates' Little League clubs and swim teams to the St. Vincent de Paul thrift shop, from volunteers' hands to his mother's. True, the circumstances of his own birth and his years of poverty had only made his classmates more impressed with his buoyancy, intellect, and wit. Still, even now those memories felt to Hernandez like a personal affront, a wound he had had to forgive God for inflicting on him. As a teenager he felt he would have done anything to rise out of that dependence, even if he had to become one of those men on billboards barking on about INJURY, ACCIDENT, YOUR RIGHTS—men wearing hairspray, men in red ties and white French cuffs with blue pinstripes. He had thought the seminary would shelter him from the need to consider such base motivations as worldly security, public image, self-protection. As it happened, the seminary would, but the priesthood wouldn't.

Through minor seminary to major and into the clean, cool, generous spaces of the rectory, sacristy, transept, nave, marble altar—*Qui laetificat juventutum meum*: was it God, or was it the bishop, who had given back the joy of Hernandez's youth? Not given it back, even, but bestowed it for the first time? Patronage. *Pater*, father. The bishop had grown up in rough circumstances, not unlike Hernandez's own. Both men's fathers, *migrantes*, had vanished when the sons were small and had left no word. Had they been killed, incarcerated, driven along in search of better pay, lured away by any of the thousand deceptions the canny practice on the vulnerable? Neither of the two priests, as adults, ever knew. Both of their mothers had died relatively young, too; Hernandez's had passed away during his studies at the North American College in DC.

The bishop never spoke about his own mother, other than to recall her on the anniversary of her death: but he had sent Hernandez condolences when his mother passed, he had said Masses. In November of that year, when the bishop came to town for the plenary assembly, they met for a votive Mass in a side chapel of the Basilica of the Immaculate Conception. Hernandez, then a transitional deacon, had been invited to serve: spicy incense rising in geysers, clouding the eyes, a valid pretext for tears under the watchful gaze of the Black Madonna.

It wasn't unmanly at such a time to weep, the bishop had told him afterward in the crescent-shaped room behind the cathedral's great baldacchino, where silver light slanted in on them from a row of arched and mullioned windows. The bishop's warm hand had sat heavily on Hernandez's hunched shoulder. *Christ wept at the death of a friend. How much more when St. Joseph passed? Any other day, I'd say: buck up, save your breath. Not now, hijito, now it's all right. Give it to Our Lord. He knows.*

So Hernandez's dislike looked, through his own eyes, impossible, inexcusable. The bishop understood, truly understood, Hernandez himself. But that was just it. Hernandez disliked to be so thoroughly understood. Their origins, their rises, so similar: both of them scholarship boys, staking their claims against irrational prejudice, present by what felt like others' sufferance. They had both made their names on their ability to overcome adversity. That Hernandez knew he would likely be tapped as the bishop's replacement did not assuage any of his fears about the future.

It occurred to Hernandez to envy Fr. Donner, as he pulled his black BMW up the rectory's gravel drive at St. Margaret's, where he made the mistake of parking it under an unpruned Bradford pear that shed oppressive scent and littered light petals all over.

Hernandez sneezed.

Donner, a company man but not a careerist, bore the twin blessing and curse of having no future worth worrying about. In seminary Donner had made himself a local name as an outspoken critic of the previous bishop. Only when, under the auspices of spiritual direction, Donner was told outright—no hints—that continuing such lines of talk would not only compromise his candidacy for ordination but make him, upon dismissal, liable for all of his own student debt, had he quieted down.

Now for years, under the present bishop, Donner had been a pillar of his parish's stability. Success stories in the diocese had become vanishingly rare; Donner's tenure told one of them. Even if Donner's adult parishioners did tend to vaporize in and out of existence according to liturgical season—though less so after the merger with nearby Holy Family, which had the people to fill the empty halls St. Margaret's last generation had left behind—the parish school tumbled with life, and revenues rose steadily. Over the last half-dozen years, Donner had transmuted into a man who did not upset boats. If only, Hernandez wished, the barque of Peter could always be so smoothly sailed.

As Hernandez parked, his rearview mirror afforded a view of low-slung brown brick buildings of slapdash 1990s construction. The children of landscaping crew chiefs, of construction foremen, of enterprising restaurateurs lined up, chattering, uniformed, precocious: all round brown cheeks, all bright dark eyes.

Hernandez met Donner coming from morning Mass and confessions in the church across the street. Donner—pink-faced, out of shape—stepped up to the foot of the drive, opened the mailbox, and took out its contents without looking at them.

Hernandez quipped, as he and his former classmate climbed the steps of St. Margaret's marshmallow-colored Victorian rectory, that Donner had his hands full.

"Of good things," Donner shot back. "Keeps me out of trouble. Come in, come in."

The great room of Donner's rectory could hardly have differed more from the bishop's sepia-toned, brass-studded furnishings, his long shelves of the classics perfectly bound in red and green. This room, rather, parish women had made what it was. Microfiber sofas the light brown of toasted meringue topping, a seventy-five-inch flat screen, potted ferns, and prints of an icing-sugar nineteenth-century Virgin suited their ideas of what befit their priest's vocational dignity and domestic economy.

The two stood side by side in the entryway. Donner explained to Hernandez, by way of an opening gambit, that he found the majority of his students' parents a constant marvel: never complaining (as he himself surely would have, in their place) about the cost of tuition or the pressures of volunteering. On the contrary, they displayed energy to spare; though they worked long hours and lived on strict budgets, they seemed to feel only too happy to be given the chance and freedom to leave their children, at seven-thirty each morning, at the foot of an educational ladder the height of which the parents would never traverse.

"They were me once," Hernandez said in response. "Those kids, I mean. I was once just like that. Makes me nostalgic. And—protective."

"Protective?" Hernandez seemed unaware of how his words might be taken amiss. Wasn't it Donner's job to be protective, if it was anyone's? Was he implying that Donner was doing a poor job?

"When I hear things." Hernandez looked sidewise at Donner. "So you haven't heard things? About Fr. Mortimer?"

"Only rumors about a misunderstanding in his old diocese. But I thought those had turned out to be unsubstantiated."

"It's not in your nature to be suspicious, is it, old friend?" Hernandez smiled, but Donner suspected a judgment lurking under the smile.

"I'm not in the habit of looking outside myself for someone to blame," Donner told Hernandez, as they walked inside. Donner flung the junk mail on a credenza below a mirror. "Some folks aren't so much concerned with real purity of heart as with ferreting out bad news that makes their own failings look not so dire by comparison."

"They've been sending you letters too?" asked Hernandez, and when Donner looked blankly at him, pressed on: "*You* haven't been hearing things? Some priests have been getting—"

"Getting what?"

Hernandez's eyes flickered to the pile of junk mail. "Warnings. From an anonymous group in your parish, they claim to be a group of men, self-appointed to watch out for priests they think are bad news. And I'm sorry to say the name that keeps on cropping up in their warnings is your assistant pastor's."

"I don't think that sort of thing often amounts to anything more than malicious gossip," Donner said, though as he spoke an image from a recent parish dinner floated into his mind: two mothers of second graders, their heads inclined toward one another, whose conversation had quickly ceased as Donner approached. True, this could have been about anything or nothing. Who was to say it wasn't a confidence about some private, feminine mystery to which Donner neither had nor deserved any access? Yet Donner now feared their sudden silence had meant something far darker.

"Do you have any sense of who might have something against Mortimer?" Hernandez asked.

Donner shook his head. "He's so quiet. Not the type to make many enemies."

The two priests moved to the kitchen, which was

sunny and well-scrubbed. A giant spiky aloe plant in a terracotta pot glowed green in the windowsill.

"I'm sorry to say there was more than gossip in his last diocese," Hernandez confided, over the steaming coffee Donner set in front of him. "There was a process to investigate him."

"A legal process?"

"No, just internal."

"Unfounded?" Donner demanded.

"That's how the process concluded," Hernandez said. "But the fact of its ever having started puts me on the alert. Along with these letters, it raises real questions."

Donner frowned. "What do these letters claim Mortimer did?"

"That's the trouble. There's no clear claim in them. Nothing specific, nothing actionable. Lots of dire insults, though."

"Hmm. What was the claim against him in the last diocese?" Donner asked.

"There was a concern he might have said something—highly inappropriate. Explicit, even. It was a group of children who said they'd heard him saying it. The problem started when those children were heard repeating it. A lot of parents were unhappy. But Mortimer claimed they'd misheard him—that he had never said *that*—that if they knew what *that* meant, it had to be because of some contagion they'd picked up from the media. That maybe those parents should be more careful what devices they let their kids access from now on. Anyway, the process found he had done no harm."

"What exactly did they say Mortimer said?"

"That I can't tell you. The substance of the complaint is supposed to be kept confidential."

"But—it was bad."

"I wouldn't want to have the words in my mind if I could keep them out of there."

Donner looked frustrated but didn't press. Hernandez changed the subject. First, he tried again to find out what Donner knew about the unofficial parish watchdogs, but this turned out to be a dead end. No one had told Donner a thing, and from what Donner said about his daily round, he certainly hadn't had time to put anyone up to any watching.

Then they chatted about the parish school in a way that seemed trivial to Donner. Hernandez started asking questions about curriculum: math, language arts, sacramental prep—by the way, who was covering those First Communion lessons? Hernandez had asked, and when Donner told him:

"Ah, Mortimer again. What a help he must be to you, even after all that trouble he's been through," Hernandez had said. "Well. You also know how people can be, especially when they're afraid. How easily these hyper-cautious parents are spooked by nothing. As long as it's really nothing. I'm hopeful it is nothing, here.

"But you'll make sure of it, that's the kind of good man you are; I've known you a long time, haven't I? Long enough to remember all the kinds of things you used to say about *wolves in sheep's clothing*, aha ha ha, ahh. Didn't you make the place almost too hot to hold some people?—or was it that they made the place almost too hot to hold *you*? Ah, well, look out for those First Communion kids, my friend. Find out what you can, and let me know what you hear. And I'll see you when I see you."

Then Hernandez stood up and checked his watch.

"Someone's expecting me," he said. "An old teacher who's been in for gallbladder surgery. I said I would bring him the Sacrament."

Not until Hernandez's BMW had sailed halfway back to town would Donner, standing over the sink washing out the *Stingray Soccer #1!* mugs they had used, realize what Hernandez had really been saying about Mortimer. Then the crash between Hernandez's flippant tone and the gravity of his meaning jarred Donner at the skeletal level. The phrases ricocheted in Donner's skull, like children's calls at recess, their vocalizations at first stripped of meaning and then, tauntingly, horrifically, freighted with it: *Look out for those kids—find out what you can—*

Donner dried his hands, picked up his cell phone, and dialed Hernandez, who answered on the car speaker.

"What now?" Hernandez half-snapped, leaving Donner unsure if Hernandez was truly annoyed or just unaware of his own brusqueness.

"Wait. It just occurred to me. Were you saying that you think the earlier claim about Mortimer shouldn't have been let slide? That you still have some reason to worry about whether he's—safe? If that's true, then don't we have to get Mortimer out? Away from St. Margaret's, away from the kids?"

Hernandez hurried to respond: "No. Listen to me. I told you the internal process found no harm. All I meant to say was—it's unfortunate, but these days we have to be extra cautious. So I'm trusting you to keep an eye on Mortimer from here on out. And if you find out anything more about who's behind these letters, let me know right away."

"Well, but why? Either he's a problem and needs to go, or he's no problem and deserves to be left alone."

Hernandez sighed. "I wish it were so clear-cut. It's as much for your own sake as for anyone else's that I want you paying attention to what he says and does. Of course I hope to God it's all smoke about him being some kind of—the word the letters keep using is "predator." I don't want to find out that it isn't all smoke. Unless—it isn't. You ought to understand by now that what we don't know can hurt us. Just keep an eye on him, please. And speak up if you see or hear anything that isn't right. Report to me.

Don't hesitate."

Donner heard the beep that terminated the call. Though the mugs were clean now, he stayed at the sink, staring out the window. He realized he had forgotten to turn the water off; he reached out absently for the tap.

So Mortimer could stay put; he just had to be watched. At best the bad news would turn out to be untrue. Either way, Donner told himself, he could not be held responsible. Bad things might happen, but not bad news—not in Donner's back yard, or Hernandez's, or the bishop's: the rot not uprooted, not burned, just transplanted. One bad apple. Weeds in the wheat.

What if the worst was true, though? Donner felt a sudden Dantean surge of flame flood his imagination: Mortimer's face on a lizard body, roasting on a spit. If anything, the need to conceal this thought made Donner hold it closer. Publicly he toed the party line about *mercy, forgiveness, nonjudgment.*

The air conditioner balked and coughed. Last October, when it started to falter, he'd ignored it, thinking it could wait until next year. Now it was only April, but already close to ninety degrees out. And then Donner had the curriculum oversight committee, and the leak in the church roof—the school was newer, but this construction dated back to the fifties, long overdue for maintenance—and then the Annual Fund, and then the contractors for the new classroom building, and then the women's and men's nights of reflection, the hours in the stifling velour-curtained box. He had liturgy planning meetings from here to next spring; he had the floods of people needing the St. Vincent de Paul Society: bus fare tokens, meal coupons, help with utility bills, the whole time-and-mind-draining business, all carried forward against a backdrop of mountains of donated t-shirts and sneakers . . .

No. Donner could not take one more complication. He had to get this one off his plate. Even if he could reorganize the whole parish's life around keeping Mortimer busy far away from families—no catechesis; no bazaar or spring festival; no volunteer coordinating, clubs, or associations; no confessions or Masses; only financial paperwork, engagement prep, outreach to isolated elders—even if he could manage all this without raising any further suspicion, Donner couldn't continue to look at Mortimer, suspecting, not knowing, not exactly *not* knowing either. He couldn't be everywhere; he couldn't prevent everything. He couldn't be responsible.

But—what if he could find some backhanded way to push Mortimer out of the parish? Not the way Hernandez would do it himself—Donner didn't have those gifts of subtlety—but perhaps he could do it in a way artful enough that Hernandez might even approve. Maybe he could tweak Mortimer's ego, drive him to break down in public, to throw some sort of tantrum, not enough to cause real harm but enough to justify a different kind of transfer: not to another parish but to a therapy center, albeit temporarily. Always temporarily. Just until someone figured out what to do next. Someone else, *not Donner.*

He stared out the kitchen window and across the street to the fence of orange plastic mesh strung on spiraled metal posts that blocked off an area where creek banks were being shored up. If this work were neglected, the houses across the way would slide off the ledge into the water, if not with the next rainstorm, then with one the next year, or the year after.

As Donner stood watching the maintenance workers shove their wheelbarrows of clay up the banks' slope, he thought about the most practical ways of sawing off the branch he was sitting on. He knew that, in minutes, Fr. Mortimer would roll up past the fence on his Cannondale mountain bike, clad in neon gear: highlighter-yellow vest, orange shorts, black stripes, reflective strips. Mortimer would stomp upstairs, shower, change, climb down, read the newspaper, and then make a pot of fresh coffee not in the kitchen's drip machine but with his own private imported apparatus before returning to his own room, as he did most mornings, for a couple of hours of who knew what: Mortimer had never offered; Donner had never asked. In charity Donner forced himself to presume private prayer.

*

Fr. Mortimer revolved through his rounds of parish work with the smooth, reliable constancy of a machine. Wind him or sequence him and he'd go through the appropriate motions before powering down and returning to his bed, like a robot vacuum in its charging stand. Donner had never had anything personal against the man, no. But that was just it. There was nothing personal to have against him; there seemed scarcely anything personal in him at all until now. Now Donner considered, uneasily, what there might be.

As Donner approached him on the gravel drive, Mortimer stood beside his Cannondale, peeling off, finger by finger, the complexly padded gloves he wore to prevent his grip on the handlebars from causing blisters. Who but Mortimer would mind if Mortimer had blisters?

Donner hesitated, black-shod feet shifting on the gravel. All the scenarios he'd woven about how to subtly force remorse or blatantly practice psychic brutality—humiliating his subordinate in front of the Wednesday Bible study so badly he'd feel no choice but to quit; calling him out implicitly in a homily, for something unrelated to the letters—how could Donner have even imagined these stratagems might work? True, he had seen such stunts pulled before.

But even if Donner had had the energy to start a fresh spate of petty parish drama, he lacked the tenacity to follow it through to its conclusion. Even just rearranging Mortimer's slate of responsibilities would cause disruption enough, and Donner did not believe he could handle it. Any change would raise questions that Donner did not trust himself to answer.

Squinting, he approached Mortimer, who was now about to lock his bike away in the garage.

"Message for you from the bishop," said Donner. It wasn't quite what Hernandez had said, but it was what his visit had meant. "You need to call his office. Schedule a meeting with him. About your assignment. It's urgent."

*

Above the bromeliad, Hernandez regarded Mortimer with scorn.

"Why are you here?"

"Why are *you* here?"

"The bishop called me in to deal with you when he heard you were asking for reassignment."

"I wasn't asking for reassignment. Donner told me the bishop . . ."

Only sharp eyes, if not downright suspicious ones, could have caught Hernandez narrowing his.

"Told you what?" he demanded.

"I'm not sure why, but Donner told me that the bishop wanted to meet with me. He seemed to think I might be reassigned soon."

Hernandez breathed a syllable in Spanish that might, Mortimer didn't know, have been either devotional or scatological.

"It sounds to me like Donner is taking it upon himself to micromanage his parish in ways that aren't under his authority. I'll have to speak to him about that. What I have to ask you is this: Could this miscommunication have arisen because of something you haven't told your pastor—because of a personality conflict between you two, perhaps? Is it that you aren't adjusting to the work—or to your co-worker?"

"Neither, really. I thought this was coming from higher up."

Hernandez breathed that syllable again, not toward Mortimer but out the window, as though exhaling smoke from a cigarette.

"It looks as if we're dealing with some sort of radical miscommunication." *I don't know what Donner thought I was saying I wanted him to do*, Hernandez thought, though this was not the kind of detail to confide in someone like Mortimer. *I thought I was clear enough.*

"If you ask me," he went on aloud, "Donner's brain is softening. He was never cut out for the kind of responsibility he's carrying." True enough, and designed to elicit a feeling of complicity, but here was another thing Hernandez would never tell Mortimer: if it was true of Donner, how much more of the bishop himself. Only those who worked most closely with him were aware of the missed words, the lapses in minor discourses; the forgotten names of important donors at embarrassing junctures; the kinds of reminders Valeria increasingly had to slip in the bishop's ear: *You can't use these notes; you gave this same homily three weeks ago. You left your car keys on the vanity in the powder room. Your Excellency, your zipper—*

"Can I do anything for you in the meantime? Coffee, water?"

Mortimer declined Hernandez's offer politely. Hernandez slipped out of view and soon returned in the episcopal wake. Mortimer kissed the ring on the hand extended over the desk. Hernandez left.

*

"My son," the bishop said to Mortimer. "I heard you were looking for a change."

Mortimer almost blushed. "Not on my own initiative, Father. Donner sent me. Am I being reassigned again?"

"Wait. That wasn't my understanding. Who do you say told you to come here?"

"Hernandez says Donner; Donner says Hernandez. They both seem to think you have a message for me."

"Well. It isn't anything like the business that brought you to this diocese in the first place, is it?"

The air pressure in the room seemed to drop, as on an airplane descending. Behind the curtain sheer the gray light went grayer. Mortimer raised a hand to rub his hair. The shampoo scent this motion shook loose became oppressive.

"No, I don't think it can be."

"You don't need me to tell you that nothing like that can happen again."

"No."

"It hasn't, has it?"

Mortimer's face contracted, leapt, contracted again.

"Not like last time. But I'm—I um. I need to—can you—could you—?" Mortimer mimed the placement of the purple stole over the shoulders: the sign of power to absolve. "It has to be under the seal. I can't tell you otherwise. Can't say it."

The bishop considered his options. He knew what a request like this might mean. So he could deny the sacrament, certainly. Tell the poor wretch *no.* It all hinged on what Mortimer meant by asking. What did Mortimer seek? More concealment? More protection for them both? Enough of that. It was possible to be sick of being shielded from what should be permitted to strike you.

It all depended on what he was looking at across the green-edged glass expanse: a penitent? Or a repeat offender?

The bishop wanted to believe in penitence. So under the seal, after all, Mortimer was allowed to say it: what Donner had not quite suspected but had feared, the worst that could be going on in that closed upstairs room for two hours every morning. Mortimer's dog-eyes spilled tears: real, false, who could say? The bishop couldn't.

"Let me be clear. This is not only a grave matter. It's criminal."

Mortimer didn't speak. His face told the truth.

The bishop considered his options once more. They were fewer now.

"On the computer or on—"—the bishop had temporarily misplaced the word—"paper?"

Mortimer cringed. "Some of both."

"You created it? Or—acquired it?"

"Acquired."

"Destroy it, delete it. All of it."

"I—some of it. Already."

"All."

"I will."

"And never again. If I ever hear a murmur of this from another soul, I will have to turn you in. And if I do that everyone will know. If I heard it anywhere but under this sign, you know I would have to report it."

Mortimer only wept.

"I don't pity you. You've defiled yourself."

Mortimer only wept more. The bishop couldn't bear it; he looked down. Eighteen minutes of this already now. How much more? His own eye blinked back at him from his glass watch face.

"It is possible to take care of this. To get you the care you need to stop. But for that to happen, it has to be voluntary, on your part, not forced by me. Do you hear what I'm saying to you? When you check in to the treatment center, you will have made a decision on your own. We will never have spoken about this."

Mortimer's throat had stopped almost anaphylactically. He eked out a weak, convictionless *yes*.

"If the least proof of *what* you are being treated for ever surfaces, the least suggestion of proof, I will leave you at the mercy of civil authority and you won't surface again. They'll conduct an investigation. You'll be charged and, I should hope, tried, and sentenced. There won't be any protecting you anymore. You are going to suffer in ways you cannot imagine. Ways you'd better start imagining, if that's the only way you can help yourself. God help me."

Mortimer could not speak, only nod.

"Get treatment. Fix this. No healing otherwise. No salvation. None. You hear me?"

The bishop had begun to lose hold. He railed on:

"You shame our Lord. You make a mockery of his Body. A byword. Haven't we all had enough?

Haven't *you*? No, you had to go and do this. Again. This—filth. And drag every good priest and every pure child, every innocent soul, down with you."

The bishop spat the syllable Hernandez had used. This time there was no mistaking the curse. Like a charge of thunder, it cleared the air. The bishop then heard himself, heard his own voice, saw the spectacle he made: wire rims half hanging off, bulk hoisted over the desk's glass top, stole slipped to the side, loose jowls, yes, quivering.

Mortimer's eyes, red and dry now, took it in, terrorized.

Poor wretch. Just days ago, the bishop had sat in front of a screen's cold white glare to audit a training on the very topic: *Neurons that fire together wire together*. Sad cases. Addicts, essentially. Not much to be done for them but sorrow. *Sorrow*: seven silver swords piercing a red heart. *That the thoughts of many hearts may be revealed*.

He could deny absolution. Part of him wanted to deny it. Let the wretch roast. But here, a still older training laid hold of the bishop's own thoughts. He could be looking at both neurons and a soul: a soul more real than the body it made breathe, more permanent. This moment might be that soul's last chance at recovery.

"Well. Your conscience can say more and worse words to you than I ever could. Forgive me, child, if you can. In Christ's name, I forgive you. Remember there is no sin so foul he cannot cleanse it. No wound so infected he cannot heal. You see even I, here—I lost my—lost control. If you can find it in your heart, forgive *me*. He will have to purify us both."

Mortimer made a wordless sound: inchoate, vowel -laden, keening.

And the bishop assigned him a penance, and he pronounced the words of absolution.

*

Later that afternoon, when Mortimer stumbled into the rectory slamming one door after another, Donner was not there to see his mouth twist or hear the frames shudder. But when Donner came in from after-school meetings with teachers, he saw Mortimer's car keys sprawled on the credenza. Donner had to wonder, but he didn't have the energy to worry.

He sorted through the junk mail next to the keys, almost every piece some sort of request for money: donation pleas, cellphone ads, furniture-store flyers, even an ask from a religious order with a brass-plated third-class relic stuffed inside. Donner rescued the relic and dumped the rest. He had heard of a woman, living not far away, who'd made an art installa tion out of all the junk bulk dozens of companies had shunted to her doorstep. It had filled whole rooms.

Then Donner, undone, parked himself in an overstuffed meringue-colored recliner. His whole body contained a sensation of not-quite itching, perhaps a low-grade fever coming on, some sort of histamine response to pollen, or a toxin in food, maybe? Vainly, Donner tried to recall what or whether he'd eaten yesterday, or the last time he'd walked farther than to the school and back. The feeling lent credence to what one of his parishioners, a regular at confession yet also a diehard New Age syncretist, persisted in calling *stuck energy*—as if one's Krebs cycle could suffer constipation.

Donner tried to laugh at himself, but it ended in a wheeze. He felt some invisible weight on his chest. The recliner cushion seemed to rise up like sticky bread dough around Donner's thighs and shoulders, to be pulling him into itself, smothering him in a softness that terrified him. If he yielded—if he yielded—

When his eyes next opened, the room was filled with the blue of April's long twilight. Donner had dreamt he lived inside an aquarium: couches and Virgin, plants and flatscreen, all underwater. The impression dissipated. Someone was banging on the rectory's front door, much too loud.

Donner groaned out of the chair, crossed the room, and pinched the lock open. He hardly had the door open when Hernandez shouldered his way in, his face contracted with worry. He made straight for the back stairs.

"Sorry, friend, I need to know. When did you last see Mortimer?"

"I—didn't. He was home when I got in. I fell asleep."

Hernandez made a wordless noise of vexation. "So you didn't get my voice mail?"

Donner prodded his shirt pocket. Where was the stupid—

"You ignore your phone, I'm not surprised." Hernandez thundered up the staircase. "But Mortimer always answers his texts. Always. I got a voice text from him an hour ago that didn't compute. Garbled, incoherent nonsense. Crying. When I texted back, asking what all that was about—nothing."

Donner clambered up after Hernandez, breathing hard from the effort. "Who knows. Maybe he was at prayer, and he tapped the mic by accident. Should we really—"

When they threw open Mortimer's door and stood in the frame side by side, Donner could only see what he'd feared and had not wanted to know, what he wished he could set fire to. *Burn it all*—but no, they would have to leave it the way they found it. Investigators would come, and they would need to see. Not only the note from Mortimer telling how he'd been caught—in a chat-room sting—and spilling his insufficient apologies. Not only the belt and what swung from it, hung above it: the well-tended cyclist's body broken, the once-handsome face discolored, distorted.

Car doors creaked and slammed in the drive. Blue and red lights flashed on the branches of the Bradford pear and turned its pale blooms lurid. Hernandez unpocketed his phone and began to dial. Donner, eyes clenched shut, could not even grieve his brother priest's loss, even as he felt himself losing any self he'd had left to spare. All his grief now was spent on the girls and the boys pinned glossy to the pages, at least a hundred pages, littering the floorboards, the desk, the sheets of the unmade bed. All the little lives curled around themselves *my Jesus mercy* like fallen petals, tossed aside in the breeze that shook the lace curtains at either side of the open window.

Hail Thee, Festival

The trick is not to arrange a festival but to find someone who can enjoy it.

—Friedrich Nietzsche

"The system is simple, once you catch on. Businesses sponsor us. Folks donate prizes. We raffle the big prizes off, and of course our students sell tickets. Those are raffle tickets, but—look—these are game tickets. Red, green, yellow, yes, they're all game tickets. We keep running out of new rolls and having to switch up the colors. A mess, I know, but the raffle ones are blue and orange and so you won't lose track. Yes, you pay for game tickets, too.

"Oh no, nothing's free: this is a fundraiser. They used to put FUN in all caps, leave out the D, but, you know, someone smelled the ruse. It *is* fun though. Or can be. For the children. And then, too, they earn points toward their Citizenship grade because you volunteered. It's almost like they gain back the time you lost for them. Almost. Then they'll need game tickets to spend on the games, which they'll play to earn Hornet Bucks, which they'll accumulate to trade in for prizes—not the adult prizes, not a bottle of spendy wine or a weekend at a timeshare or—did you see that burlap-and-wire sculpture of a rabbit with a bowl built into its back, between its little ears you know, and the bowl is filled with liquor-infused chocolates? I think *I* want to win that—but no, for kids we have the kind of thing they like, Lego sets, Nerf guns, plush animals: I'm sure your house is full of all that mess.

"Not that you—I mean—oh, this mouth of mine—you know what I mean, forgive me, hon. You said you had a—? Right, second grader. Oh, you have years of this ahead of you. Decades. You'll be standing in my Reeboks when I'm pushing up dandelions.

"Now over there, that's the games pavilion. We have archery, rock climbing, egg hunts, scooter derbies; basket toss, football toss, foosball tables, indoor bowling, outdoor bowling, bingo games, shuffleboard, duck pond, truck touch, fossil dig; pin-the-stinger-on-the-hornet, pin-the-curl-on-the-pig, pin-the-horn-on-the-unicorn. We have dunk-the-principal, dunk-the-pastor, dunk-the-coach; we have dunk-the-mom-of-the-school-bully (kidding, can't have that—liability—but wouldn't you love to, just once? Though the real trick would be getting her to show up). We have cornhole, table tennis, sack races, soda pong (liability), photo booths, face painters, hair braiders, henna tattooers, clowns making balloon animals or the floaty kind with strings, your choice, and always one or two people taking little sips off the helium supply to make their voices go all squeaky. Which you really shouldn't. Not that you—but someone always does, and it's a bad idea so don't say I didn't warn you.

"Over here, *just* for the adults, we sell beer, wine, hard seltzers. For everyone, burgers, hot dogs, bratwurst, street tacos; cotton candy, popsicles, cupcakes, snow cones. Over there, popcorn, soft pretzels, funnel cakes, fried pickles (mm, my favorite). Under the awning, you'll find T-shirt sales, screen-printed koozies, school hats, spirit gear. We can take cash or credit.

"There, hon, that's the spiel you'll have to give next year. There they all go—and now you're with me. Take this zip pouch, and this envelope. For tickets, use the manila one only. The pouch is for making change. Don't worry, it's easy. You'll catch on as you go. "Yes ma'am—sorry, your name's Bonnie, you said?—hi, I'm Lil—well, Bonnie, we do this every year, rain or shine. I've been at it for thirty-seven years and I've, this way or that, seen about all that can happen. Right time of year for it, too: right now, after Easter, everyone still riding high on the Exultet, everyone still feathery with hope, glossy with all that new chrism, new fire. It's downhill from here in the school year, we know, but the celebration helps. Afterward the children can coast toward summer. That helps you make up your mind to work.

"Oh, it's work, no question, and almost any little thing can mess it up. You know: *for want of a nail the shoe was lost, for want of a shoe the horse was lost, for want of a horse the rider was lost, for want of a rider the kingdom was lost?* I've seen tents fall down, I've seen those tall plywood game structures collapse, I've seen people pass out right there on the concrete, *bam.* We have to be prepared. That's why we start weeks beforehand, but the big push begins at seven a.m. on Easter Tuesday and doesn't let up till ten on Saturday night. From Easter Friday morning on, we especially need sunshine, if possible. The folks in the perpetual adoration chapel are on the case, and usually we're given what we ask.

"Just about one year in seven it rains, and that's miserable—although, you know, I kind of like it. Feels adventurous. A storm blows in off the mountains, and before you know it, we're all wrapped in clear emergency ponchos, half the games move inside, we have to put these long plastic rainproof flaps over all the pavilions . . . These little things do matter, but then at the same time they don't. Still, we're lucky it's clear today, flawless. Not a cloud.

"If you could, hon, please take this big clear bin of prizes and move it over to the games pavilion, the one with the yellow-and-white striped awning. Oh no, wait, stack those. No no, not there: no, these bins go on the dolly. That aluminum cart over there is for chairs and tables. We can put the bins four high. Take them all if you can. Right past the eighth-grade girls blowing up those pink and green balloons and festooning them all along that flexible archway over the gym door. Let's unload them here. Right, all these neon sticky aliens and rubber animals and squirmy Kooshes and fake tattoos in the bins, these slippery little bits and bites: these are the little prizes, the ones they get if they don't win the big prizes. We're all just trying to keep these kids from crying today, though we know they will anyway: all the more the harder we try, sometimes.

"We parents and grandparents spend more than we mean to every year, of course. The school counts on that. We all do. We can find our generosity for these little ones, if for no one else. Without that, the whole thing would fall apart, you know? If not for my granddaughter—oldest of eight, all the others are still babies—I'd be curled up at home with my old dog Pumpkin and my remote control.

"Okay, see there inside that *other* clear bin, sticky-tacked inside that Ziploc bag? Put these prize slips inside those plastic dollar-store eggs. Oh yes, I've run every game and sold every concession, but I'd be helpless at whatever it is the big organizers do. Truly, who knows how they do it? When I tell you I'm nobody, really, hon, please believe it. Not like the headmistress over there, whom I've known since she was born; look at that hair on her, sprayed up to here: her whole body wasn't as big as all that when I first held her. Now, *she* is someone. We've all known her all this time and it's good to see her happy, finally. She struggled, you know, after her twins—but that was a long time ago. You don't know that story? Oh, you *are* new. Well, it was just a nightmare. She was house-bound for a year, too scared to go out. Not—*sick*, not like that, you know. In the head. Just frightened. A soul problem, is how you might put it. "Heart" I'd say, but then you'd think I meant her arteries. No—a good woman. Bless her heart. All that she manages—when you think about—

"Bless *your* heart. What's your name, sweet? Maggie? Maggie, what I want you to do is hold this jump rope right here, that's right—and then you, Diego, come on up and hold the other knot—now we're a choo choo train—woo woo, go go go go—you did it—Hold up there, sweetheart—Make sure they get their sticky aliens—Oh Maggie, your *flower* crown! No—for *me*? Oh, sweetie thank you, how glorious, I'm going to put it on *right now*—

" . . . I know her, too, that mother whose three little ones just finished the game: See that monster-sized jogging stroller she's driving? She's out with that thing every morning at five-thirty, goes running with the headmistress—that's how they work off all that worry now, you know. Though what you girls all are so strung up about these days—my goodness we and our kids all walked alone to school, not so strained and stressed and pushed and rushed, not worried about all these standardized tests and abductions and school shooters and—well, when I put it that way I suppose it's no wonder—

"Oh us? Martin and I, we've been living here since before you were born, right here in this neighborhood: I live just over behind the fence beyond the Little League fields, close enough to walk. I would have walked if not for this heat. Unseasonable . . . Say, when's your shift over? Mine, too. We'll need to have some lunch along here; let me bring you—what? No sugar, no grains, all right, I can do that, I think . . . What, just ask them to leave the bun off the burger? All right, but then what's the point of the burger, hon?

"Oh, my word. Look at that glare off the tops of the tents. This heat's as oppressive, in its way, as three feet of snow. And on this concrete parking lot—it's nearly white too, in this sun—you know what's odd though, Bonnie, is I *like* it? I like *everything*. Always have. Can't help it. Even the heat, the mess, the nerves and the headaches, the sweat and the strain, the noise, dear Lord—the pocks of basketballs and footballs against shatterproof backboards and wooden circle targets, the shouts and screams of the littlest ones, the incessant chatter, the gossip. The smells—meat cooking, oil boiling, sunscreen drying, funnel cakes frying. Without it—I don't know—but this glare, it's a migraine on wheels, hon, I'll have to sit down for a while. The minute our relievers sign in, I'm gone, but I'm so glad you're here, it's been so nice to meet you—"

*

When at last this stint of volunteer time is done—which is exactly as long as it takes my companion to stop talking—I adjust my ballet flats where their gathered heels are pinching and then wade through the scrum of people to the registration tent. This is a pop-up beach canopy garlanded with molded-plastic ivy strings and leis of silk flowers, where we return our clipboards, with their click pens attached by cheap jewelry cord and their manila envelopes scotch-taped with game flyers and stuffed full of tickets. We initial the sheet to be sure our students—my daughter Ena, Lil's granddaughter Kelly—are awarded their points for our cooperation.

Next: where is Kichiro with Ena? He was supposed to bring her over from her soccer game and hand her off to me so he could take his shift, so she could earn points from both of us. He's supposed to be over at the rock climbing wall with a cluster of other fathers. Oh there—by the concessions: why is he—what—is he buying her a *soda*? But she already had juice with the pizza with the team. Plus before that, they all had some kind of syrupy greeny-yellowy resin-tasting sports drink—

"Hi hon. Thanks."

Ena takes my hand, and we circumambulate. Instantly it transports me back to when we lived in the city, when she was so new. I loved to wander out with her when the snow let up a little and she'd just begun holding her head well enough to face forward in the wrap carrier, her big eyes scaling the monuments, her small palms clutching the fringes of my scarf. Even that liberty, a modest enough claim on the world, was granted us on strictly limited terms—not for us as a family, not for Kichiro surely. After Ena was born, he started working even harder. No hope for any continuation of that coffeeshop-and-walk-up life of my last year of singlehood, that last year of grad school, still striving for the master's in economics, still planning to make better money as an international policy analyst. How we met. How Ena happened. Worth more to me than any prescient prediction, any finessed recommendation, any security or correction—no matter how many other lives those might improve—

Yes, I'm back in the office now, but only to earn enough money to make this style of schooling possible for her at all. Surely part-time accountancy in the suburbs is a step down in the world, mere counting up of other folks' earnings and dividing out Caesar's share. Would it even be worth going back, back in truth, to the city, to what I am *really* good at? Could I still be good at it now? My habit of mind remains so keyed to those days off, those days of grueling rest, of continually carrying Ena near my heart in a cushioned cocoon of gray fabric. Day after day we would take the train into the city after rush hour ended and ride back home before it started again. No one from school, no one from the office, lived near us then. Those other mothers mystified me, so tied to their soccer and martial arts, piano and violin lessons, boozy book clubs and wine-muddled girls' nights. How they made it through those Kindermusik classes that drove me into such agonies of boredom: dark glasses, woozy smiles—all self-medicated, or else as hung over as the erstwhile frat boys who'd grown up into the men they'd married, the ones who'd gotten them into this mess.

Maybe we ought never to have left the city. Of course the opportunities here, the individual attention, the class sizes . . . Still, if only Ena could have grown up near all that culture: if only we could have expanded, extended those days we'd wake up first at five a.m., and then not surface again after Kichiro had already left for work. I would pack sandwiches and water bottles, diapers and wipes, and head to the museums. Circle the fountain in the museum square off Seventh, wander the Mall, view the panoramas. After Ena turned one, I worried less about the cold. Then we'd go out even in winter, even when the same half-inch of salted slush frosted the wide walks for weeks. The sun set before five in the afternoon, the way it fell in parallelograms down the lines of the grid and turned the noble old sandstone and marble a lemon-drop yellow. Those nights, worn out, we'd fall asleep by eight, to the same lullaby rendition of *The Magic Flute*, while Ena drank my milk longer than the pediatrician thought she should—her teeth, even then—and in the morning when I worried again, Kichiro said, *well then, why don't we find a different pediatrician.* Kichiro worked late so often then that even he stood to one side of that enchanted circle. Here, things are better. Here, in a smaller, safer city two hours south, he doesn't have to be left out nearly so much anymore. His office and mine lie within the same twenty-minute travel radius as do the house, school, church, pediatrician, dentist, orthodontist, grocery, pharmacy and, yes, family therapist, and we are happier. We are. Happier?

Ena wants a snow cone; we transact our business, and soon she slurps a semicircle of ice saturated with blue syrup. I make a mental note to schedule a dental checkup. We sit down on a concrete bench, along whose riser a past decade's art students have pieced mosaic tiles to depict a sunset. Ena's two long brown braids brush the colors. In her robin's-egg soccer jersey, striped inky black, she bobs about with delight. She kicks tall-socked legs, cleated feet. We sit people-watching for a while. She is an active participant in the watching without ever having to be told what it is we are doing. She has often enough, from early enough, watched me watching that now she does it too, uninstructed. What else has she picked up so tacitly, so thoroughly? What else—chilling thought—*will* she?

"Mom, they all have the same t-shirt. Are they all on the same team?"

"You could say that. The school is like one big team, right?"

"Yeah, except not really. Like when I make a goal, it's the team's goal. When I make an A, it's my A. Why can't my A be for my class like my goals are for my team?"

The answers never come easily. People said they would. Were people lying? "People are different from each other, sweetie. People make different choices. It's good to start learning that early."

Some bodies, some postures, in this crowd make the screen-printed festival shirts look athletic; some make them look slouchy. Some have ignored the school's strong encouragement toward uniformity. One woman makes her t-shirt look as though it belongs at a trunk show, with white capris and espadrilles. Another, with cascades of freckles and terribly sunburned shoulders, slips hers on sheepishly over a cornflower-blue tank dress as she stands there by the duck pond, pressing down her stroller's wheel brake with the flat of one sandal.

An obese woman in a mobility chair carries her festival shirt draped over one quivering arm, wherein is also tucked a tiny slip of a girl dressed in dove-gray sparkles, dazzlingly blonde and so delicate she elicits an urge to run over and snatch her up out of the woman's grasp before she falls. The obese woman's shoes are flawless—smooth tan leather flats decked with rhinestone baubles.

As the woman with the child rolls her chair away, I know the shoes of the woman walking next to her: battered white sneakers over bright white athletic tube socks. No t-shirt on the wearer, just the same bruise-purple wool dress and the same fluttery crochet beige duster this woman always wears. I know the garments, but not the woman's name. Idly I wonder when she washes them. Her hair is tortured back into a comb headband that is laced into a gold thread snood that is edged with black plastic pearls. (Who ensnared those plastic pearls on the net; who twined the gold threads? Is it—uncomfortable thought—the lack of *style* that makes me ask? Inner torment over whose little fingers must have stitched the sleek brass zipper pull on to my own purse always ends in self-justification because at least the zipper pull *looks* good. To me.)—

The woman in the white sneakers and purple dress has eyebrows drawn on with brown pencil over a brow as palely powdered as an Italian wedding cookie. Her arms stretch, skeletal, a scarecrow's, out of three-quarter sleeves. Her hem drapes down over the tops of the socks so that not a hint of flesh is visible between.

I see her all the time here, waving her rosary under the teetering bulbous crown, ajangle with beads, that perches atop the Our Lady of Fatima statue. She doesn't seem to use the rosary the same way so many of us would, tucking the beads into a palm or a pocket so as to avoid being seen at the work of prayer. Instead she sways with outspread arms, she chants aloud. People give her a wide berth. I've heard she's known to show up often at the earliest daily Mass, the six a.m., but on Sunday at noon when we go, I've only ever seen her four or five times, bringing up the rear of the communion line in starched lace veil and noisy tears. No one ever seems to say anything to her. In the three years we've been here, I've never once heard her speak. It occurs to me now to wonder who here has. Who are her friends, if she has friends?

Ena has moved way on, though, enumerating team strategies—"though Coach Jill says it's every bit as important to be gray shuss if we lose. What's gray shuss? Oh and I need *ten oranges* for the game too and they have to be *sliced like moons* they can't be whole—"

Suppress all skepticism about the comparative value and culture of team sports, lay aside the preference for personal achievement—running, swimming, gymnastics—and stifle any hint of boredom. Placate her with murmurs: *uh huh, baby, uh huh, and what about next week?*, meanwhile trying to think two consecutive thoughts of my own:

Let's say a woman spends $2.75 in gas money and cuts out $45 worth of canned soup, tuna, and vegetables from her grocery budget in order to buy and drop off three sticky, corn-syrup-laden bakery cakes for $15 each, which are sold for $20 but cut down to $10 in the last hour of the sale, for a net loss of $30 over projected gains. Net *loss*. Not to mention the value of the volunteer hours, which, if each of the women (the buyer and the seller) had only worked gainfully at some skilled occupation for the five hours they'd each spent on this effort, at an hourly rate of let's say $42.25, that's an average, and then donated their after-tax earnings wholesale to the school—

Ugh.

Ena raises her arms in a V: "Coach says we can't quit."

Ruffle her braids gently: yes, don't quit. Let's say the bake sale is a loss leader. Still, they must profit somehow, or they wouldn't keep on with it, year after year—but then, maybe they would. What if, once upon a time, the gains were guaranteed and no one at the school has even thought about the doubling of food prices in the last decade? Maybe they need someone to help them, to restructure—oh no, can't think like this, where would the *time* come from? Where, out of thirty hours a week, out of all the work that home is, out of soccer and church and Citizenship points—out of my own body—

Dr. Yeh would say: *don't try to change what you can't control.* She would say: *try to find the good in the bad.* For instance, would we ever without this festival, and I mean *ever*, have purposely bought snow cones?

Would I ever otherwise have seen Ena tipping back her chin to catch the last drops of blue raspberry? No: subway rides and art museums are still my idea of a good time, but snow cones and competition are much more Ena's. Find the good. This daughter, this day, this school which she's privileged to be in, this clapboard parish church in Virginia's heart, this spring, this freshening wind—

Could do with much more freshening wind, really: the afternoon has grown hot, stagnant, and now that the snow cone is flattened to a bent triangle of mushy paper, I already regret its memory.

But Ena is pulling away. She wants to play games, and I want her—*don't you, mommy*?—to have fun. Yes I do. So with a roll of the wrist, like a Renaissance street clown, I flourish a strip of yellow tickets, already purchased, and she cheers and grabs for them.

"Not so fast. Stick close. If we get separated, let's meet under the tree." I point: right across from the games pavilion a pin oak, its trunk furred by resurrection ferns, triumphs out of a raised bed lush with impatiens, patiently waiting for the New Heavens and the New Earth in the center of the poured concrete lot. Plastic and metal folding chairs, a motley assortment scratched around the legs from many years of this routine, stand lined up beneath it, close enough to the pavilion that parents can watch. In the shade, the raised bed's scent sours the air with rotting mulch.

Ena runs to the duck pond first and grabs the duck with the gold star on its underbelly, which is easy to find as it has flipped to float on its side. She jumps up and down, waves it at me, points to the star, shrieks with delight as the volunteer hands her five Hornet Bucks printed on card stock. On to the sand pit she careens; she kneels, crushing grit into her soccer socks (more to scrub out later), and begins to dig for treasures with abandon. Okay. It's all fine. That she is having fun is enough.

Except—is it? What is she learning to have fun *with*, to have fun *about*? Life after all is not a duck grab or a sand dig. Life is not a disposable prize wrapped in a crimped and factory-sealed plastic sleeve.

Maybe we should move farther out into the hills, join that co-op we looked into when Ena was first born, whose women call themselves *wise*, where hand-woven linens, handknit woolens, spiral herb gardens, backyard laying hens, home-curated honey from beehives, and home-poured beeswax crayons serve as status symbols. (Hobbies? Nostalgic gestures, quixotic defenses, for means of production at last lost to us?) Now Ena cracks open plastic dollar-store eggs with both hands, rifling them for her paper prize slips. She collects her trash and skips on, burbling, to the next—

A splash covers the asphalt, a gushing sound like the breaking of birth's waters. The rosary woman has pushed the inflated wading pool that, moments ago, was the duck pond, off the table.

Before her, the waters rush out and down the lot's gentle incline, where they dissipate, trickle unnoticed under the walking soles of fabric sneakers and rubber sandals. Such is the afternoon's deep heat that steam curls up from the rapidly escaping puddle and visibly evaporates. The snarl on the woman's face speaks for itself.

We sit staring, the booth volunteer and I, lips stunned into stillness. No one else has acknowledged what's going on yet. Folks at other booths seem to think it's been an accident. A lone, attentive volunteer rushes over with mechanic's towels for her dress; another grabs a stack of concession napkins, all sincerity that this will do the trick. Someone else moves to take up the tarp from beneath the table the pool was laid on, to place down a dry one. Someone else seizes the buckets and runs for the hose: refill duty.

The woman sees all this and shrieks without words.

Ena is five tents down the gallery by now and doesn't turn from her game.

The woman shouts out the first words besides the *Hail Mary* I've heard from her in the three years we've lived here. She has a rasp in her throat like a smoker's:

"You! None of you love God! Not a-one of you does! You all only love mammon!"

Not to worry: in the old days, would-be prophets

bellowed nonsense like this out the mid-car door at L'Enfant Plaza or off the platform at Woodley Park. Back then I would have gotten off before my stop and taken the next train to avoid them.

"Trash," the woman screeches, "worthlessness!"

I stand up and step slowly sideways while looking at my phone screen, in a defensive grapevine designed to thread me closer to Ena, only hoping I look nonchalant enough. The volume of conversation from the crowd, of music from the main stage, does not diminish at all. Ena? Ena throws another ring at the pegs: flash of robin's-egg blue as her shoulder blades flare forward.

"Trumpery! Frippery! Scraps of plastic, scraps of cardboard . . ."

An oscillating fan behind the striped awning flutters her hair, her skirt, wafts toward the flowerbed the cloying scent of her powder.

"Fiddly little scraps. Who done took the time to mark 'em—fives and ones and twenties, even? Eh? Cain't believe you even *want* this trash. Your hearts all full of scraps. Stinking slinking plastic toys. For baby or you or who, now, who now—c'mon. What for? Where will you put it all? You know those grabby hands gon' freeze stiff one day!"

Out of a clear prize bin atop a white table she snatches up a backscratcher, a pair of plastic Halloween skeleton hands compared to which her own are hardly any broader, any fleshier. She bends down with the toy; she makes it smack the spilled duck pond again and again, as she stomps her Keds. A rip opens in the fallen pool's vinyl. Her dress hem shakes.

"Why? Why? It don't even please you. Do you think it pleases God?"

A little circle of quiet has, finally, cleared itself around her, though it is broken by the vaporish grumbling of the gas-powered generator that runs the air pump that inflates the bouncy house. The duck pond volunteer, one hand half over her mouth, uses the other to unfold the backup pool from the clear bin behind the table—as if the woman might try to stop her.

And Ena? Ena stands in line, oblivious, for another turn; Ena grips a wooden ring in knuckles that knead her nonexistent hip; poised like a little David, she is ready to deliver a slaying shot.

Behind the unhinged woman, still other volunteers are quietly refilling the new kiddie pool and placing the weighted ducks in it, carefully, each one flat side down, so that the color-coded stars painted across their sealed seams once again sit watertight against the pucker of surface tension. The metallic tang of spent petroleum hangs in the air. The sun's heat continues to flood the lot.

"Gimme a drink, guzzlers!" the woman screams. She makes a break toward the generator, throws the plastic skeleton hands, and grabs the cord. She begins to tug but gains no purchase. Who is this woman risking electrocution, ready to generate sparks? Her convulsive clutching has managed to loosen, almost enough, the three sturdy prongs in their black-taped outlet.

Just then a crackle of static announces Security, who stash their walkie-talkies on their belts before they kneel around the woman. As they wrap thick hands around her brittle wrists, they exchange a comradely look of mutual irritation over her head. One of them pushes the loose plug back in. They escort her, now limp and unresisting, to the first aid pavilion.

Someone somewhere pops a balloon, but it sounds precisely like a gunshot. At the sound, a child cries out. This unfreezes me from my spot under the resurrection ferns; this frees me to rush to Ena's side, where she still stands at the blue painter's-tape line and takes aim coolly.

"I'm okay," my daughter says at my advent. That she knows she needs to reassure me is, somehow, more devastating than any of the rest.

"Mom, will you hold my bear for me? I won it but it keeps falling out of my pocket. Mom, I'm really good at this. Look. You can't put your toes past the blue tape. Can. *Not*. You have to throw this ring and loop a peg with it. I can do it a lot. I can loop the ten-point peg again. Watch! Mom! Mom Mom Mom Mom Mom Mom Mom. *Look—*"

Rock climbing has wrapped up, and the fathers

who were spotting harnessed children have dispersed. Contractors have arrived to lower the wall on a winch, angling it down and down until it fits on the flatbed of an eighteen-wheeler. Volunteers have twirled the harnesses into tight rolls and zipped them into reusable waterproof casings for the next borrowers. The Eagle Scout troop has heaped a tower of firewood high in the soccer field adjoining the parking lot and stuffed it full of brushwood and wastepaper, a leaning tower of potential mayhem. When dusk comes, they will douse it with acrid barbecue starter and then light it.

At the edge of the tower, there rests an irretrievably broken picnic table, which the boys have also dragged over to be burned after an unsecured basketball goal fell on it and split most of the boards. Fortunately, no one was sitting there when it happened. The table lists slightly as the Scouts perch on the one remaining unsplit bench on its far side. They half-joke about staying there to self-immolate on the pyre as a live alternative to taking Monday's calculus exam. Shadows stretch out already between the tower's slats. The low light yawns in long bars between the poles of tents and the flailing limbs of stubborn grade-school-aged game players still unwilling to pack it in. Yellow fills the horizon above the tree line. The sun's angle purples the mountains in the distance.

It is well past Ena's dinnertime. In the concessions

line, she chooses fried chicken strips, applesauce packets, juice, water, and one giant pretzel; I pay cash for it all. Kichiro is wearing a wobbly paper crown that Ena has crayoned to look like it carries clusters of jewels. He secures a fan of napkins for her. Since all of the tables are completely filled, the three of us sit down together on the grass at the lot's outer corner.

Music still streams from the main stage, though by now the DJ, too, has packed up his equipment and gone home. Two high schoolers with guitars and an amp have taken over. The three of us straw-poll ourselves and concur: we prefer the high schoolers.

The raffle winners have been drawn, announced, and awarded. The games are being swept up, mopped up, binned up. Volunteers don cellophane gloves and begin to pick up shreds of torn wrappers, scraps of spongy white bread, popped balloons, popsicle sticks lick-stripped of flavor, white paper lollipop sticks chewed to pulp, emptied juice boxes and foil packets, and plastic straws, plastic straws, *so many* plastic straws, long white ones with red stripes, short sharpened ones, clear or yellow or milky. Loose straw wrappers skitter end over end across the square.

Children's skin and clothing run with sunblock, sweat-salt, syrup, and grit. Hours of soaping, scrubbing, and rinsing loom ahead. The faint haze that tomorrow will be dew begins to gather in the grass blades.

Every face, every limb, every downy hair pale or

dark and every fold of clothing, each line is limned in gold. The light picks up chips of mica in the concrete that catch and spark. The light shimmers the vinyl outlines of awnings, glosses the ribs of table umbrellas. The light glints on the teeth of laughers, on teenagers' braces, on glasses' lenses; it traces the curves of bare shoulders and chins and glosses the gossamer of Easter dresses; it gilds the five o'clock shadows on fathers' cheeks; it aureoles mothers' tousled chignons and illumines the queenly, tall satin coiffures that the members of the Nigerian women's group all wear. In the folds of one headwrap, a lone peacock feather nods.

The air is so clear it hurts, and the guitar notes twine themselves in it like fingers in smooth hair. A breeze picks up. A child in a green gauze dress flits barefoot across the lot, wearing glitter-lined bumblebee wings. A cheer floats over from the basketball goals, which have long been taken over by high schoolers.

All of the children have won prizes; few of the adults have; this is the way of things. We don't dispute it; we don't *want* our kind to win, anyway. Better to watch these children carry, so lightly as they do, the groaning burden of this inescapable excess. The only question left is: how can we propitiate these children, so that one day they may be able to forgive us for all we've given them?

The sun melts, drips down behind the tree line.

Below the tower of brushwood and wastepaper in the field, a flame blooms into view. It is as though the mossy grass is no more than a bolt of tapestry in which the sun has punctured a hole so that its heat continues to burn into the flat of the picture, to pour through, to consume flower and feather, lion and unicorn. The Eagle Scouts raise a cheer.

Ena whines in a perfunctory way for Kichiro to carry her to the car. For once, instead of correcting her, he enthusiastically scoops her up into a bundle as though she were a newborn, nuzzling his nascent beard into the nook where her neck meets her shoulder. She squeals in feigned indignance but watches my eyes all the time, telegraphing her joy.

Kichiro secures her in the booster, shuts the door, and turns to me; he hands me the keys and then places one hand on the door handle as if to open it to me, but doesn't yet. First, he slyly catches my waist in his other hand; as my earlobe receives the heated crescent imprint of his lower lip, his construction-paper crown falls off.

"Hey," he says. "You okay after all that?"

"Yeah. You heard?"

"Who didn't?"

"Well, everyone else around me acted like it didn't happen."

"Well, I don't miss a lot."

He grins close to my face, causing momentarily to falter my habit of doubting that this world is worth all its trouble, all it costs, all it wastes, all the wait.

And it is true that Ena will carry no memory of that woman—I will ask her, years and years later, when she has been working so long at the embassy that she has risen to a place of trust there. She will not remember, though as I dwindle into the crone years, as mind fades and yields to body, as body yields to place, I will remember. Every time I donate another toy left unused by the children Ena will never have, I recall that skeleton woman being led away by security guards: her black-pearl eyes, the tears in them like the specks of white in the eyes of a prize plush toy bear falling to the flat concrete. I pick up the bear and place it in the box, feeling an uneasy kinship.

Omnes Habitantes in Hoc Habitaculo

Great-Grandmother ran the house from beyond the grave. Against Mignon's mother's distinctly expressed wishes, Great-Grandmother demanded that the furniture be arranged in a specific way, that crystal lamps be perched where little girls must sit in tense fear of knocking them over, that mirrors be polished and porcelain bells dusted daily, in the one room Great-Grandmother had reserved to her own exclusive use. That room held only creaking pointelle-cushioned princess chairs, their stippled embroideries too sharp to relax against, and one sofa, upholstered in cloth the color and texture of burlap but with tufts of scratchy white wool, beige cotton fluff, and an unsettlingly slippery butterscotch sateen ribbon woven between the fibers. Great-Grandmother would not permit Mignon's mother to get rid of this furniture or even to slipcover it, no matter how Mignon complained that she could never sit comfortably enough to read or fall asleep there, that the couch as a couch was unsuited to its purpose. *Who said it was your job to be comfortable, young lady?* demanded Great-Grandmother. *Keep watch and stay awake.* The question of guests' comfort was as moot as that of Mignon's own, since Great-Grandmother had convinced Mama that the house was unfit for guests and, therefore, no one ever came over.

Then in the family room there dwelt Mignon's grandfather, who howled and gibbered in the night about the soldiers who, he claimed, were on their way, who'd tortured him and told him they would use the address on his bead-chained aluminum dog tags to find and to behead his family, in vengeance for what had been done to theirs. Daytimes, Grandpa only grumbled about the soggy cornbread and the stringy roast beef and the absence of decent scotch whiskey in this part of the country, despite his lack of any place to put such matters, had he found any he'd approved. A great-great-aunt sat in the corner with her ring-decked hands folded on her black-clad knees and simply did nothing at all other than lace and unlace her fingers, making a soft clinking sound of gold and gemstones that only Mignon could hear.

By contrast, Mignon could easily handle the occasional skeleton that chased her through the rooms of the house or the set of disembodied teeth that pursued her out the door and down the block. The specters of her dead relatives vexed her much worse. They congregated in the back yard, warning her that the vines on the fence were poison ivy, that rabid rats lurked in the compost heap. They stood, admonitory, at the top of every climbing tree, every ladder, every staircase, prognosticating the likelihood of a fatal tumble. They stood at the edges of pools and streams and ponds, instructing her about drowning and snakes and waterborne diseases. When Mignon began to learn to drive, they sat in the passenger seat. Sometimes they climbed right into her lap to grab her hands off the wheel and scream that they were all about to die—or, worse, become liable for the payment of an astronomical insurance claim.

The specters accompanied Mignon to college, which she discovered that first night after her roommates had gone to sleep. Mignon lay awake in the cinderblock room, listening to ambulance sirens wail away thirteen floors below. Then she heard the whisper.

—If you had a stroke tonight, it said, now I know women your age usually don't, but let's say you did, your roommate probably wouldn't even wake up.

—Who is this? Mignon asked the air.

Mignon's grandmother answered questions with questions: —You got that lil phone a yours close by?, it said. Let's put 911 on speed dial.

Mignon obeyed and then put the phone on top of the microwave that served her for a bedside table.

—Put it closer, her grandmother urged.

Mignon put the phone on the mattress beside her pillow.

—Closer, hissed grandmother's voice.

Mignon complied.

—Not under your pillow. You're not gonna be able to reach under there if you're blacking out and you know you only have a second to react.

Mignon sighed and laid the phone on the mattress next to her hand.

—Better, said grandmother.

That night the dorm room was visited by a lost and drunken fraternity pledge who mistook her roommate's beanbag chair for a public urinal.

—Let's get a single room, muttered grandmother in Mignon's ear when they woke up and scented the damage. Your roommate forgot to lock the door. You won't make a mistake like that.

So Mignon applied at the housing office and was transferred to a single, which had gone unoccupied only because the window-unit air conditioner didn't work. Reluctant to bother housing staff again, Mignon made friends with a boy who promised he could fix the air conditioner, but who, once inside the room, seemed more interested in Mignon's body, an interest Mignon didn't share, than in making any repairs. He told her so. She told him no. He didn't listen. Crashed into her. Left.

After, the ghost of her grandfather made its presence known.

—My little girl, he said. He didn't ought to have done that. Hadn't you better look for an apartment off campus? You might be safer there.

The apartment Mignon found was just a studio; she couldn't afford more space on her own.

—It's enough, said her grandfather, and brought

in more relatives: grandfather, grandmother, great-great-aunt, a man in glasses and a camouflage cap Mignon didn't recognize, a pair of immensely fat twins, and a tiny, wizened woman in a high-collared black dress who identified herself as Aunt Vicky and informed Mignon that she was there to give lessons on deportment.

—Staying still, Aunt Vicky said. Going unnoticed. Being ladylike. Sit right here next to me, she ordered, tucking her many layers of petticoats under her bony thigh, patting the cushion on the floor. Mignon sat down next to her and stayed there until dusk fell, when Grandpa sidled up to her with a Swiss army knife in his hand, saying:

—Let me teach you some self-defense tactics.

He became her jailor. He lectured Mignon about attackers, terrorists, biochemical warfare. He enforced masks, a curfew; he forbade visitors. He had her hang thick rubber-backed privacy curtains at the windows.

—Situational awareness, hissed Grandpa, crouching beside her as she squinted into the thin sunlit bar between the curtains. —Stay here until the coast is clear.

The coast was never clear. Grandpa considered everyone a potential threat: delivery people, bus drivers, professionals, the homeless, parents with strollers, youths with earbuds—especially students. Mignon stopped going to class. Then she stopped going out, even to the store around the corner. She could keep soul and body together with what she could find in her own building's first-floor bodega. Even if she couldn't, it seemed to her that nothing she was doing now couldn't also be done after soul and body came apart. So she ate Doritos from cellophane packets, drank orange juice from little plastic barrels. She sealed up drafts in her window and door with strips off an $8 roll of duct tape. She bought tampons in travel packs, $3.59 for six, until she stopped needing them due to poor nutrition.

—Better that way, murmured Aunt Vicky, in case that air-conditioner boy ever comes around again. He don't know where you live, does he? Suppose he found out and you ended up with another kind of unexpected guest, get my drift? Much better this way.

Mignon began taking lessons from Aunt Vicky on invisibility. She began to slink downstairs at night, take goods from the closed store, and check herself out at the register, leaving cash in the drawer. Then she ran out of cash and, with no job and no apparent way to get one (how could an invisible person be interviewed?), just took goods from the store. The bodega manager expanded his hours, posted a night worker.

Now Mignon only stole in the daytime: lunch hour, rush hour. She got to know the cashiers: a business school student with sky-blue rectangular glasses; a tall hawk-eyed girl who walked and dressed like an athlete out of training. Both, when not busy with customers, absorbed themselves in other pursuits behind the counter. Blue-glasses read books on quantitative easing or how to appear empathetic. Hawk-eyes constantly texted.

Mignon never knew which cashier had spotted her the day she fainted—she must have fainted, to have woken up no longer invisible, in a hospital room with an IV in her arm, but she remembered nothing except looking at the shelf in front of her—gummy worms or peach rings? She woke to the sound of a triage-room TV blaring news of a school shooting at already traumatized patients.

People in scrubs challenged her: —What have you been eating? Is that all? For how long? Where have you been living? How? Why?

Mignon could say only that Aunt Vicky had told her to be careful. —Who is Aunt Vicky?

Gold rings, she told them. Clinking. She couldn't say more.

They put Mignon in a room: one that, she noted, had straps on the bed, though these weren't used on her. They presented her with a tray heaped with turkey, candied sweet potatoes, green beans, canned cranberry sauce, white rolls, butter. At the sight of the heaped tray the relatives descended all at once, shouting contradictory orders. Grandmother begged her to remember the starving children in the Third World. Aunt Vicky yelled back at Grandmother that Mignon's not eating it couldn't hurt anyone a bit. Grandfather barked back that for all they knew, it might have drugs in it, mightn't it? The fat twins drooled, complained: they missed having bodies, missed food, it wasn't *fair*. Aunt Vicky stood up, walked across the room, pointed a knife-sharp pearly nail, and pronounced right into Mignon's face:

—Just how do you plan to *pay* for that meal, young lady?

Mignon lost her patience. She began to scream, to throw dishes at the wall, to kick the bed, to crush handfuls of food into the sheets. Orderlies came; a new needle went into Mignon's arm.

Aunt Vicky stroked Mignon's forehead. She whispered in her ear: —Don't tell them about us.

—Why not? Mignon asked.

—They'll say you're crazy. They'll say we aren't here. They'll say you belong here. You cain't afford it here. You cain't afford how long you already been here. You got to get out. We'll help. Now listen. Here's the plan.

After trying to carry out the plan Mignon lay strapped to the hospital bed, and no matter how patiently bland-faced people sat and explained her rights under the Subsidized Care Act, she screamed her throat raw. Never mind the things her relatives were telling her now. They were her, now, or she was only what she had seen and heard them be, what she surmised it was necessary to become.

All along, Mignon had assumed she was doing the right thing by imitating them. But imitating them had led her here, imprisoned her here. She felt a victim of circumstance, although simultaneously she blamed herself, unable to point to any one action the relatives had asked of her that she hadn't believed she was freely choosing. She felt a rightness, a sense that what was happening to her was happening the way it should be.

And the relatives crooned to her.

—We always said you was crazy, girl.

—Shut up Margery; you ain't crazy, Mignon, world done gone crazy. Just got to let it roll off you, like water off a duck's back.

—Shut up Harold, girl's upset. You want to disappear now, don't you girl? It's okay. We'll teach you how.

—You want to go away now, don't you girl? Look over there. Now here's what you do . . .

—You want to go home, don't you? Come with us. Come be one of us. You're just like us. Be just like us.

And they told her stories, and they forbade her to recount the stories they told her: of infants born deformed and buried hours after birth, of toddlers locked in cupboards, of children beaten with belts or with branches trimmed off saplings, and the relatives averred their firm belief that the world would be better if more children were locked away or beaten sooner, oftener, with more focus and conviction. And Mignon threw up over the rail of the hospital bed, because now she had shrunk to three feet tall and they were all sitting around her in a circle watching her play with hollow plastic blocks that slipped about and wouldn't stack or stand contiguous to each other, blocks with corrugated convex sides, blocks that hurt Mignon's small hands. Meanwhile the relatives discussed in no uncertain terms the dreads and terrors of the world and she had begun to cry, because nothing would stay together and she didn't understand how anything was supposed to fit, and now Grandpa crouched down and went very red in the face as he began to shout at her to STOP THAT CRYING OR I'LL GIVE YOU SOMETHING WORTH CRYING ABOUT, as tears filled his own eyes and he screamed at her about little girls her age found dead under leaves in the jungle, without their heads, without their dresses, and worse, and worse, AND YOU KNOW WHAT I MEAN BY WORSE DON'T YOU?, and she didn't know, she didn't know, but her body knew and it vomited. And now only a little bit of greenish scum, then nothing at all but still every muscle was cramped and locked and the room was full of spiral-dancing stars and then of grayness and then of unholy quiet.

When she woke up, she didn't know how long it had been, but she assumed she was dead because of the way the relatives were standing around moaning and keening. Only she counted one too many of them. Crouching on the floor, cleaning up the green scum with blue disposable cloths, was a man she didn't recall having met. He seemed vaguely as if she ought to know him, though: like they had been introduced sometime, but she had forgotten his name. Embarrassment stuck like an ice chip in her throat.

—Don't worry about that, she said, or thought she said, but the words didn't echo on the air the way they should. —I'll get it: but again, no sound came from her mouth.

She tried to get up, but the straps . . .

"Don't worry, I'm almost finished cleaning this up," he said, and the vowels of his speech were long and warm and round and slow. He got up and put the cloths he'd been using into the trash can. The lid flapped shut again with a barely audible pop. The man washed his hands with soap at the sink in the corner, lightly hitching up his black cuffs, then turned around and smiled.

"You need some water?" he asked her.

—Yeah.

He brought a cup and a straw from the bedside tray.

"Looks like about time they brought you more. I'll tell the nurse as I leave."

"Are you a doctor?" She found the sound startling: her own unfamiliar voice.

"Er. Not really. In a very limited sense only."

“Don’t worry about me.” She turned away. “I don’t plan to be here much longer.”

“I can see you’d rather not stay. Also, I notice you have a lot of visitors. I’m afraid I can’t get the staff to discharge you until they feel you’re ready. But maybe I can help you get some privacy.”

He had a book in his hand and a tray with two small jars: water, white powder.

“What’s that?” Mignon asked.

“Salt,” he said. “Here, taste.”

She did. It sharpened her tongue.

He sprinkled the flakes around the room. The door seemed to open, though Mignon could see it was still closed. In came seven orderlies dressed in white scrubs and white sneakers. In their hands they held what seemed to be bungee cords, woven through with copper and steel wires.

“They can bind them,” the man said, nodding around at the relatives. “Is that all right with you?”

Mignon couldn’t find her voice anymore, but she nodded agreement. The men stepped up to the relatives, marched them out through the closed door that was somehow also open.

—You can’t let them take me away Mignon, I’m a helpless old woman, I’m depending on you, squealed Aunt Vicky. The man in black shuddered. He could *hear* her.

“Close your ears,” he whispered to Mignon, laying his hands over the sides of her head. Mignon closed her eyes and lay very still until the whole group disappeared. Then Mignon and the man in black were alone. She cried out with fear.

"Be not afraid," he said in a voice like wind over still water.

And she was not afraid.

"Be healed."

And he read from the book in an unfamiliar language while his fingers traced shapes in the air, gripped and shook the water container, traced the letter t on the damp petalline skin of Mignon's forehead.

The book closed. A moment passed.

"How do you feel?" the man asked, and seemed to want to know.

"I . . . don't think I feel anything," Mignon answered. "I think that's an improvement."

The man gave a slight smile.

"Don't be afraid," he said. "Whatever you are expecting when you go back into the world, it will be different."

Mignon nodded. "I've never been alone like this before."

"Never?"

"Not since I can remember."

He nodded again.

"Why don't you do what your caregivers tell you," he said. "And when you're ready, think about coming around for a visit. You are free, but free doesn't have to mean alone."

He paused, handed her a small white card. Then he asked her:

"Do you *want* to be free?"

Then he left. The air seemed full of a silence like a series of sung notes, a harmony blooming with overtone.

Mignon lay back on the pillow and asked the harmony:

"What's next?"

Only then did the place's rightful inhabitants begin to speak.

The Convert

On the evening of the first snowfall, the convert stood on the steps of the rectory. He took the brass door knocker between two fingertips and tap, tap, tapped on the plate under the hinge.

The convert, a former fan of *Fight Club*, had been reading the desert fathers. This left him half-hoping a burly priest in full cassock and collar would stick out part of his face, one eye showing under biretta and bangs, and shout "Too stupid!" before slamming the door in Tyler's face.

Instead, a woman in late middle age, sporting a short silver crop haircut, stretch pants, and knobby sweater knit with large pink reindeer whose hooves pranced upon her bulging hips, flung the door open wide.

"Come in!" she cried. "Just up the stairs, if you're here for RCIA. You're lucky tonight, too. Monsignor Cartwright is speaking on the Church's theology of marriage and the family—his thesis topic." Aunt Reindeer smiled without showing her teeth.

"Don't I need to start with something a little more . . . intellectual?"

Aunt Reindeer showed her teeth this time. "Oh no, dear. It's all connected up. You'll learn as you go."

So Tyler took a seat in a deep red cloth chair, drank mediocre coffee with gritty powdered creamer out of a Styrofoam cup, and ate a homemade brownie bristling with walnuts. He tried not to think about how much soap Aunt Reindeer's thighs could supply if she underwent liposuction.

Monsignor Cartwright, by contrast, was a pleasant surprise to Tyler. A tall, broad-bodied man in black, with weightlifter's shoulders and a Durdenesque buzz cut, he didn't look like someone who had been emasculated by years of chastity and parish dinners.

As the priest detailed Church doctrine, Tyler listened for any gleam of salaciousness when he spoke of men respecting women's bodies or about pleasure in the union of spouses. Part of Tyler felt disappointed to the pitch of anger at not being able to find any. He had had two hopes, at cross purposes with each other: he had wanted to be titillated, but he had also wanted to edify his newfound faith by eliminating from his mind some stomach-turning historical imagery he had encountered in online forum discussions. No one, he knew, would be a priest if it had involved literal castration. Vowing celibacy wasn't the same as becoming an actual eunuch for the Kingdom of God. Still, there must be literal pain in abstinence. Tyler knew it with a wince. He had gone without Delia, without so much as a tour of the internet's offerings, for a week now, and already he was blue as a whale.

The unplugged ethernet cable, coiled under his desk like a grey snake, taunted him.

Thought and passion churned in Tyler's mind, but somehow the words got through and went home. He had read just enough to see the foundation of Monsignor's arguments. He had to admit, the progression from Christ and Church to groom and bride went logically and smoothly.

The problem didn't lie in the logic. Tyler met with bewildered hesitation in other people when he—at least he thought he was doing this—tried to spread the doctrine to them. Tyler had drunk down Monsignor's lecture like wine, and it had burned in him like fire. He couldn't understand why he failed to spread the flames. After a few weeks, he had decided that his poor track record probably reflected the faults of others and not his own.

Not his fault, for example, that Dan and the other housemates had not taken well to his quoting Proverbs on the evils of strong drink when they asked if he would drive them to the package store. Until six weeks ago Tyler had been well known for his capacity to put away Miller and Jack Daniels, so from a certain angle he could understand their accusations of hypocrisy. In truth, though, he thought, those accusations were just evidence of their own lack of understanding. Which of them, he asked himself, had ever taken a thing in life seriously? Which of them had ever been through a conversion? Not his fault that no one understood. Not his fault, the eye-rolling of professors at his fervent classroom rehabilitations of the Crusaders and Savonarola. Not his fault, the shocked stares of his former Ethical Society discussion group when he strolled in sporting an elaborate crucifix and began to argue about the value of human suffering—not of reducing human suffering, but of allowing human suffering. Not his fault that Christians were a stumbling block and a folly (that was the way Tyler recalled the verse, and he hadn't felt the need to look it up: it was Christians, he felt sure, not the Cross).

Most of all, it was not his fault that Delia had reacted as she had to her encounter with the stumbling block. Who, Tyler asked himself with his heart in his shoes, who could have expected her to react so emotionally to such a clear line of reasoning as he presented?

Lying crushed against her warm sweaty skin in the narrow single bed of her dorm room, Tyler had whispered, "Baby, you know if I'm taking this becoming-a-Catholic thing seriously, we have to talk?"

"Mmm." She had laughed, rubbing her cheek against his chest, shaking her long dark curls so that they tickled him. "What's to talk about?"

"Baby." He had shifted his body back from hers, put his hand on her shoulder to move her slightly back too. "I'd still want to see you, of course, but we couldn't keep on doing this" (he had waved his hand back and forth between their naked bodies), "not unless—"

'Unless we got married' had died on his lips. In a moment like that it seemed too serious, almost too good, to say.

Delia had laughed again. "Plenty of Catholics do this all the time. My roommate and her boyfriend freshman year, be-he-leeeve you me. She told me later that she thought it was no big deal and that it was her conscience that counted."

"Right. Whatever. But—baby, stop that a sec. Look at me."

Then he had caught a good look at Delia's eyes, glinting darkly in the nearly lightless room. He stood up from the bed. He didn't see her throwing his boxers at him until they had already hit him in the stomach. Gormless, he crumpled the shorts in his hand. She sat up with her back against the wall, arms folded across the blanket that covered her body up to her shoulders.

"Well," she said eventually. "You've gotta do what you've gotta do, then. And if that's how you feel, you better start as soon as possible."

*

After Delia stopped returning his calls, it was, no doubt, his body that bothered him most. He took to lying in the ice under the bushes outside his apartment complex, feeling the chill tighten his muscles and shrink his scrotum. Each night, staring at his phone timer with teeth chattering, he tried to increase the amount of time he could stay on the ice before reaching for a cigarette, inhaling the smoke slowly to warm himself, then slowly letting it out.

When his roommates asked him where he'd been, he always said, truthfully, "For a smoke." They saw the cold damp patches on his jacket and jeans, but Tyler felt that if he explained, his tactic would stop working.

Even with the ice, even when he rolled over to lie on his face, took off his coat and gloves, pressed his bare palms to the ground, even then it sometimes didn't work. Once he was warm again, alone in his room and falling asleep, fires would kindle and burn unquenchably until he quenched them himself.

Afterward he always felt humiliated—less of a man, not more as he had in early adolescence—it wasn't at this point as if he didn't know what his body was capable of. What he needed now was not proof of what it could do, but proof of what it could do without.

*

Three weeks after Tyler's first catechesis, one week until he was to drive home for the winter break, Monsignor Cartwright spoke again. The marriage talk had been the conclusion of a series on the sacraments and from there they had passed on to grace and to human dependence on God. People needed grace for everything, and everything culminated in grace, Monsignor said. And the pretty young wives, the graduate students, the grandmas, and Tyler all nodded.

Although Tyler could already feel the edge of the confusion that would clamor up inside as he stepped out into the frosty night, here, now, it all made sense. That night as he lay on the ice, Monsignor's words echoed in his head like chimes in a belfry: "All of this, it's all about a gift of ourselves to God, which is the only real response that makes some small echo of His gift of self to us. All these rules and laws and regulations that seem so stupid to other people make sense to us. We know these are where we find our freedom. Through the grace we receive when we try to keep God's commands, we are made free to become the kind of people we wish we were. It's the only way we can give ourselves, the only way we can be truly happy. By ourselves, we can't give ourselves. By ourselves, we're broken. It's grace that makes us whole, and grace is the fulfillment of the Law. Everything God asks of us, He gives us first. The only things he asks of us are those he also gives us the grace to do. Period. It's that simple. And it's ours for the asking."

It sounded so good to Tyler. He wished he could find his freedom in it.

*

That same night Tyler was discovered in the snow. His roommate, Dan, came out for a smoke, lit the lighter, then sniffed the fireplace scent, the cold, in the air. Dan turned; a tar-scented cloud was billowing up from behind the shrubbery. Dan followed the smoke. Tyler looked up, grinned, and waved.

"Tyler, what the hell are you doing down there?" Dan reached a hand down to him. "Are you drunk? You better not be drunk. You've got an exam in the morning, don't you?"

"Yeah, history. Going to be a motherf—" (Tyler cleared his throat) "—one of those. But I already studied." Tyler waved Dan's hand away. "I'm just incensing the temple, you know, clearing my head."

"Incensing the temple." Dan shook his head and lit his cigarette. "Napping in the damn snow. Whatever floats your boat, I guess."

A pause insinuated itself into the conversation like a snake uncoiling. Tyler sat up, the cold under his hipbones so fierce it made his body ache.

"What a dumb-ass phrase. 'Whatever floats your boat,' hurr hurr." Tyler chortled in a deep goofy voice. "Whatever buoys your dinghy. Whatever creams your twinkie. Whatever tickles your pickle. Whatever—"

"Dude, shut up." Dan shoved Tyler a little. "It's

stupid, all right? So is sitting in the snow, turning yourself into a frozen corn dog."

"Yeah, I guess so."

"So why the smart mouth?"

Tyler just shrugged.

Dan stood up and walked around. "Eh, it's your ass. Freeze it if you want."

They both looked anywhere but at each other: at the cold ground, the brown scattered leaves, the grey concrete squares of sidewalk.

Tyler spoke first. "Hey Dan?"

Dan just looked at Tyler—not really at him, but in his direction.

"What would you think if I told you I was going to become Catholic?"

" . . . What do you mean, what would I think? Why should I care? Do whatever you want. 'Right you are if you think you are,'" Dan began to sing in the same low goofy voice Tyler had used a moment ago.

Tyler stood up, put his hands in his pockets, and walked into the house. "Never mind."

*

Tyler didn't feel sorry, at the end of that week, when he stripped his room of every last possession and crammed it all in his car before the two-hour drive north to his parents' house. It wouldn't be fun trying to find a new place to live after Christmas. Still, it felt necessary. In his mind he had jumbled annoyance with his housemates, desire for friends who also understood faith (he figured they must exist somewhere), and suspicion that his current friends prevented him from making the good decisions he meant to start making, but never managed to make.

His housemates followed him back and forth to the car, occasionally carrying a box or some clothes, but mostly hounding him with questions.

"Why didn't you say anything to us before?" Mike asked as they climbed the front steps. "Seriously."

"Seriously? Because I knew that if I did, you'd try to talk me out of it," Tyler snapped, slamming a box into Mike's arms. "So shut up and make yourself useful."

Tyler pushed the full trunk shut. Mike threw the box into the back seat, on top of a pile of full Hefty bags. There was a slight crunch, as of mugs breaking, which Tyler tried to ignore.

Then Dan spoke up: "Look, T. We gotta respect this, all right? You gotta do what you gotta do. But you can't just leave us in the lurch on the rent."

"Use your beer money," Tyler said. A couple of guys chuckled, not sure whether he was kidding. "Eh. I'll keep an ear out and help you find someone to take my place."

Dan sighed. "All right. Fair enough."

As Tyler swung himself down into the driver's seat, Dan kept his hands on the door; when Tyler was in, Dan pushed it shut after him, companionably, then thumped on the window. Tyler rolled it down.

"Drive safe, all right? And hey, don't be a stranger. Swing by when you're back in town."

"I will," Tyler said, smiling, knowing that he wouldn't.

They fist-bumped, knocking their knuckles together.

*

Alone on the winter highway, speeding so that the sun flickered faster over bare silver branches and brown hills, Tyler felt more like himself again: not the pitiful uncontrolled self, but the strong masterly self somewhere inside, the person he wanted to become, the kind of soul he figured the saints must have been.

Once upon a time Tyler had bought into the fairy tales about how real men had fistfights, used women, blew shit up with fire. He had been terrified for some time that conversion would take him to the opposite end of the spectrum—the crying, hugging, nametag-wearing, IKEA-haunting specimen lampooned in his favorite movie. Now, though, Tyler understood that the only real men he knew were Christ and the saints. He loved the desert fathers. He loved Athanasius: "If the world goes against truth, then I go against the world." He loved those five thousand St. Johns: "A penitent is the inflictor of his own punishments; repentance is striking the soul into vigorous awareness." Tough, enduring, virile, and supplied by an unlimited Source of all these qualities.

*

"That's fine with us, dear. I don't know why you seem so worried," said Tyler's mother, sitting in her soft blue armchair and sipping green tea.

His father spoke up. "My only worry is the suddenness. You said you've been thinking about this for a while, and I trust you. I guess it's just the way this seems to me. You know I've never been religious" (his mother bobbed her head), "but this is the kind of choice you have to make as an adult, I suppose. It's not something to take lightly. You know it means you'll have to believe—? Where do I start? — Any number of things. Don't put a chain on your brain, is all I want to say. Don't fetter yourself. Don't commit to anything until you've thought it through."

"I won't. I promise."

"Let me feel your temples, sweetie," his mother put in, setting down her matcha. "Let's see. Ooh. That feels negative to me. Unfriendly, anyhow. And your muscles are very tense." With cool fingertips she began to rub Tyler's forehead. "That better?"

"Please, stop it." Tyler stood up. Suddenly he felt woozy. "I'm fine, really. Thank you," he added, seeing her injured look. "I think I'm going to go read for a while."

Tyler went up a set of narrow back steps to the dormer room above the attached garage. His parents had given him the room when he turned fifteen, "because we can't give you a car for another year," they'd said. Originally meant for a bachelor renter who might share meals with the family, it was a suite composed of bedroom, bath, and living area. It even boasted a fireplace. It had been built with independence in mind. Tyler loved it.

He drew a crisp new copy of Augustine's *Confessions* out of his backpack, sat down with one leg flung across the arm of his easy chair, and tried to read. His concentration had been dulled by the drive, and his mind soon began to wander. His eyes followed, never dwelling on one part of the room more than another, given over to distraction.

Tyler had no idea how much time had passed before his father knocked softly on his door, then prodded it open.

"Thought you might appreciate some new reading material," his dad said.

"Thanks," Tyler grunted, not looking to see what his dad had dropped inside the threshold. Whatever it was had fallen with a soft slick thufff. For the moment, the outer distraction called his attention to the inner and gave Tyler fiercer determination to focus. He read for about half an hour in this mood, up to the fourth chapter, before getting up and investigating the stack of magazines.

As soon as Tyler looked at one of the pages, he looked away as though confronted with the mangled flesh of car crash victims. Outside it had begun snowing again. Tyler made himself not think about what he had seen.

Meat. That's all these are, Tyler told himself. Like Monsignor said. Lust is treating a woman like a piece of meat. Like she's just a body. Just something to satisfy your hunger, not something to house a soul that demands respect. That's how I was treating Delia: like meat. That's why I had to leave her. And that's all these are. No different.

"No different," Tyler repeated out loud. He crammed the magazines into the trash can, curled up in his chair in the far corner of the room, and went back to Augustine.

But his concentration was badly shaken. He watched snowflakes fall on the thickly whitened lawn; he pressed his hand to the dark window, then opened it, letting the cold come in. He could, if he wanted, leave his room through a second set of stairs along the outer garage wall. It seemed such a long way, though, and his parents might see him, and how would he explain? Mom, Dad, I need to roll in the snow, because if I don't . . . Gross. He couldn't.

He kept on trying to force and kick and drag his mind back to Augustine, where he hoped to find descriptions of the strong wine of delight in God's truth, a fire to burn his mind clear. But these were still the early chapters, where Augustine detailed the slick-talking Manicheans and his own desires, sins, exploits. Tyler began to feel a delicious torment instead. He tried to stop or ignore his memories, but he was fighting himself, and he was losing.

Even Augustine prayed for chastity but not yet, a voice said in his head. With a groan Tyler threw the book aside, went to the trash, and fished a page out. He did what he was going to do, filled with nausea at his own sense of weakness. Tears of futile rage burned in his eyes, but he didn't stop—couldn't now—and it was over, leaving his body feeling slimy and heavy and dead.

Tyler split the spine of the magazine in his hands. He fished the other magazines out, ripped their pages, crammed them back into the metal bin—and it still wasn't enough. Confession. But confession still might not stop him from uncrumpling those pages, piecing them back together, degrading himself again and again and again.

Why—he raged—had God not given him some other failing, something more spiritual? Why not malice, envy, wrath? Why this desperate dependence on pleasure? Why had he been given this?

He took out his cigarette lighter, emptied the contents of the bin into the fireplace, made a strip of kindling from some glossy pouty lips, and soon had a blaze going. He cracked a window for ventilation—he was already sweating.

The voice said again: Everyone who looks at a woman with lust has already committed adultery with her in his heart. If your right eye causes you to sin, tear it out and throw it away. And if your right hand offends you, cut it off and throw it away. It is better for you to lose one of your members than to have your whole body thrown into Gehenna.

Of course. In reading about the desert Fathers, he'd read about Origen—of course. But he'd also read that Origen's self-castration kept him from being beatified. And then how would you live? Let alone marriage: even a monastery wouldn't take you unless you were physically whole. It wasn't sex or even desire that was wrong, but selfishness. But, Tyler asked himself—and he took out his pocket knife, eased the blade slowly open with his thumb, looked at his reflection in the blank steel—could he ever have one without the other, desire without selfishness?

Another voice: Go on. You need to do this. You'll probably go to hell otherwise. You can't get away from yourself otherwise. Don't you want to be free?

Bitter bile rising in his throat, Tyler unzipped, brought the blade against his skin. A horrible stench of ash from glossy paper filled the room. Tyler pressed the blade a little closer. He looked at his own eyes in the mirror on the wall. He stared himself down; he said aloud, "Shut up! Leave me alone! I'll do it! I swear to God!"

A roaring wind whipped through Tyler's open window, lifting the shade, blowing the curtains parallel to the ceiling. Tyler heard a crackle. Slowly he turned to see the fire in the fireplace blown past the screen and out onto the carpet. It ate its way along the floor and up another curtain, began to gnaw into the wall, to spread to his desk, his chair, his books. At first Tyler sat frozen, watching: only slowly did he begin to act. He had to move slowly in order to avoid doing by accident what, moments ago, he had intended to do by force of will.

No extinguisher, no water: the blaze had grown too large and hot to control. Tyler had enough presence of mind to shout down the stairs: "Mom, Dad! My room is burning! Get out of the house!" He grabbed his still-packed suitcase, threw it out the window, and jumped after it.

A foot of snow broke his fall. He ran around to the front door and banged on it, wishing fiercely he had kept his car keys in his pocket. No idea where they were now. "Mom! Dad! Get out!" he screamed again.

He heard the sound of rushing footsteps, the door of the coat closet slamming open and shut. "Tyler, honey, are you okay?" his mother shouted.

"Oh my God, smoke:" his father's voice. "Hon,

call right now . . ."

The doorknob turned. Tyler couldn't face them. He fled, wading coatless through the snow, away from the house, up the road, toward the town.

*

Tyler had barely given the Gothic building behind the fence a second thought before. Now he scaled the chain links as though his life depended on heaving his body over them, flailing his way through the drifts to the inches-thick wooden door, pounding his fists, shouting till somebody came.

Tyler still felt fuzzy about the details of the sacrament of penance and reconciliation, but he remembered this much: absolution wiped away the sins of the baptized. Well, Tyler was baptized. He and the others were supposed to have had their first confessions together before Easter. But now Tyler couldn't wait. It had to be now, tonight. He'd been called to perfection all his life: everyone was. He burned now with the knowledge of the call: its weight, its heat, its terror: the terror of falling short. He saw now that he had been falling short his whole life. Still, none of the things he'd done wrong before had he done with such knowledge of what he was doing, such drive and intention to do them for their own sakes. And he could have died in the fire. He could have died at any second before this second, now, shivering in the snow. He could still die at any second afterward. A new question, one that had never had meaning to him before, rose in him: what if he lost heaven? What if he died on the outside of this new love that spasmed and sparked like a sputtering Roman candle within him, hotter, brighter, heavier than any fear or any pleasure he had ever known?

Nearly half an hour passed, counted by Tyler in trembling, shivering seconds, before a panel at eye level opened to let out a chink of candlelight. Grey eyes, red-veined with age, squinted out through a little screen.

A gruff voice demanded: "What the hell d'you want at this hour?"

"Anything but hell, Father." The old monk didn't even crack a smile. "I need to confess. Please let me in."

"No more priests here, sonny," the monk growled, not unkindly. "Come visit on Sunday when Father's in from the Cathedral. All the old priests died, or else they went away forty years past. None of us was young enough to learn it all, even then. Hell, you want the truth? None of us had the vocation. Try the Cathedral. Good night." The monk shut the panel.

"Please! You don't know—" but pound and scream however much he wanted, it was no use. Tyler turned his back to the door, but he didn't take a step. He felt lightheaded anyway; hadn't he better call a church in the morning? Wasn't he being rash? He shivered violently. What if he killed himself trying to get to confession before he died?

Then he heard another growl behind him: "Didn't I tell you to go away?"

"Oh, thank God." Tyler turned. "Which way is the Cathedral?"

The monk pointed. "North. Eight miles." He didn't shut the window but kept staring at Tyler while Tyler stared back at him. Finally, he opened the door a crack and shoved something bulky and soft through the interstice: a waterproof parka. Then he held out something that steamed: a white Styrofoam cup, full of very black coffee. Tyler put on the coat and took the coffee gratefully.

"Hot," said the monk. "Watch yourself. Don't get burned."

The door shut and, again, so did the panel.

Tyler kicked the snow ineffectually from his shoes. He reveled in the delicious warmth of the coat's fleece liner, its tough shell. He brushed off his jeans, his knees, the top of his hatless head, and then pulled up the hood. Eight miles. He couldn't do it in this snow. Not alone.

Then again, Tyler thought, picking up his suitcase, there were always taxis. If one happened by before he died. He put his head down against the snow and began trudging east, until his forehead made contact with cold hard metal.

He looked up, smarting. Snow whirled down into his eyes, but he could read the sign if he blinked. "BUS STOP," it said.

Tyler thrust his hands into his own pockets. Nothing. Then, breathing fast, he explored the pockets of the coat the monk had thrown to him. The right-hand pocket held a dollar bill, plus a little change.

Allie

After Jack left the house in Enterprise Hills, taking along with him the organic cotton sheets on which they had so often slept together and the expensive French press that had been an un-wedding gift from friends, Allie had breathing room. For the first time in months, months that felt like years, she had time to think. And what she thought was: Never again. Never waste her time like that again, ever. Never wake up in the purplish black of the night, allowing the one street lamp to pierce her retinas and further scramble her blue-light-fried cerebrum, to listen to anyone's anxious soliloquies on global warming, as she had listened to Jack's. Never again, never endure the faint grassy odor of sweat, the prodding of knee and ankle bones, under the percale duvet. Never live with another human, another *body*—as if her own body weren't trouble enough.

What had possessed her to do it? Her salary had supported them both. And Jack hadn't been much help, either—rising at noon, frying up some sort of garlicky vegetable skillet in the kitchen, going for a bike ride without showering afterward, then retiring to the sheets with a book until it was time for Allie to walk in from work. The leisure of it had appealed to her in the early days, when a wave of delight and relief would pass through her on seeing his relaxed form there in the covers, when she would drop her things and her clothes and join him. Afterward, he might go for a run while she made dinner, and then he would leave her to deal with the dishes.

"I'm going to write," he'd say, but would instead read news articles on the Internet for several hours at a stretch, muttering under his breath at the words on the screen—"idiots, fascists, criminals"—until long after Allie had put down her knitting and her earbuds and gone to bed.

He swore to her whenever she raised the question that, at some point while she slept every night, he sent in flurries of submissions to journals, toiled away at drafts of chapbooks, planned to make his mark. One day, he swore, she would see.

"Will you show me?" she would ask.

"The work is in progress," he would reply, sadly shaking his head.

She rose again at six; she was on the interstate to Charleston by seven, driving east, to arrive before the interns did. In her first weeks she had striven to arrive before Janet, the director, whose job Allie wanted. Before long, Allie had understood that Janet would never arrive before ten no matter what, and never at all on Fridays. Janet scarcely cared what happened in the office; Janet didn't really have to care. Caring was what she paid Allie to do.

Both women were in their late twenties, but so far, no friendship had grown between them. Allie had made overtures; Janet had smiled and said thank you but had not really seemed to know what to do with the book Allie proffered or with the hand-painted mug with sachets of lavender tea. Her hands cupped the gifts awkwardly, as if unused to grasping things on their own.

What could Janet really need from Allie, what could they hold in common? Janet's family owned vacation homes, plural, on Myrtle Beach and Isle of Palms. Green Spaces South was her parents' philanthropic outlet, their "passion project," Janet liked to say. The only passions Allie could detect in Janet aimed at girls' nights out, weekend flights to Atlanta or Nashville, interpersonal drama within her circle of friends and the strictly limited pool of men they condescended to date.

On these topics Janet held forth at length, during office hours, on her cell phone behind the closed door, in the front parlor—not quietly enough to prevent Allie from overhearing. Janet's true work at Green Spaces was to manifest occasionally at fundraising galas: gown and heels, hair and golden shoulders, surrounded by a cluster of equally golden, unapproachable women.

Allie maintained the office, hired and fired cleaners and handymen, suppliers of coffee and houseplants and printer paper, editors and graphic designers for pamphlets and posters and annual reports. She met with lawyers on current regulations and with lobbyists on new, stricter ones. Allie helped schools and scout groups submit project proposals. Allie kept the files in crisp order. Allie made the interns put down their phones and do work.

Even as Allie sweated for promotion, she wondered what kind of chance she had. Janet's parents were major donors to Green Spaces: the Beauregards, a gracious and personally temperate couple Allie had met exactly once, at a benefit dinner. Over spinach salad, in dim shadow outside a ring of candlelight, Allie had gleaned that they worried—correctly—that Janet lacked direction and purpose. They felt better about their daughter's life and their own if they could tell their friends that Janet headed a branch office, never mind whether Janet was suited for the work.

The Beauregards felt more justified in their square footage, in their yearly budget, in their travel plans, in their chef and housekeeper, when they were *making a difference.* By giving some small percentage away, they felt they earned the right to keep what had been passed on to them. Allie saw all this in the yellow candlelight gleaming on the carefully maintained smile of Janet's mother, the little gold line of light darting between the two bone-china front teeth.

Allie too, in her way, was trying to earn by giving. All she had to give, though, was her competence. Was it possible that she had reached her level, that she should remain there, rest content? If the organization were to pay Allie three times more, confer a fancy title, what would she do differently, do better, than she did right now? She would remain a good manager only. She would never be as capable or comfortable in Janet's world as Janet was in it or as Allie was in her own. Allie would never be able to trade as Janet did on the commodities of good looks, good humor, impeccable grooming, dismissive wit. Allie was not beautiful. With great effort she could be made presentable in the kinds of rooms where Janet shone. She had made an effort before the benefit. Still Janet's parents had not seen Allie at all except as a sort of distant echo of Janet, a receptacle for their thoughts about Janet.

Allie was clever but not with the sago-palm quality, lush but cutting, valued most highly in Janet's circles. Allie's cleverness was valued for its reliable invisibility. Without it, Janet's glamor had no substance below its surface, no justification for all the resources it consumed. Allie ran her fingertips over the satin of her evening bag, the tulle of her skirt, and considered quitting. Find somewhere else, somewhere better, to work: why not? Who needed this?

"You should quit," Jack had said, as Allie had curled into the sheets later, resting against his body. "I'm serious. They don't deserve you. The capitalist bastards."

Allie had at that time found Jack's political angst

amusing rather than worrying. She had laughed. "They have no self-awareness. You know Janet drives this glossy new chartreuse Prius? And on the back, she's stuck this hideous bumper sticker? Blue with gold text. 'Nobody with a good car needs to be justified.'"

Jack writhed in an ecstasy of irritation. "She thinks owning a hybrid makes her a virgin martyr. All the time she's screwing the whole planet. In more ways than one." If only he had not gone on to add, "Look at me: I don't drive *at all*," Allie could, maybe, have felt as comforted as he had meant her to.

Well, now he was gone. If only he had had more to show for his sacrifices; if only they had not fought endlessly over the trivial duties and desires of their days and nights. If only. Oh well.

In this broad June morning, in its humidity heavy as the box of papers she bore in her arms, Allie wove her way under the Spanish moss, under the wrought-iron balustrade, through the newly installed swinging glass door printed with a live oak and the words *Green Spaces South–Tomorrow's Glory, Today's Gift* in arching serif font Allie had chosen herself. Over glossy pine floors, past brass fittings and white wainscoting, into the gray-and-white working monotony of the back half of the building, Allie passed. Not for her the front parlor, not for her the reception room with its foliage, its tapestried sofas, its sepia pineapple prints in mahogany frames, its ivory textured wallpaper soft as a blanket. From time to time Allie met visitors there—mostly the lawyers and lobbyists—but most of the time it was Janet's kingdom, while Allie sent the interns out to serve her and her visitors with trays of water and coffee.

Allie's own desk in the former servant's quarters was a pressed-wood monstrosity from the 1970s, warped from the second drawer to the footboard from when the last hurricane had flooded the building three years ago. She had refused to have it replaced, although Janet had offered, because it still worked and Allie hated to think of it sitting in a landfill. The floor had been redone at that time, though, so that it no longer creaked at each step or smelled of mildew as it had when Allie first started.

"Long overdue," Janet had insisted, as Allie wrinkled her nose at the smell of the off-gassing carpet.

Allie had insisted, too, over Janet's protests, on bringing back all the same furnishings she had inherited from the previous office manager: metal file cabinets, stacks of decades-old bankers' boxes, a second industrial desk in the corner where an intern sometimes sat in a folding chair. In the back room, too, Allie had rescued a set of wicker deck furniture cushioned in nautical stripes and strung with cowrie shells, which no one else in the building had wanted to claim, which Janet had called "hideous" but Allie found nostalgic.

"If you want it, you can have it," Janet had

shrugged, wrinkling her nose in her turn.

On the corkboard above the desk Allie had hung a photograph she had taken on a hike not long after she and Jack had moved together from Raleigh to Charleston. Along a boardwalk trail over wetlands, she had stepped into a clearing beside a long low pond, almost the size of a lake. Cream iris flags had leapt toward her like spatters of paint out of wild grasses. Overhead, a row of cumulus clouds the color of unpainted canvas yawned between the watercolor blue above and, beneath, the deep blue of a coming storm. Their bellies had been a deeper golden-grey like the unbleached wool of sheep. In the foreground, low over the indigo water, swept a white egret.

The photograph did no justice either to her memory of the moment or to the light already betrayed by the flattening effect of the phone camera lens. Yet she hung it anyway, an aide-memoire, a focal point, a window into a place where time flowed differently.

*

"An order to restructure? What kind of restructuring? Whose order?"

Janet looked much farther down-market perched on the wicker basket seat than in the commodore's chair in the front parlor. Her hair's texture and exact shade of yellow now reminded Allie of a potato chip:

Allie obscurely wanted to bite it.

"Oh, nothing you need to worry about for now." Janet's voice was breezy, beachy. This irritated Allie, who wanted details. "Just moving some seats around. Maybe, you know" (Janet cast her eyes around the room) "revamping some offices, overhauling some roles. When the dust settles there will be plenty of time to talk it all over."

It wasn't plenty of time. The following week Allie knocked on the frame of Janet's open door; when Janet murmured "Yes?", Allie held up the slip of paper that had come in with the mail, in a plain business envelope, bearing Allie's name in an assistant's perky hand-printing.

"You expect me to be able to read that from here?" Janet went on—not bothering, as usual, to extend to Allie the elaborate courtesy she expected to be handled with herself.

"You don't recognize it?" Allie struggled to hold control of her voice.

"'Fraid not."

"'We at Green Spaces Corporate work hard to support our branch offices, which do the vital field projects,' blah blah blah, things they say but don't mean . . . 'We regret to inform you that due to recent feedback and budget cuts, we have made the difficult decision to *eliminate. Your. Position.*'" Allie shook the letter once, hard, and it snapped in her hand like a flag in the wind. "I *am* this office. Where will you find someone to do everything I do? At the salary I do it at?"

Janet was unmoved. "Actually, remember my friend Sabine? Who interned last year? Recent graduate? Needs to gain some experience, is willing to volunteer her time, is asking a buck a year for tax reasons. This is a nonprofit, it's not like the office is made of money, you know? If you needed more money, you should have been looking for new work anyway, a long time ago."

Allie swallowed tears. "But I love—"

"Yeah, everyone loves something. You get bad advice for just that reason. People want their work to affirm them. But work isn't built for that, you know? Work isn't made to be loved. It won't love you back. My advice? You want to be loved, get a dog."

Janet set her latte down—a disposable cup, Allie couldn't help noticing—on Allie's geode coaster. The hollow at the bottom of the cup sounded a crisp tap on the surface. Behind and above Janet's yellow head, on top of a metal file tower, the *Phalaenopsis euro*, which Allie had carefully watered every other Friday for years, nodded in the breath of the air conditioner vent. Allie kept her eyes focused on the petals of the orchid. The lines blurred, wavered, but by force of will she kept the image sharp.

Later that week Allie was to remember the color of the orchid, the exact magenta pink of its petals, when the color appeared before her again, this time in two straight small wet lines: an equals sign tipped on its back, a pair of towers destined for destruction, or rather the twin lights shooting high into the fog in commemoration of a way of life that had had its glories, true, but could no longer, in view of the situation, be sustained.

She called Jack the next evening. He told her he was sitting on the balcony at his new place in Nashville. A faint twang of guitar strings sounded in the background. He'd been trying to write lyrics, he said.

He sounded surprised to hear from her, still more surprised to be told what she was telling him. "What do I want you to do? Why ask me? I would have thought that was up to you."

"Well, it's yours too. Ours."

"Nothing is 'ours' anymore."

"This is."

"Well, I give you my share in it."

Allie counted silently to ten. Jack waited.

"Meaning I'm on my own with this," Allie interpreted, correctly.

"You're strong. I believe in you," Jack said at length.

Allie hung up. She knew this kind of support, knew exactly what it was worth.

She found a new job right away, an administrative assistant position at a trendy dentist's office in downtown Charleston, a place with its walls painted black like a club's, the same trance music jittering from the speakers. She had quit by the following Monday: it had taken only a few days to figure out that the office was scamming patients, charging for treatments it hadn't delivered, recommending expensive superfluous work, administering "laser therapy" that was hardly more than flashing lights and theater. That week Allie put the blue house in Enterprise Hills on the market. She sent out handfuls of applications, set up some interviews, and, working against a sense of heaviness in her muscles and her skull, followed up ads in the *Post and Courier* to find a studio apartment for herself.

The new place, a loft over the garage of a dandelion-yellow Victorian gingerbread place off St. John's Avenue, was owned by an energetic grandmotherly woman who occupied the main house. An illustrator of children's books, Violet was delighted to be bringing in the modest rent Allie could offer.

"As long as you don't put meat scraps in the compost, darling, we'll be fine," Violet said, smiling as she tucked Allie's white envelope with the small security deposit into her apron pocket.

Allie wondered if Violet might make a good confidante. The children's books, the quaint house, the sweet garden, led her to pigeonhole Violet as a sentimentalist: fresh rosebuds, doilies, Lady Grey tea, that kind of thing. Then Allie invited her over for a drink. Violet smiled and asked for whiskey on the rocks. Allie learned that Violet had worked for more than two dozen publishers since retiring from her day job in administration at a charter school. Violet had had no family of her own, had saved up considerably and invested wisely, had become familiar with contract law in the process of learning to ask for what her work was worth. Her warmth, her triumph, washed over Allie like a wave, pulled her low.

Allie's loss of the Green Spaces job came bubbling up out of her before she could think. Next, in a rush like a wave of nausea, out tumbled the truth of her pregnancy: worse and worse, Allie thought; no way will she let me live here now.

Then it emerged that Violet had been a volunteer doorway guard at a downtown clinic in Atlanta in the early eighties, when Allie herself had been only a small girl. Violet had given up the work after a few years of it, not so much, Violet quickly assured Allie, from a change of heart as from a lack of time.

"I'm not here to tell you what to do," Violet confirmed; Allie heard a false note in Violet's voice but couldn't have said why.

"I wish someone would," Allie admitted. Violet looked puzzled and offended; Allie then described Jack's indifference and self-indulgence, his unearned sense of *wu wei*. Sympathy and irritation replaced Violet's confusion.

"In general men tend to be useless," Violet asseverated. Thinking of Jack and only of Jack, Allie couldn't but agree.

"What do you want to do?" Violet persisted, and together the women sketched out a plan. Violet would keep the rent lower than normal for Allie for up to a year after the birth: "It isn't as though I *need* the money, darling." Allie would do light gardening and odd jobs, saving Violet "just boatloads, in this old rattletrap: you can't imagine what I pay a year to contractors." They could share cooking sometimes, she suggested, "although you don't have to if you don't want." Mainly, Violet would let her stay and would charge only nominal rent.

"You'll have time to figure things out," Violet comforted her, "plenty of time."

Not fourteen days later Allie began to bleed. At first it felt like a relief; she thought she might let things run their course. Yet she never felt cramps. The flow simply continued, a red line through her days. When she mentioned it at her next checkup, the midwife's eyes went wide.

"No, it's okay," Allie said. "If it won't live, it won't. That's just nature. It happens sometimes. I'm not worried about it."

"I'm worried about *you*," the nurse said. "Hemorrhaging isn't a non-issue. Let's get it checked out."

Allie checked herself into the hospital. A blood clot had formed in her cervix, placing pressure on the placenta. The consulting doctor recommended a simple procedure that would heal Allie and make sure the baby—she said *baby*—was saved, if that was what Allie wanted.

Was it what she wanted? she asked Allie. Her mouth formed a flat line, communicating no emotion, no slant.

Allie felt small, irrelevant. Who and what was she, she asked herself, to be wanting things, not wanting things? She asked the doctor how urgently the decision needed to be made. The doctor's eyes narrowed, and she sighed.

"Obviously, the sooner the better," the doctor said.

Allie asked again: how soon? Meaning, not saying: If I take time to think will I die? Will my thinking have killed me and the little amphibian too? She laid her hands flat on the strange blanket, its breath-mint color, its cotton pilled from many washings, to wait for the answer.

There was time, the doctor told her, but not much. They would leave the room, would come back in a couple of hours: doctor first, technician after, like a hawk followed through the marsh by an egret.

Allie's eyes slid closed. She lay there she had no idea how long, not awake, not sleeping, aware of the room, aware of cold air on her cheeks, a loop of plastic on her wrist, faint beeps, the spinning alienation of a strange bed in a strange city—Charleston wasn't her hometown; her hometown was the place she had left with Jack, a nowhere between Raleigh and Richmond off I-85 in the shadow of old-growth pine forest: the Walmart-and-Lowe's side of town, the

Jack-in-the-Box and Checkers side, the mall side; not the fountain-garden, stone-walled subdivision, green golf course side.

Was there a way from the wrong side to the right side for her; would there ever be? Did she have the sides marked out correctly on the map in her mind? Did the map in her mind match the map in fact? On which side of the map, anyone's map, lay the pool in which the little creature swam between her hipbones?

Allie didn't remember sleeping, but when she woke her head felt clear. The doctor looked the question at Allie, and Allie nodded.

"I want it."

*

Allie's body became an exoplanet, an unfamiliar world. She developed capacities she wasn't sure how to classify: subhuman, superhuman, inhuman? She could smell microbiomes; she could taste insincerity. She could hear, like a radio transmission, what to eat when; could feel the proteins sliding into her bloodstream, building the mysterious presence. She had thought a host organism should seem defeated, overthrown, consumed. Now she felt surprise at her unthought-of power. A lioness, an apex predator—shaping the web, yes, but beneficently, splendidly.

Tautness and softness counterbalanced themselves in her. There formed in her an estuary, a quiet habitat, a whole ecosystem.

The little creature grew slowly out of its tadpole tail, out of its alien elongation, into mammalian recognizance. In Allie's dreams the birth took place bloodlessly: little creature transposing itself through her abdominal wall; paranormal, painless caesarean. Sometimes it emerged already five or six years old. Sometimes it sported scales or talons. One time a tawny griffin slid forth, seven pounds, perfectly formed, with velvet paws and small white wings.

In another dream the child, this time human, was stolen from her and she leapt into the driver's seat of a car to find it; when she caught the kidnapper, a hairy convict dressed in only the lower half of a prison jumpsuit, she branded him on his bare chest with a red cattle iron and woke to a smell of sizzling flesh that was really only the smell of Violet's coffeepot. The villain's scream became, for a moment, her own until she rose from the water of sleep.

All summer Allie trimmed azaleas and hydrangeas, thinned daffodil bulbs, spread mulch, planted impatiens. One August day, it was already too hot to work by ten. The heat shortened Allie's breath, hobbled her steps. A tightening of muscle began at her left hipbone and spread around her pelvis. She parked the wheelbarrow under the fire escape, letting the work-rounded ends of the wooden handles slide one after the other out of her sweat-slick palms. The tightness receded, then returned, spreading from her sacrum into both hips, down her thighs and away.

She sat in the shade of the spreading oak for a moment, in a folding camp chair left there by Violet for the purpose, but the weight of her belly pushed her backward into the chair at an awkward angle. Her discomfort rose sharply. She stood again and walked in little circles.

She wanted her room, her bed, but couldn't face the thought of the stairs. Her belly seemed to weigh half again as much as the rest of her body. A pulse of fear like a shadow of hawk's wings passed over her. She made her way to Violet's screen door, avoided the place where the wire mesh cutout had begun to fray at the edge. The black plastic latch gave at her touch. Allie swung the inner door open.

The kitchen, at midmorning, lay full of greyish gloom. Light filtered through a lace-lined window over the sink; a cloud passed, darkening it, as Allie entered. Once her eyes adjusted, Allie noticed Violet's sink cluttered with last night's dinner dishes, this morning's teacup and pinwheel plate on the counter. The coffeepot sat cold at the side of the range. Otherwise, there was no sign of Violet: maybe she was working.

Allie walked around to the back office: turquoise walls, rolltop desk, typewriter, Macintosh with large monitor; easel, paint jars, pastels; landslide of art books, newspapers, periodicals, old printer's proofs, new sketch pads. No Violet. The vintage pickup truck and the bicycle nestled side by side in the gravel drive. She must be upstairs.

But at this hour Violet was almost always working. Images from television, of elder women in billowing nightgowns being hoisted on gurneys, filled Allie's head. What if—? Allie didn't want to think about what she would do, how lost she herself would be, if something happened to Violet. She passed through the living room—fringed drapes, velveteen upholstery, polished wood, porcelain behind glass—grasped the newel post, fixed her foot in the center of the carpet runner, and began to pull herself up the stairs.

Seven steps on each passage, one turn at the landing, yet Allie had to stop four times in the process: how absurd. As she lay curled on the landing, she could only make herself keep moving by reminding herself that Violet was missing, might be ill, might be in trouble, had to be found. And now Allie too—but she knew she shouldn't try to drive herself to the hospital, and she couldn't leave without her phone, which she'd left upstairs. For both their sakes, for all their sakes, she at least had to get the phone.

Allie had heard a contraction described as a pain or a stab but what it really felt like was an exercise, an exercise without end. The center of her body had become a runner's calf or a gymnast's arm; the muscle had cramped but the cramp was everything and as soon as it left it came back again, endlessly back, until Allie was no longer even a single muscle being strengthened by use but a rag being wrung out again and again, hot and limp and motionless.

When she reached the top, she found herself at the end of a long hallway. She had been upstairs in Violet's house once before, when Violet had been giving her vintage sheets to be remade into receiving blankets. The whole of her life refashioning itself around this weight, this ache.

At the top of the stairs Allie had to stop again. The curtains here, substantial in drape and heft, were made to cocoon sleep or illness. Illness—but Violet was so healthy, so active. But things could hit people so suddenly. Allie had to find her. Allie seemed to be stepping now through thick mud, though the pine boards shone with polish and breathed a faint scent of oil soap. This was absurd, absurd. Allie had to laugh, and did so, loudly. The sharp bark rang down the corridor, and Allie fell to her hands and knees.

She heard the warm splash before she felt it. The warmth on her thighs seemed to be coming from somewhere else. Her fingertips pointed toward Violet's bedroom door, the door at the end of the hall, but that was as far as Allie could advance. It was through her fingertips that she felt the vibration in the floorboards, the vibration of footsteps, of the door opening and then slamming again, of the old rotary dial jangling, the shrillness of its demand, the urgency.

"Yes, please, it's my tenant"—Violet was fine, then, but how about this tenant? It was as if Allie had never heard the word before, couldn't recall its meaning—and then she could hear nothing at all because of the noise, a sound like a kettle whistling, but the coffeepot had been cold; a train coming, but the tracks were miles away; a noise that stretched on and on, higher and higher and swallowed her, *was* her, subsumed her body and all its sensations: she burst, a pop and a surge like nothing she had imagined, and then she heard a little thud, and a wail like a crow's call, and then silence.

Allie felt a wave of relief like breath after a brush with drowning. Instinctively she reached down. Where—? Where was—? She felt a tug.

Violet, in jeans and t-shirt, knelt behind her. Violet held something violet in her hands. Violet said, "I'm so sorry." Violet handed her, tenderly, a little something wrapped in a towel. A little wet slippery something with eyes and a nose and a mouth like a doll's, but indigo blue as the egret's lake. A little body which, all the while the EMTs were turning and lifting and hooking up tubes and wires and loading her and it—her and *her*—onto the gurney, into the ambulance—she held and held and held, repeating over and over, until her throat and tongue ran dry, *Please let her be okay, please let her be okay, please let her be okay*, pressing the little body close and closer to her until they gently pulled it away and even then reaching out as if holding the little body still, as if not knowing what on earth else, any longer, her hands and arms were for.

Jack

He couldn't say how he had lost Allie's favor. And once it was gone, he couldn't give a good reason for staying with her. They had gone around and around, night after night, until Jack understood how she felt and decided he had burdened her enough.

He rambled through a utility room drawer until he found the key to the gray Cadillac he hadn't touched in months. He eyed the rust lining the wheel wells and then unlocked the car and got in and cast up a vague wish that the engine would start. It coughed and spat and turned over. He tried again. This time it roared to monstrous mechanical life. Soon he was ripping his way down the silver zipper of the state road toward the highway out of Charleston, headed back to Nashville in June, while all around him the hills breathed like women in green dresses. The wind pressed down the grass with the insistence of a kiss. How could the place where he had become who he was be anything but kind to him? He would find someone new before long.

*

Days later, he sat on the beech-shaded balcony of his new roommate's mid-rise in a gentrified neighborhood near Vanderbilt, twisting the frets of his guitar and imagining that he was thinking publishable thoughts about American exceptionalism. In truth he was only remembering a fight he'd had with Allie, in which she had argued him out of a belief in his own illusive personal exceptionalism but then had made it clear that she still expected him to live as if he bought that lie. Against her claims that he should get a real job, should pay rent, he laid the claim of his art, a claim to uninterrupted, protected time: the kind of tribute the goddess deserved, a desert that the commercial market would never, never understand.

You imagine yourself as a poet, she'd said to him, a frown twisting her beautiful golden face, *but you're missing the mark, you're wasting the real talents you do have in a chase after ones that you don't*, and he'd replied *Oh really? What real talents am I wasting then?* Her mouth had gone flat in a way he couldn't interpret. *Salesmanship*, she'd said, *persuasion.*

He had no idea what she meant by that, or he had chosen not to understand. Now on the balcony, though, as the breeze and the sound of cars filled his ears again, he remembered a moment on the road when he propped the wheel on his knee to roll down the driver's-side window with its ancient hand-rolled crank. As the window dropped, a gust of hay-scented wind like wild fingers had pushed his hair about in several directions at once. A thought without a body had drifted across his mind then but had not rested there. Now the thought returned to roost.

The thought was this: Allie had never really wanted him around. She had been glad enough to find a warm body in her bed at the end of a stressful day of crusading, but anyone could have given her that. His body, as he understood it, was just a machine he rode around in. His voice, his talk, his stream of language, was who he was to himself. Now he understood all these words of his to be meretricious patter, a veneer of intellectualism without its substance: persuasion, mere salesmanship.

Although he already had a Ph.D.—well, *most* of one—Jack for the first time proposed to himself that all his previous training might be useless. What could he do now to be useful? Jack resolved to apply to a new program at the university right away: tomorrow, definitely, or by next week at the latest. Next, he decided, without wasting a moment's time, he'd start a mindfulness practice. He put down the guitar, went in, shut the sliding door of the balcony, and lay down on the tapestry blanket, which now covered a battered and slightly musty brown microfiber couch—there was no bed in the spare room and Ben, the student who was subletting to him, had said up front he had no plans to acquire one.

Jack closed his eyes. He tried to center his mind. First, he saw darkness. Next, small spirals whirling at the edges of vision. Afterimages, parhelions, burnt in. The midday glare crept through the blinds. With a grunt of anger Jack stood up and shut them and lay down again. *No, sit up,* said a little voice in the back of his brain. He crossed his legs. Closed his eyes. Tried to center his mind. This time he tried picturing something. A lotus, naturally. But what sprang to mind was first one lily pad and then a whole pondful, each as long as his forearm, each supporting a flower the size and shape of his outspread hands placed together. Curling white petals, obscenely pert seedpod. Allie in his bed later, as pale and spreading as the flower. No. Empty. Empty mind. Lotus. The lilies came back. Empty the mind. Come on. The mind. The lily. The flow of the deep green water, in which the lilies' roots were mired, bore him solemnly away.

Try something else. His gaze traveled up and out the window. A cloud, good. Better. Obscure, gleaming; grey at the center, edged with glare. The glare was too bright. He squinted. This is stupid, he told himself. I'm getting nowhere. His neck craned back; his crown hit the wall. Popcorn ceiling, fan creaking lazily around its flywheel, pendulating to one side and then the other: he imagined its center as the sun's dark circle left on his corneas after staring too long.

Once more he closed his eyes, pictured a lotus. Now. Soft azalea pink. Sun on the green leaves. Floating in pure water. No real water was that blue; he saw the blue of water bottles banked for sale in a convenience store fridge. But then on the mirror-like surface there flashed the wings of an egret, all curved neck and wingspan, a dart of light. His eyes flew open. He scrambled to his feet, fumbled for a notebook, a pencil. Sight, flight: a good one, don't lose it. He scrawled down a few lines, then stopped.

He stared out the window: commuter cars flashed by, mirror-bright on the afternoon road. He wanted to go on, but when he looked back at the page it was empty, dry. The short, penciled lines looked awful, adolescent; he couldn't remember why they had seemed so good a moment ago. Truth hurt. He wanted some weed, but Allie wouldn't have liked the smell, but who cared now.

Blank moments passed. A thought occurred to him. He ripped the page from the notebook and tore it to shreds and flushed the shreds down the rusty-bowled toilet. Then he clattered down the stairs and unlocked the old bike he'd just bought secondhand down by the college. He pedaled down to the package store and bought all the cheap vodka that would fit in the panniers. Back at the house, he hauled the panniers up to the kitchenette. He wedged a few bottles into the freezer between bags of tater tots and frozen pizzas. The rest he lined up on the counter like toy soldiers. He searched the cabinets for clean cups. Finding nothing, he took from the pantry an extra-long green plastic straw, still in its paper wrapper from a chain coffee place, and unwrapped it.

Holding the straw between two fingers like a chopstick, he wrenched the red metallic cap of the first bottle and heard the threads of the seal give way with a complicated, satisfying crack like a spine being realigned by a chiropractor. He set down the cap with deliberation on the counter, placed the straw in the bottleneck, and carried the resulting setup with him to the brown couch. There he sat scrolling through bad news for a while, until it occurred to him that the couch was low enough, and the straw tall enough, that he could perhaps set the bottle on the floor and still continue to drink. He tested the thought, flattening himself as nearly facedown as he could manage while leaving one eye free for scrolling and reading. He read until his eyelid felt microwaved to limpness. Then he read some more, forcing the lids up and up again until sheer exhaustion forced them down. Even then he continued to reach out to the green straw for sips until consciousness eluded him.

He woke to pain. Morning glare, sheen of sour sweat all down his neck and torso. He looked in the mirror and pronounced himself pathetic. He couldn't go on like this. For one thing, rent was steep here. For another, he couldn't face the futility of another night spent like that. After all, Jack told himself, he cared, he really cared; he loved things so much it hurt. A fence of barbed-wire irony was the only boundary fierce enough to protect the soft warm trembling creature that was his heart, curled inside the fence for refuge. The creature demanded protection, its pathos its only justification. Jack resolved to build a stronger preserve, a more invulnerable habitat.

Time to get to work, he said to himself. He showered, standing resolutely upright in the rusty tub. If Allie is doing it, so can I, he continued to coach himself, as he soaped his hair with something that smelled like melons. But this is about growing up. Becoming a man in the world. No rites of passage, that's what's wrong with me. I should have been made to sleep in the underbrush. Survive with a knife and my wits. Eat crickets alive. Lost all that. Chased it away with the native inhabitants. Own damn fault. (Jack could never forget that he had had an ancestor in the colony at Jamestown, Virginia: a fact that occasioned him as much pain as it had given his grandparents pride.) Still. Their genes. A man like them. Even if they were evil, I still came from people who could starve on a rock for two winters and still raise up crops and a family, descendants and a social contract, from destitution. From nowhere. Now those were adults. It's time I adulted. Patient application. Obedience of body to brain. Jack realized he had been absentmindedly soaping his hair for several minutes now. He rinsed off and stepped out and realized he had nothing with which to dry himself. Naked, he ran across the hall and used the tapestry blanket and dressed himself before hanging the blanket on the balcony rail to dry. *Now,* he self-coached, *time to earn the right to continue existing.*

He biked downtown to the coffee shop where he had found Ben's number on the bulletin board. Its handmade benches, artfully warped, gleamed with polish and care. Its hand-painted murals spoke to him of culture, vibrancy. He did not think of either fact as an advertisement or of himself as its target market. He bought a triple espresso that cost several dollars and took out his notebook again, this time to record job postings, contact numbers. He stepped outside, sat on a glossy bench, and made some calls. Now he need only wait.

He locked his bike to the rack, walked down to the Frist Museum, and stared at Turner paintings for a while. The smudgy strokes, the contrasts, cheered him. Yes, Jack thought, Turner knew the way to see the world. Light and darkness, inexplicable fires, stormy seas. Danger and trauma. Jack left the cool of the museum and stepped back into the light and heat of the sidewalk.

There hove into his mind's eye—in his own handwriting, tucked away in his pocket, but to him as visible, and as glaring, as the neon signs of Broadway Street at night—the signposts of his own likely near future. *Barista, bartender; art handler, tutor; assistant, intern.* No fishing in a midnight sea for him, no brave rescues from burning buildings. No carving out a living from chalk hills, no riding on dusky chargers. No more opportunities for heroism.

Jack considered his education, considered everything he knew about police crimes and about the history of injustice: could he, for the hope of living for a few moments once in some thrilling atmosphere of smoke and fire, stand the mindlessness of that training, the brutal physicality of it, the boredom? Could he follow orders given him, watch others perpetrating aggressions small and large—in short, could he get through it, in the hope that in some obscure corner of some city or town it would be granted to him to save someone, do something noble?

Where would he begin? Who would he call? Jack had no idea. It was hot and humid, and he was tired and bored. He walked on a little farther until he found a poured concrete paling around a trucked-in garden of dirt and mulch, planted in tidy rows with plumes of feather grasses. He sat down on the paling, which was shaded by an overhang of more concrete, and scrolled through missed calls.

One from the tutoring service: he wasn't going to answer that. A hatred of teaching had been one of his main discoveries in graduate school. One from the business office that had been looking for an assistant: too many early mornings. One from the coffee shop: same. Five a.m. and Jack were not friends.

He wished, fleetingly, that he had kept in better touch with more of the people he had known when he lived here before, when he had gone first to college and then to graduate school at the university. People who graduated from here were not supposed to end up in this sort of fix. Yet here he was.

If only he could go back, could start again. Nostalgia took him. He remembered in particular one concert, one evening: he had gone to check out this wild gathering at some famous musician's house—his buddies Hank and Terence, who now both toured with bands, had known the singer-songwriter, had worked for him as unpaid interns on his crew. At the gate of the hedged-in yard of the mansion it had turned out that security didn't want the interns there, but Hank and Terence had fast-talked the guard—had possibly plied him with the goods; Jack had scrupulously not paid close attention to what was going forward—anyway, they had made it inside, and the evening had reached its high point for Jack when he found himself floating and floating on an air mattress in a pool filled with rose petals and surrounded by candles, holding the hand of a nearly naked stranger on a nearby float who couldn't stop giggling, and certainly the goods had come from somewhere because both he and the woman on the float had been high as kites in a tropical storm.

Jack had never seen her again. And, anyway, all that was over now. He was determined to stay clean or at least off the harder substances, which for him meant staying away from the music scene too. Even so, it would certainly all be dredged up in whatever dreary background check would accompany the effort to be accepted into the ranks of Real American Heroes: so Jack rejected this possibility. He rose off the concrete bench and continued down Ninth Avenue, making for the green space behind the museum.

As he walked back the way he had come, past the tall white sweeps of wall and window, he ruminated. From a major in music at Vanderbilt he had switched to a major in English at the last possible moment. He had done a Ph.D. program but had quit three-quarters of the way through writing the dissertation, over a disagreement with his advisor, the substance of which he couldn't now recall. He had lived with Serena, his undergraduate girlfriend, most of that time, before meeting Allie; he had flowed along with that relationship, had even been engaged to her, had balked only when it became clear that Serena was serious about all the middle-class economics of marriage, the wedding registry, the hard gold rings, the pillows and thick towels, the curtains and sheets and napkins and tablecloths, the heavy, heavy furniture. He was sure of few things but was certain he did not want to live like that, while she had been quite sure that she did.

Lack of clarity had been his enemy, that and a series of terrible trips, the last one of which left him hospitalized at the end of senior year, every vein burning. He lay there missing convocation, knowing it was going on, seeing in his mind's eye his classmates crawling in slow gowned rows across the platform. At that moment he had made a strong decision, rare for him: He couldn't continue to live among his current friends and yet also say *no* to the things they enjoyed together. This was the only thing he had known for sure as he lay there in St. Thomas's in midtown. That fall he had cut his hair and bought new clothes and applied to the graduate program in English with a vision of being the next Robert Penn Warren. A few semesters of rejection notices, secondary literature, and interdepartmental contretemps had burned this out of him too. He had slogged along through sheer inertia until he had come to a point when the work no longer seemed worthwhile. He had flowed past the point like water past a rock and had been borne by the current all the way to this place, here, now.

Where was this place? He stood, confused, in the shadow of a stories-tall parking garage where none used to be, a decade ago. The heat staggered him: by now it was almost one p.m. He was looking for the Flying Saucer, and by turning in the opposite direction and walking several blocks he happened upon it and went inside and asked for a table for two. From there, he thought, he would call his former advisor to catch up and then maybe even, who knew, Serena: it didn't seem impossible. All the lightbulbs on their long wires reached down generously toward him, their filaments shaped like the nibs of fountain pens, ready to disclose secrets: dozens of little touchpoints of optimism.

Jack ordered a Saint Arnold and a chickpea burger. He opened his notebook and made a list of his positive traits: He could hold up his side of a conversation. He could repair bicycles. He was a respectable vegan home cook. He could discuss multivalent ideas into the small hours, including his self-taught expertise in climatology, provided he didn't get too bored or annoyed or drunk. He could teach a class if necessary but didn't want too much to do with actual students. He could—sometimes—write a decent poem.

He stopped writing and scratched his hair with the green metal band around the pink eraser and smelled the pencil's cedar scent. He could (he wrote it down) wash dishes. He could compose and, to an extent, edit papers. He had dealt in a minor way in weed once, had learned that he had an eye for the likely client and the vulnerable moment, but he wanted no more of that because of the risk factor.

What could someone like him do for money without feeling dead inside? Who was he kidding? Would they even take him back at the university: a failed scholar, a washout? He threw the pencil down on the notebook; a stranger at the next table frowned at the *pock* it made.

Back at the sublet, Jack's phone rang. He saw the number on caller ID and went into his room and closed the door. Before answering, he picked up his guitar and laid it in his lap. As he answered, he strummed a few chords to soothe himself.

"Are you listening?" said Allie's voice.

"Yeah, just doing a little songwriting," Jack said, convinced as he said it that this was indeed what he should do with his life from here on out. If it were meant to be, he would find a way.

"I need you to listen carefully." Allie explained her situation. When Jack asked for clarity, she simply groaned.

"All I want is to make sure I understand. You're sure it's ours?" Jack asked.

"Whose else would it be? Are you accusing me of cheating?"

"No, I suppose not. But—I mean, you're sure you're . . . ? It's not . . . ? Like, you didn't just miss a cycle?"

"I've been to the doctor. I've had a blood test, an ultrasound. It's not a missed cycle."

Around and around they went. Jack finally told Allie that he would support her whatever she decided to do. For some reason, this caused her to cut the call short.

When Jack came back to the main room, Ben had flipped on the television to reruns of nineties sitcoms. Jack stayed to watch not because he enjoyed television—he enjoyed complaining about the banality of television—but in this case television happened to be on and it seemed good to be near another human, doing the things the other human was doing.

Gold shifted toward blue and then black in the windowpanes. The men ordered sub sandwiches, which arrived late, soggy and limp. They ate them anyway, courting food poisoning, and then also ordered and split a pizza. Several colorful pull-tab cans seemed to mushroom up on to the counters already empty, so distant seemed the agency that had drained them.

Jack recalled emerging at some stage from a cloud of bloat and sloth into a fountain of mental energy. He pounded the tempered glass of Ben's coffee table with the flat of a sweaty hand—with each slap the palm stuck and smacked with the slight slurp of its rising. Jack was not clear enough in mind to tell that this sound was not the cause of Ben's disgusted look but, rather, Ben's well-founded fear that the table might shatter under Jack's onslaught—slap, slap, slap, as Jack demanded that they turn off the fucking Big Bang or whatever and watch the debates, fuck yeah the presi*den*tial debates, yeah man it was a travesty but *cui bono*, man, who *benefited* from their ignoring the spectacle? Fuck right not them, where was *their* benefit?—slap, rattle of fragile bottles, uneasy shifting of the nearly empty pizza box out of which Ben now liberated the last slice. As he did so Ben stole a sidelong look at Jack, who this time saw in the look both disgust and fear, which he chose to ignore.

Ben scooped up the remote and flipped to the debates. Yet soon the debates could barely be heard anyway, over Jack's snarls and curses. Before long Jack spiked the remote into the couch cushions and then snatched it up and shut the screen off. The two men then poured more shots and smoked more weed to get back on an even keel. Jack stuck two twenties in Ben's freezer where one of the bottles of vodka had made its tunnel between bags of frozen foods, apparently forgetting that the bottles had been his own to start with. Then, in the afterglow of his own act of generosity, Jack noticed Ben's growing sullenness, his lack of response. Jack slapped the younger man on the shoulders; Ben shrugged Jack's hand away, ambled to his room, and shut the door. Jack went to bed, first stopping by the bathroom to brush his teeth with elaborate drunken meticulousness. He set his phone alarm for five-thirty.

Jack woke to pain. Oh God his head: why, why. His eyes could barely open. He cursed and imprecated them, shut them against the glare, forced them open again. Necessary pain: today absolutely had to go well. Oh hell: last night Jack had left the new shirt crumpled at the bottom of Ben's washing machine. He washed it again and, while the shirt dried, took a punishingly hot shower. Shirtless, he made coffee in the French press and eggs in the skillet. Then he swallowed a few of Ben's ibuprofen, stole a little of his Visine, and finally put on the new dress shirt. The American RediSmart Temporary Employment Services Agency Network had better get ready for him, he thought, and called a Lyft to take him to his interview.

This interview, as it turned out, couldn't have been more of a cake walk. Behind a metal desk in a cubicle a weary-looking high-school-principal type of woman asked him why he wanted to work as (she squinted, took off her wire-rimmed glasses, pressed a manicured fingernail to his application) "let's see here, an . . . administrative assistant?"

"I don't, really," Jack threw out casually. "I just need money to stay in the city so I can be connected here. What I really want to do is write. To be a singer-songwriter?"

The woman's face had lit up. "Oh! Say more." The romanticism of it won her instantly. She made up her mind that she wanted to help him almost before she knew she had done so. He left two hours later with a manila folder full of schedules which he slid into his messenger bag. He would look at them later. He didn't have to be anywhere else until tomorrow morning. Now he threw himself onto a bus going downtown. When it stopped on Broadway Street, he leapt from step to curb—no idea what time it was, didn't matter—swam through the white-hot humid haze, the sidewalk a river of it, into the dark cool doorway of a pub.

He tested, surreptitiously, the feel of his back pocket: the new wallet swung there quietly, causing a little hitch to the lift of the fabric. Inside, the new card waited quietly to know what he would ask of it, like the genie in the lamp. Jack felt a relief beyond words, a sense of belonging in the dim smoky room with its tall windows and potted palms and plantation blinds: the only real church, his blood hummed, for a soul like his. He took a seat at the bar, ordered a whiskey on the rocks. There was never any need for him to have been a washout; there was, at this moment, no need for him ever to be one again, no need for anyone to know what had happened. He could snap right back from his Dionysian life into his Apollonian one. Nobody knew him here anymore; nobody would have to know who he had once been. The past was a fever dream; this was the future.

Three places down, there sat a woman tracing circles around the base of her glass. Jack checked his watch, another new purchase, so as not to be caught staring at her. Although it was midafternoon, she had on a black lace cocktail dress, demure enough not to be a sales pitch, flirtatious enough that he might have a shot. She looked about his age and had night-shadow hair like Allie's, a string of pearls around her throat. In front of her on the counter there lay a small sparkling wallet, the kind with a wrist loop that dangled from one corner. She stopped tracing circles and started twisting the wallet's clasp open and closed, looking at the license inside as if to check that the face on it still matched her own.

The drink in front of her was two-thirds gone, so

Jack signaled the bartender and sent another one her way. Told of this, she looked over and returned Jack's smile. So he moved down to the chair next to hers, all according to plan.

"Old fashioned? Classy." And immediately regretted the words out of his mouth: the very fact of the compliment was patronizing, the drink name making it still worse, and the use of the word *classy*, he could hear his mother telling him in his ear, denoted anything but class. True, it had worked before. But it had been awful, and the result had been awful, and here he was, true to pattern, being awful again.

The woman blushed, though, and smiled. His feelings seemed to him irrelevant, at least to the degree that they were invisible to her. The attempt was working, at least so far.

"Thanks," she said, raising her glass an inch or two. "'Prechiate it."

"Long day?" He leaned a degree closer.

She rolled her eyes, but she was smiling. "You've no ah*dea* how long. You?"

"Endless. But over now, finally." He smiled a slow deliberate smile of relief, suggestive of more relief to come.

"Here's to the end of the day." Another slight lift of her glass. So far so good. Very good, Jack thought. Could it already be time for Swinburne? He took a breath. The lines seemed to tumble out on their own.

"'We are outcast, strayed between bright sun and

moon; / Our light and darkness are as leaves of flowers, / Black flowers and white, that perish; and the noon / As midnight, and the night as daylight hours.'"

Her eyelids flew wide. He shrugged and closed his briefly: no big deal, this is how I talk all the time.

"You write that?" she asked, almost red in the face now. He considered telling her yes.

"Wrote my dissertation on it," he said instead, trying to look modest. Her face changed at the word *dissertation*: a lower degree of delight, but still she was pleased, he thought.

"Wow. Must have been a lot of work."

He nodded.

"What made you interested in doing that?"

This brought him up short. What had made him interested? So long ago he had begun, so long ago walked away. At the corner of his vision something pale flicked into view, like the wing of an egret. When he turned his head—toward her, never away—he saw it had been only folded napkins on a tray, borne up by a server's outstretched hand.

"I was after . . . a certain sense of life," he said, feeling with his tongue the words' smoothness, their grandiosity: but also feeling through the air-conditioned coolness, through the light on the leaves, through the glint of ice in her drink, that the atmosphere was working in his favor. He felt he would be able to carry off what was coming next.

"A sense that life is fleeting and complex and

marvelous. That in the little time that's granted to us we should be able to do what we find most compelling, most—glorious. A sense of—of glory."

She was compelling, she was glorious. Jack was leaning so far toward her that he felt vertiginous, a meteorite pulled by her gravity. He wanted to ask her to go somewhere alone with him—the card loomed again into his mind; they could go wherever they wanted—but to push the issue now would be to jeopardize it; wait, wait. Look. She had been more pleased by what he just said than by anything else that had come before. Her face, already a sunset, had passed into starry peace: quiet, triumphant. She had him, and she knew it. She was going to make him wait, though, make him figure out whether he had her too. He thought so, at least, but he also thought that to rush it with someone like this would be to lose it. You could expect that, sometimes, still, here: people didn't move as fast as they did elsewhere.

She reached across the bar to take his hand. Gently, she smoothed her fingertips across his palm, the bases of his fingers. "No ring, no lines either."

"Married to work, you could say." What a lie, but maybe not such a lie, either. A short time ago hadn't he considered it his *work* to write poems about global warming and send them off to little magazines that would maybe, once in a while, publish one of them?

Her lips pushed out a bit. She dropped his hand. She seemed to be thinking carefully about how to say what, in her mind, had to come next. He heard in her voice an effort to keep the sound light. "Anyone—important? Before?"

"One. A while ago." He didn't, he reasoned, need to say how long a while ago.

"Kids?" It sounded as though she could barely push the syllable out: and who could blame her for feeling self-conscious, if she had the restraint to ask questions like this in the first place before getting involved? Lots of women would be in the taxi on the way to the hotel by now.

Her hesitation made him hesitant, too. At the meeting of Jack's lips was *no*—no kids, no involvement—it wasn't necessarily an untruth, if Allie had done what he expected her to do. But then, what if she hadn't? He imagined the possible future: Allie keeping—it; Allie asking him for support; this woman catching him in a lie, this woman hating him for it.

He decided quickly: "Complicated. The mom doesn't want me around. Not sure what I did wrong."

"She's—a strong person?"

"A force of nature."

"You like that in a woman, then." He still didn't know her name, he realized, now worried, as she sat studying his profile, considering his preferences.

"Yes, I suppose I do." Her smile had now spread a bit too wide. Jack wasn't sure when or how.

"I've been strong as long as I could," she said. "Longer. It's time for me to try something new."

She picked up her wallet in her other hand and made for the terrace. He considered following her, even making a scene; but what kind of person would that make him, what kind of effect would that be likely to have on her?

No way. He slammed two twenties he could scarcely spare down on the bar and strode out the door into the still brighter heat of rush hour. No romance, then, but it wouldn't be hard to find the other thing in this part of town, at any time of day, and he found it and used it and came thundering down the back fire escape of the derelict building, the iron rattling underfoot, his heart still racing. He paced up and down the blocks in the falling shade, watching magenta and orange and red and blue signs cut on and filaments flare up in marquees. Letters on the headliners stood out crisp and black against the warped cream of the lightboards. Abstractly he found himself thinking of barbed wire, of bullets, of fire. Cut something, shoot something, burn something down. The heat of his own flesh shocked him. His readiness to do violence. To whom? To—himself? No. To the woman? The women? No. To whatever threatened—whatever came close to, whatever had so hurt, so exhausted—the woman in the black lace dress. To whatever had forced her into that sad renunciation, into an endurance beyond endurance.

He. He himself. He had forced Allie. Not to bear the child, no. But to bear the consequences. Cut, shoot, burn down: himself? No. But whole forests, if necessary. To build a shelter for the soft thing, the small thing. Build it from his own bones if necessary. He had to find her, find Allie, find them, do something, something. What? The amber streetlights in rows reeled overhead; the concrete floor under him, the bars to both sides, felt like a prison. Dizzy, he stumbled (two drinks in? Three? Had he eaten today?—perhaps not: and so what?).

He walked down off Broadway and started to call himself a ride on the smartphone, but when he reached back in memory for Ben's address, it was gone. He began to walk instead, heading to the bus stop, but he soon remembered he was out of cash and so he halted where he was. But he was nowhere, and so he started walking again.

Like a bored child looking for a toy that still holds some interest Jack cast his eyes about: cinderblock apartments, cereal-box hotels—even if he could have pulled them down like toy bricks, what could he have built with them, except more of the same? No water anywhere to throw himself into, no grass on which to lie down.

Jack walked on until he found himself in front of a lattice of ironwork at the intersection of two residential blocks. Behind the lattice was a battered and scratched plastic playground, freshly floored with mulch that smelled of pine sap, the hearts of shredded trees. Jack walked around behind the slide and lay down underneath the bridge that connected it to the ladder. He fell asleep there and woke to pain and knew, when he sat up shaking the shards of broken wood out of his hair in the morning, that the pain would be his close companion from now on, that it would not leave him until it had told him what it had come to say. As his fingers combed through his hair again and again, there came a sharp jab: a splinter in his palm. He looked closely at the splinter, which had lodged in the skin near the base of his thumb, where it stung with each pulse of his heart.

Sequatchie Valley

Thus we went on like true idealists, rejecting the evidence of our senses . . .

—Henry David Thoreau

I

When Ward Tarrant decided he wanted to farm, having already chosen the westernmost edge of the nearby Sequatchie Valley for a place to take his stand, his wife Lucia had questions. She supported him, naturally. Still, she felt they might be moving too fast, on the hot May afternoon in their Birmingham apartment when Ward handed her a thick folder of real-estate paperwork bristling with sticky-flag arrows.

"*Dar gato por liebre*," Lucia said, "is what Grandma would have called this."

"*Dar gato por* what?"

"It's about the same thing as *a pig in a poke*. Meaning if you can't see it, you don't know what it's worth. How can I sign to say I'll pay for a farm I've never seen?"

"I've seen it," Ward said. "It's beautiful."

"How, though? What would it mean for me to say I'll be *co-responsible*? I haven't earned a steady salary since Quinn was born. What little we've saved is all we have. Or are likely to. For a while."

Quinn, just turned two, toddled from the children's room into the open-plan main area of their apartment. Peering into the small recycling bin beneath the bar area, he discovered a clean, empty mayonnaise jar. He crowed and began attempting to twist its lid off.

"But see?" insisted Ward. "We have to make changes. And the faster the better. Our whole life is artificial. Plastic."

Lucia looked around at their supposedly plastic life. She found it satisfying, clean, quiet: a sixth-floor, midtown condo near the Galleria, recently updated in fresh paint, granite, and hardwood. The recessed lights in the ceiling were almost not necessary, given the amount of natural light that came through the sliding balcony door. If she looked over her other shoulder she would see, through plate glass, the modest downtown skyline hunched in a smudgy blue haze.

True, the closest playground was miles away, the preschool coordinator was a snob and hard to take, and groceries cost too much. But Lucia could hardly imagine how they could be doing better, given the circumstances. She had struggled enough already; she felt she could now expect to enjoy herself a little.

"The entirety of American middle-class life is a rigged game," Ward said. "The more you play, the more you lose. The house always wins."

They had started out in a much smaller studio as newlyweds, but when Olivia was born, they decided to find a place closer to Ward's job. Now, though, with Ward fired last week from managing Archon Books in the Galleria—not only because he couldn't stomach modern publishers' ways of catering to mass appeal, but because he couldn't stop emailing the CEO massive screeds and needling links about it—any talk of saving had come to an abrupt halt. In Lucia's mind, they only had to manage not to run out of money before she and Ward figured out new jobs. But to move down the economic ladder, to make themselves poorer on purpose: this to her was unthinkable.

"Would a farm even possibly run a profit?" Lucia asked. "I keep stumbling across nightmare stories online about agricultural debt."

Lucia smoothed down her hair, not because it needed it but because her mind felt mussed. Quinn began to smack the plastic jar on the slick floorboards and cry, quivering all the way to his tangled curls, because his hand was too small to fit around the lid's top. Ward went to him and started to loosen the seal so that Quinn could spin it the rest of the way by himself. Quinn instantly quit crying, watched quietly, giggled, and reached for the jar, which Ward gave him.

"It's doable," Ward said. "I've been researching,"

which Lucia knew meant he had been tapping terms into a browser search bar.

"You never told me before that you wanted to do this," Lucia hedged. "I mean it doesn't surprise me. But, well."

"It's time to stop dreaming about the life we wish we had and start living it, you know?" Ah, here was how it must have come about, Lucia thought: In the evenings for the past year or so, the two of them would listen their way through audiobooks together while they did the dishes. Each book took them about a month to finish at that pace. Last month's book had been a brand new, chart-topping release about the devolution of American food ways—everyone, the author said, needed to eat more plants—sandwiched between a president's memoir and a physicist's classic study of the cosmos' evolution. Lucia and Ward had talked idly at the time about how cool it would be to grow their own food, how much purer and healthier, but Lucia had had no real intention of acting on this ideal. Who knew Ward had been taking it all so seriously?

"We're going to be paying how much for this?" Lucia pried open the folder and squinted at the number, which looked out of all proportion to her. Quinn's crowing, his clutching, cut into her calculations as his little fingers began to wrinkle the page. Ward took the folder back from them and closed it quietly.

"We can borrow," he told her. "For a while. It's

not that much when you divide it out and see how much we're paying per acre. And when you compare it to the lifetime cost of, my God, rent. Land today is—well, it doesn't ever go for less."

"Well, this is an—enthusiastic—amount of land," Lucia said, reopening the folder, tracing the acreage with a smoothly polished fingernail. "Acres *plural.* Can we really manage all this on our own?"

"Once we start making money, I think we can. I mean, it's a business proposition, which means risk. We'll have to hire folks to help. But until we can do that—what have people ever done? We'll manage." Ward plowed fingers through his pale hair, leaving it a tumbled but not unappealing haystack.

"Manage how exactly?"

"I'm looking into getting an organic certification. We'll earn a lot more that way, plus it's just better for the earth and for our bodies, honestly."

"Well, I agree with you there," Lucia granted. They'd been shelling out for organic applesauce packets recently, and now Quinn had discovered a cache of the packets' twirly little green tops in the recycle bin. He screeched happily and stuffed two twirly tops into his mouth at the same time.

Ward blanched and made a sound like "eck" as he wedged a finger between his child's teeth to scoop the tops out again.

"It'll be a ton of work," Ward said cheerfully, dropping the damp green tops back into the recycling with a clatter over his son's protests. "No, yucky. Not for mouths. —But then, so is what we're already doing."

Lucia smoothed her face with her hands. "Speaking of work. We really could take this slower. You could take agriculture extension classes. In the meantime, I could find a middle school that's looking."

"I don't want you to have to do that." Ward frowned.

They had had this one out before, many times. Was it worth having out again, Lucia wondered. Did she really have the strength left to wrangle a fresh pack of thirteen-year-olds already struggling with adult-sized addictions?

"What if I want to go back?"

"You don't, really."

Lucia couldn't quite bring herself to lie that the prospect of middle-school campus counseling still thrilled her the way it had when she was a student. Then it was only an ideal, an idyll. Now she knew the hard practice.

"Well, though, that's not the only use I can make of my training. Clinics need—"

"But didn't you tell me there are all kinds of barriers to—"

"Okay, just say you don't really want me to do it."

Ward shrugged in the way that meant the opposite of indifference. "I don't."

"Okay," said Lucia in the way that meant it was not really okay, but also not worth it to her to start an argument.

The steps of Olivia, five years old and constantly busy, made a crescendo in the hallway. As she bustled casually between the couch and coffee table, her skirt hem caught at the corner of the real-estate folder and pulled it off the couch's edge, splaying papers everywhere.

Lucia bent down to pick them up and sort them back into order. Olivia picked up Quinn, squeezing his chest so that his plump arms dangled over her slim ones. In one small hand Quinn held a palm-sized battery-powered music player decked with bright plastic beads.

Ward reached out and swiped the toy. "No more of this kind of thing," Ward said. "Bad for the earth. From now on only wood, wool, cotton. Toys we can compost."

Olivia gently dropped Quinn, who landed catlike on hands and feet. He bear-crawled to the bookshelf, where he began methodically to pull down one volume after another. The pages splashed open on the floorboards.

"Dad, what's compost?" Olivia asked, as Lucia quietly checked page numbers and tidied the stack.

"Old things that turn into new dirt. Vegetables, leaves, food scraps. Also, animal poop."

Olivia giggled. "Daddy, don't say poop," she admonished with delight.

"I'll say *poop* if I want to," Ward countered, and sang the monosyllable until it lost meaning. The room filled with Olivia's shrieks of laughter; Ward swept her up and plumped her down in her plastic playhouse. Quinn followed her inside. Olivia issued some instructions, and the children noisily began to make a pretend compost pile together, using all the plastic toy food they could find.

"See, there you go, we're already homeschooling," Ward laughed.

Lucia closed her eyes briefly and sighed.

"What?"

"Nothing."

"It's something."

Lucia shook her head. Strands of dark hair were falling in her face; she brushed them back again with her fingers. "You're right, it is something. What is this whole plan you seem to have already? Without ever telling me? This is the first I'm hearing about any homeschooling. How primitive do you want us to be? Are we talking *off the grid*? Are we going to have health insurance?"

Ward drew his breath in through his teeth. "Not unless we want to pay for private. We can probably afford to skip that for a few years at least, though, while we're getting on our feet. The kids have seen the doctor enough by now to last until they're teenagers, don't you think? Besides, the countryside is a healthy place. And maybe, before too long, the universal plan will finally pass . . . And then, well, yes. Maybe getting off the grid is aspirational. But I want us to experiment. To see how few unnatural resources we can get away with using. To walk lightly on the earth. To harvest our own, human power."

Lucia made another and, she felt, sincere effort to tamp down her skepticism, but she couldn't resist challenging Ward's idyll just a little more. "You didn't read the Little House on the Prairie books growing up, did you?"

"Nah. Those are girls' books." Ward stood up and stretched so that a strip of pale skin feathered with blond hair showed between his t-shirt and his belt. "But now that you mention it, there's another plus. The children will love country life. We would have a kitchen garden, and they could have their own little corner of it. They can plant and weed with you and, when they get older, fish and hunt with me. Feed the chickens, milk the goat."

"Chickens? *Goat*? You didn't already . . . ?"

"The animals come with the property."

"Who's feeding them now?"

"Neighbor. Just until the place sells."

Lucia took a moment to imagine the neighbor. She saw a jolly, rotund woman with a short haircut, sporting an Auburn sweatshirt and dowdy denim: someone kind, someone who could teach Lucia how to tend chickens and how to grow something that wasn't overpriced, pre-sprouted basil in a fancy ceramic pot.

"And we *could* homeschool. You're smart, smarter

than me. Always have been. Better grades, better test scores. Hell, you have a Master's degree. I had to go to work when—"

"You're sweet." Lucia wanted him to stop talking about the reason he had had to go to work. They had rushed to get married when she was in the first trimester of her first pregnancy, with Ward all the time claiming it was not just an old-fashioned stricture but a genuinely new depth of passion, sparked by admiration for her genius body clever enough to grow another human. Neither of them had expected her to suffer a stillbirth at thirty-five weeks. That sorrow always stood on the shelf of references between them: a volume that by common, tacit consent they didn't take down and re-open.

"Anyway. The place also comes with some secondhand equipment the previous owners couldn't sell."

Ward's face took on the half-secretive, half-proud look it wore whenever he made a unilateral decision that he expected her to love.

"We're probably never going to have another opportunity like this again," Ward said. "It's a great deal. And look, we've never really been satisfied with city life—"

"We haven't?" Lucia said.

"You complain," Ward pointed out.

"About the preschool. We can switch preschools. Olivia starts kindergarten next year anyway. That'll be free."

"And about the driving? You hate driving."

"*You* hate driving. There won't be tons more driving in the country?"

"Not city driving. No madmen, no speeders with a death wish. Lucia, okay, *I've* never really been happy in the city. You know how close the decision was, about going to my dad's place."

Around the time Ward went to college, his mother had left his father, at which point Drew Tarrant had sold the house Ward grew up in and moved to a ranch in a stunning, flower-studded valley near Yellowstone. Before he met Lucia, Ward had strongly considered moving out West to be with his father, who regularly sang the praises of his new rural life, but Drew had encouraged Ward to stay where he was and finish his degree in economics before making another big decision. And Lucia was glad he had, because otherwise they would never have met at the graduation party, and Olivia and Quinn would never have been born.

"If you want to change anything you have to start by changing yourself. I just—I feel like," and Ward stretched his chest again in the way that Lucia knew meant he was getting to the point, "we've both been becoming something artificial, something we were never meant to be, just because that's the way the city is set up to make us pretend."

He reached over to caress Lucia's hair, disarraying the cheekbone-length cut she spent an hour each morning styling and two hundred dollars a month maintaining. He cupped her cheeks with his palms, traced her closing eyelids, showed her the dark sparkling dust that flaked off on to his thumbprints.

"There's so much we have that we don't need, that we might actually be better off without. Like this—glitter. You never did any of this when we first met, and you were always beautiful without it," he said in a low voice. "I don't know, it seems to me like you just keep trying on new faces, looking for better ways to be in the world. Just like all my fake professionalism was something I put on to try to be the right way: for you, for the kids. But there has to be a way that's—I don't know. Truer. Cleaner."

He ran his fingers slowly along his wife's arm in the direction of the fine dark hairs that lined her skin. His touch traveled to her wrist and then to her palm. From the direction of the plastic playhouse clattered the noises of Olivia teaching Quinn how to stack towers of plastic food, paired with squeals of delight when they fell.

"There are deeper laws. Of nature. That if we trust them. Will make us happier."

Lucia tilted her chin up to look at the ceiling. Ward, seeing an opportunity, kissed the base of her throat softly.

"You know?"

Lucia picked up the pen and signed where the arrows pointed.

Ward scooped her into a hug, stood up still holding

her, and swung her around, his face festooned with a grin of relief.

"I can do anything as long as you're with me," Ward said. "I'm not afraid of working hard if we're in it together."

"I've never been afraid of working hard," Lucia returned, flustered but laughing. Ward should have known that she could never have made it this far otherwise.

Ward put Lucia back down gently. Olivia emerged from the plastic playhouse and tugged at Lucia's t-shirt hem with a book in her hand.

"Hansel and Gretel," Olivia demanded.

Lucia sat back down and obeyed her daughter.

Lucia's mother's mother, Asuncion, had come to Birmingham from Puerto Rico by way of Houston. Asuncion had grown up on the island and, guided by the wishes of parents who hoped she would become a nun, trained as a nurse. Once she married Eleazar, the surgeon who had most often requested her help in the operating room, he became concerned about the risks and complications of living where they did. (Lucia, imagining her grandfather from the secure vantage point of a childhood spent seated at smooth new desks or soft couches in air-conditioned rooms, always wondered if he had been unduly concerned; Lucia always believed that her life would have been essentially the same, protected and placid, regardless of where it unfolded.) Whether it made sense or not,

Eleazar paid thousands to a lawyer and an accountant to set up his affairs in the contiguous States before Asuncion delivered their child, Paula, Lucia's mother. Paula was born on the mainland; she grew up attending public schools and speaking English. Though Lucia's grandfather never quite regained the career security and the community trust he had left behind him in San Juan, he often told Paula that he considered her education to be worth any sacrifice.

In time Paula grew up to marry a cardiologist who, working at the Houston medical center in the seventies, had learned new surgical techniques that made hospital administrators in Birmingham eager to invite him to join their staff. Paula also finished medical school herself, and she went into practice as a psychiatrist, though she cut back her hours when, in the early eighties, Lucia was born.

When Lucia's father died of cancer three years after her college graduation, Paula sold the quiet red-brick place in the Birmingham suburbs where Lucia had grown up. Then she moved to the California coast to stare at the waves, sun herself, and do what she described to Lucia in rare letters as *heart work*.

Lucia had nothing to say against that. She also craved, if she were truthful with herself, a more placid and less strained way of living. After her initial resistance, she started to praise Ward in her mind for having seen that craving and acted on it, though she still would not admit that to him out loud. As she put the children to bed on the evening of the day they'd finalized the farm purchase, she scrolled through her phone and imagined herself as the long-haired woman walking in a flowing pale dress, in pictures of flowered meadows that glowed with sunset heat.

After the children fell asleep, Lucia put aside her phone, pulled Ward into the empty master bedroom, peeled away her clothes, and described to him what she wanted in no uncertain terms, with a directness that startled and delighted him.

The next morning, a Saturday, Ward got up before the children. He made coffee, scrambled eggs, and pancakes before disappearing to the library and returning with a stack of books that stretched from his palms to his chin.

"'Before you get down to work on a farm, you must learn what kind of land you have,'" Ward read aloud from a volume eight decades old. "'Only then will you know what it can be asked to do, what acts it will reward, and when you can expect it will rebuke you for your presumption. All land is not the same.'"

So they researched the Sequatchie Valley together and found that it was an extension of the Tennessee River watershed, extended into the northeastern corner of Alabama where thousands of years ago a glacier had pinched together low mountains and smoothed wide valleys. When ice melted and weather warmed, indigenous tribes settled down: Cherokee, Chickasaw, and Choctaw, with whom early settlers warred to make settlements. Later planters with their households of enslaved persons never made it quite so far west, preferring to seek out less demanding land in Georgia, the Carolinas, and Virginia. Those of European descent who stayed in the area tended to be of scrappy temperament, German and Scotch-Irish, habituated by history to expect less of their environment and to exact more from their flesh.

To their immediate west, but separated by about ten miles of pine-forested hills, there lay a pick-your-own apple orchard. To the east, separating them from Tennessee and Georgia, were state parks and Civil War cemeteries. North of them was the bend in the Tennessee River whose creeks fed their land; south lay little hamlets and, if they kept going, Birmingham, where they'd started.

Laid out along the river that had carved the valley, the current community looked to have farmers' markets, state parks, campgrounds, and plenty of churches. Neither of the Tarrants was a churchgoer—Lucia's parents had regarded their ancestral faith of star-crowned virgins and bloody martyrs with the casual scorn of children who know their education to be many degrees superior to that of their parents; Ward's parents had no ancestral faith and never said anything that would hint they felt its lack—but Lucia did not judge. She knew that the people who clustered around such places tended to make community and to be generous with their time. Maybe it could be to the Tarrants' benefit, as they learned to farm, to get to know people like this.

Coal industries had once dominated the area, so that Ward worried about pollution, and a decommissioned factory nearby was being destroyed and converted into a satellite campus for a global tech giant. He wondered aloud, half joking, about emergent androids equipped with murderous rogue AI. Lucia laughed, but some nights when she couldn't sleep, she perseverated on the thought, just a little. Of course, it was ridiculous. They had both watched one too many movies. Then Lucia remembered childhood stories of a panther that tracked a little boy through the woods, of wolves that howled through the wilderness all night long and kept a little girl awake. The world they lived in now was at least as wild, in different ways.

She rolled over and planted her lips on Ward's bare shoulder.

"Hey. You awake?"

He stirred. She kissed him into consciousness, warmed her cold hand against her own skin before running it over his.

They broke the lease on their apartment, scheduled a move-out date, and reserved a big truck with enough room for their furniture and some boxes of books and clothes. Lucia packed up the children's rooms at night so that they would not realize right away how many of their beeping, jangling, bright items were not going to join them in the countryside. She sold her commuter car and banked the money. Ward traded his in for a pickup.

"We've got to save as much as we can so the start-up costs don't bite us too hard," he told her. "We need specific breeds of wheat, and specific fertilizers—only the ones on this list. Look at those prices and then multiply them by how many acres we're trying to cover."

Corn grew well but often sold at a loss, so Ward opted for wheat, figuring that everyone needed bread. He also planned vegetable plots, with the idea of selling CSA boxes to offset their expenses.

"Community-supported agriculture's the wave of the American future," he crowed, handing Lucia the stack of library books he'd taken out about gardening.

"As for the wheat, we'll need to build new fence lines to keep deer out of it," he elaborated. "That means wire and posts and probably new tools. There's a chicken coop, but it's dilapidated too. And I'll want to build a pen for when we get a pig."

"When? Not if?"

"Yeah, why not?"

On their last night in the apartment, she settled Olivia and Quinn down in sleeping bags—their bedframes already sold, only the bare mattresses packed—and then stood alone on the now-empty balcony to look out for the last time at Birmingham's summer night, burnt brown with summer's heat, lit amber-pink with strings of streetlights following the hills' swell and ebb and filtering through leafy branches along the tree-lined streets. Her fast pulse clashed with the placidity of the sight. Her breath began on its own to leave her so that she had to grasp it back with force: *what are we doing what are we doing this is out of control I can't I can't.*

"You can," she said out loud, "and you will. Stop." She clutched the cold metal railing, its edges slightly crusted with rust, until her hands felt ready to crack with the pressure. When she let the railing go, she felt more settled. She let some new breaths arrive of their own accord before she went in and lay down. After all, thousands—no, millions; no—how many people? —had lived in the countryside throughout history, and had not panicked, and had not died of preventable causes? Preventable, farm-related causes?

The next morning, they loaded up their last few boxes, gathered what they'd need for the first few nights—bedrolls, suitcases, diaper bag—and set off. Ward drove the rental, Lucia the pickup, hoping to prevent meltdowns between Olivia and Quinn by the sound of her voice.

The edges of the city fell away, giving place to walled suburbs, to gas stations and cheap hotels and fast-food drive-thrus. Then came fields, rocky hills, thick swathes of trees canopying leafy undergrowth, stretches of green grass on which barns and grain silos and bales lay spaced like a child's carefully aligned toys.

Along the road, the foliage glowed green and golden and smelled of fresh hay and clover. Lucia felt lulled by the lush length of the drive, by the rich fertility implied in smell and sight. To wonder the whereabouts of the nearest store, school, hospital, didn't consciously occur to her: they were healthy people, right? They could manage? By themselves?

They spun past the place Ward had told her belonged to their closest neighbor: a tilting red-and-gray structure topped with an oxidized tin roof. Lucia lost count of how many minutes passed after this. They were well out past the interstate now, mile markers a mere memory.

Then she saw what Ward had told her to look for: a thick tangle of greying boles and green-and-brown leaves that filtered the sun down to a flashlight's aluminum-refracted bulb.

So here was the pear orchard. The trees were alive, Ward had said, but they had suffered a bout of fire blight this spring—those rusty, withered branches made up at least a quarter of the foliage. Because he had been told fire blight was curable if treated with copper sulfate and calcium hydroxide, spraying was one of the first tasks on his list. He would later find out that this could only prevent the blight from spreading further. Damaged branches, and some whole trees, would have to be pruned.

The dusty road wound through the lane to reach their own single-story red brick habitat, slung down in the center of the valley. The forested hills, the barn, the abandoned and encrusted beehive, and the other outbuildings lay to the house's east. Box gardens and fields stretched out to the west.

While Ward carried their possessions inside, Lucia sat with the children at the table left behind by the last family. She read them nursery rhymes illustrated with wistful art-deco pictures. Olivia took these in with hungry attention while Quinn sat wrapped in a green crocheted afghan that Lucia's father's sister had made for Lucia years ago. He poked his short fingers in and out of the holes between the looped stitches, ran them through the yarn fringe.

Without warning and without knocking, the neighbor walked in. There was no Auburn sweatshirt, no radiant smile, just grey hair and brown teeth, pale skin and a musty smell.

"Came to collect my pay," the neighbor said. "For caretaking yer animals."

How had Lucia, how had Ward, not realized this person would expect to be paid? Lucia could not even tell if it was a man or a woman and could not scrounge up the courage to introduce herself so as to harvest, in exchange, a name.

Lucia parked Quinn in the playpen—where he complained until she threw him the green blanket—and retrieved Ward from the toolshed because she didn't know where he had packed the checkbook. Then she haggled the price down, because they surely didn't have on hand the thousand dollars the wraith asked for.

While writing the check for six hundred, in an effort to shrug off her own tension, Lucia poured out a stream of empty and, sure, she could admit it, pretentious chatter about how happy her whole family felt to be here in this beautiful land, the *skirt hem of Mother Appalachia* she called it, this *emerald jewel of the Sequatchie Valley—*

"This ain't the Sequatchie Valley," the neighbor said.

The map flashed into Lucia's mind, and she opened her mouth to protest, but the neighbor insisted.

"Sequatchie, now, you're talkin' over toward Tennessee, up to the east like."

The neighbor took the check and left.

Later that evening, Olivia came running in from the yard, offering up two handfuls of black-eyed susans mixed with what Lucia thought was Queen Anne's lace. Lucia took them with exclamations of gratitude as she locked the door.

In the middle of the night the rash awoke Olivia and then Lucia, an azalea-bright violence on their palms that no washing and no lotion could slake, followed by a bout of vomiting. By the light of a candle in the dining room Ward rifled his backpack and dug out his plant identification guide to discover that what Olivia had found was a patch of wild hemlock.

"That could have killed her if she had gotten any more into her system," Lucia gasped. "God, if she'd found it before dinner and she'd eaten with the residue on her hands . . ."

"Luce, don't worry. It's a fluke. It isn't the kind of thing that will happen every day."

"So I should trust nature, huh?"

Ward looked pained.

"You are nature. So am I. Do you trust us?"

Lucia didn't answer. Ward went out and mowed up the rest of the hemlock in the dark, using an old-style rotary hand mower. Then he burned the plants beside the compost pile, putting on a respirator and staying at a safe distance so as not to breathe it in. But he still went in to bed smelling like the smoke.

II

"Why," Ward fumed coming in from the fields at the end of their first month, "is there this belief people have? That farmers in the past stayed on farms because they were idiots? Farmers would have to be geniuses; this work is so damn complicated. I would need to get about three Ph.D.s before I could do it the way it's really supposed to be done."

He had spent the day with the certifying agent who would have to sign off on their organic systems plan before they could get federal approval and start earning higher rates. The agent had given him more than sixty criticisms—Ward clutched the list on a clipboard—ranging from the direction of the irrigation ditches to past weed control methods to concerns about pesticide residue from the conventional apple orchard nearby.

"We have to draw him a map," Ward sighed, "of the whole farm. Lucia, do you have any idea where we put that folder from the real-estate place?"

After dinner, with Quinn clinging to her shin, Lucia dug through box after box until she found it. Ward thanked her absently and left the table to trace the property lines on a large roll of paper the certifier had handed him. Lucia did the cleanup alone and then put the children to bed, more than an hour late.

The next day they went over the whole property

together with a digital camera and a notebook, Lucia pulling the children in a hand wagon behind her. The children demanded to hold the notebook, to draw pictures in the notebook, to hold the camera, to take pictures of crickets and grubs, to take pictures of each other's teeth and nostrils.

Eventually Ward said, "Honey, why don't you let me finish this on my own."

Lucia pulled the wagon home, full of whining bickering sweaty limbs and tangled hair.

Later she caught a look at Ward's list, which read in part:

- Dig new drainage ditches
- Mend paddock
- Put up signs on main road saying Owner Will Maintain
- Build new greenhouse
- Write notifications to neighbors
- Plant hedgerow along west property line for buffer zone
- Solarize fields

"How are you going to find time to do all of this?" Lucia asked.

"One damn thing at a time," Ward said, but to Lucia's mind he said it with a trace of bravado that didn't fully convince her.

Ward consulted with their grey neighbor, who had no visible means of support and might have been willing, but the neighbor claimed joint pains that ruled out manual labor. On an afternoon spent in Danton, Ward found, somewhere, a handful of workers willing to do any job for any rate, but he hesitated to hire them because he didn't even know yet what to tell them to do. He was learning everything as he went.

Because they had no idea how the land had been managed before, Ward had to get the soil and water tested for pesticide and pathogen levels. While he scheduled the appointments, Lucia set up one Excel file and banker's box for managing their CSA subscriptions and another for the certification paperwork. So much for reducing dependence on the grid, Lucia thought, as she used the 3G on her phone to figure out how to install the Internet router and extender they had had to buy to stay in touch with their certifying agent and with their CSA clients.

First on her list, once this was done, was building a website. She'd never done this before, but how hard could it be, she asked herself. She was no longer asking at two a.m. after a week of late nights. It would have been nice if they had had a budget to hire themselves any proper help. Ward couldn't really afford assistant workers, either. What little expense they could afford had to be directed toward their hopes of a successful transition to organic status. Everything cost more and took longer to set up this way.

"It will be worth it in the end," Ward assured her.

"It's a long game."

Because Ward spent most of his time on controlling weeds and pests in the wheat crop and the pear orchard, not to mention negotiating for the best harvest price and checking off his endless lists for the certification, managing the CSA fell wholly to Lucia. After she harvested each week's items, Lucia counted them out into crates: volunteer potatoes that must have been there since last fall, greens fresh from the cold frame, eggs from the new flock of hens Ward had just settled in.

Daytimes, she planted and weeded and kept their vegetable gardens, while Ward managed the main crop plots. Lucia learned how to tell whether topsoil was dark because it was full of manganese, full of weathered rock, or full of decomposing organic matter, and what to do about each of those problems. She learned to take the compost pile's temperature, to turn and aerate it with the pitchfork until her ribs hurt. Gardening turned out to consist of endless squatting and kneeling, thrusting and lifting: her body changed, taking on a leanness and a mobility the other mothers at Quinn's old preschool would have envied.

To organize the CSA boxes, Lucia had commandeered the whole front room, which she had lined with old folding tables Ward's church had been giving away. Because upon moving they had decided no one needed a couch to live well, they had plenty of space in there. The locks on the table legs were broken, though, and she constantly worried about a table collapsing on Quinn, who liked to crawl underneath and fiddle with the free-spinning metal parts. The tops of the tables were freighted with old crates. Lucia had alphabetized signs posted along the wall, each customer's labeled crate set below their Sharpie-printed name.

Even so, much more of her time than she'd believed possible when they were in day programs, was subsumed in the little round of the children's days: breakfast clothes yard cleanup garden lessons lunch cleanup stories rest snacks cleanup cooking cleanup dinner cleanup bath cleanup songs stories bed.

What little overlap there was in their mutually shared labor always had to give way to this little round, into which Ward did not enter anymore at all. Her arms ached from lifting, and her throat went raw from talking. Quinn's toilet training and Olivia's schooling soon consisted of little more than a handful of half-helpless instructions Lucia issued over one shoulder with her hands in something else.

Then she also had to deal with the irrational animals. The goat lived in their yard, in what had once been a horse paddock. The creature hated Lucia, and the hatred was mutual. Even if it had been a nanny rather than the billy it turned out to be, she would not have dreamed of letting the children near the thing.

It regularly jumped the fence to get at her herbs and her sheets, both of which it chewed to oblivion.

The goat also hated the chickens. Their coop had been built too close to the paddock, so that their presence and smell constantly tempted the goat to mayhem. It terrorized them and they pecked at it. It ate their feed until they were driven to eating the bugs in the grass and in each other's feathers, in pursuit of which they would peck each other bloody. Then one night a fox came to the coop, which Olivia had left open by mistake. All that remained, in the pillowy pile of mangled wings and red-streaked feathers over which she wept, was the oldest pair from the flock, the ones that had come free with the property: one a stringy hen past laying, the other a rooster with a sour temper.

After this, Lucia nicknamed the goat Lucifer. Ward frowned at this (and since when, she wondered, was Ward against a joke of this kind?), which only meant the children picked it up that much more eagerly—though they distorted it to *Loofah*. This version stuck until, one day, Loofah escaped altogether into the forested hills and was not seen again.

Every time Lucia went outside, she worried about encountering the beast, now that it was loose. Loofah's first act of freedom was to eat the wild blackberry brambles—leaf, vine, thorn and all. This was too bad, Lucia felt. She had wanted to try blackberry jam again next year, though her first attempt had failed so spectacularly that she was still finding shards of glass and purple splotches in the floorboards and the shelves from the jars that had exploded.

For a while her only evidence of Loofah's continued existence was that the creature had moved on to eating all the poison ivy in the underbrush. Lucia almost felt grateful to it then, for the little extra mental space she could now spare when the children played outside. But when the night-prowling beast knocked over her cold frame to devour her tomato plants, gratitude died.

Finally, one day Loofah discovered a fresh patch of hemlock Ward had missed during move-in. Ward found the animal near the edge of the deer fence, bloated and staring. He lost a whole morning's work burning the remaining hemlock and burying the shaggy body near the compost pile.

That same morning Quinn, gazing out the window, noticed the empty paddock.

"Where Loofah?"

The child knew the answer to this, but Lucia told him anyway. "He got out."

Quinn persevered. "Where Daddy?"

Lucia said, "Working."

"Where Loofah?"

Lucia didn't answer. She was not about to explain bodily demise to a two-year-old. Besides, she was busy reading about how to isolate the old hen and dust her with diatomaceous earth, to prevent the bleeding from her peck wounds from attracting the rooster's further aggression. Quinn had already asked about the goat's blood in the last remaining lace of blackberry bramble, and Lucia had had enough gore to last her a while now.

The next morning, she walked out to find that the rooster had finally pecked the hen to death. Lucia beheaded the little brute with Ward's firewood axe. Plucking the two birds' feathers took her most of the rest of the day.

She shoved the two birds in the refrigerator and, later that week, turned the bodies into an attempt at soup. No one ate the results, except for the pig, who they had moved into the paddock in Loofah's absence; the job of building it a proper pen, like so many other things, had to take second place to the work in the fields.

By the time their first harvest had come and gone and they were ready to slaughter, the leaves had bronzed, reddened, and goldened, jeweling the hills. For the last several weeks Lucia had had her hands and head submerged in gathering, dividing, and delivering produce for special holiday orders. The pig was the one project that she and Ward were going to take on truly together, and she had been looking forward to it.

"Right time of year for the work, if you don't have a dedicated cooling room," Ward said, sharpening for Lucia the long knife she would need when she cut the pig's jugular. He had already sharpened another to have nearby in case the first broke. "A cooling room would be good, and maybe one day we'll build one. Till then we'll hang it in the shed."

He had cleared rusty tools out of the smallest outbuilding and fitted its ceiling with a gargantuan iron hook, which looked to Lucia like something out of a torture dungeon. Another hook like it was affixed to the tractor, which they'd use to transport the pig to the shed when the job was done. Ward took the knife and his hunting rifle, because he had read that a shot between the ears from behind would make the process quicker and less brutal than a direct attempt to "stick" the pig, which meant slitting its throat. The slitting had to be done so that the blood would drain. Without this step, two hundred pounds of meat would quickly spoil.

"Between the shot and the slit we'll have one minute," Ward warned her. "No more. After that the animal starts thrashing. It's not alive then—no breath, no pulse—just nerves firing, but it can hurt you all the same. Ready?"

They had agreed that Ward would be the one to fire; Lucia's job would be to slit the throat while Ward held the body. After, they planned to run away until the thrashing ended. Then they would pick up the pig, hose it down in the yard, and hang it to drain for a day before bringing it into the tub to scald it in preparation for butchering.

She cast a look at the children, who stood watching outside the paddock fence. Between this and paying their grey neighbor to watch them, Lucia had preferred this.

"Ready."

Ward fired. The bullet sang forth from the barrel and struck the pig in the cheek, stripping the face's flesh and shattering half the teeth. The pig screamed and began to charge in wild loops. Lucia screamed too, but she held her ground. Ward ran closer and fired again. This time he hit the pig between the eyes, splintering skullbone and spraying blood. To Lucia's horror she heard that the children were laughing. Then she found she was laughing too, with the shock.

She hurried toward Ward only to see him wave her off— "get back, back," he shouted as he grabbed the long hunting knife. He lunged for the pig's neck as it writhed its head upward openmouthed. His back was turned to Lucia so that she could not tell how his arm got in the way of the ruined jaw, but when he leapt back to run away, she saw blood, his own, pouring down his forearm. He dropped his knife on the dry grass and swore.

"I missed," he shouted, "I missed. Stay where you are, no, don't," he called. But he was already headed back toward the gate, his arms spread wide in a guarding gesture, and she was already in forward motion, her own knife out.

As Ward reeled away, pulling his sleeve down to

keep the dirt out of his bleeding arm, Lucia narrowed her focus until she could only see the slashed but not slit wrinkle of the bristled skin. She recalled the diagram that showed how to find the vein. In went her knife as the thrashing animal kicked hard in the opposite direction. Had it arched toward her with the same force it would have lashed her shin and broken her femur as she knelt.

She rose to a squat and pushed the blade into the pig's neck with all her force. Then, leaving the knife in the convulsing flesh, she scuttled back, shuddering and crying, all the way to the paddock fence. With gasps of breath, she climbed over to reach the spot where Ward and their little ones stood, afraid that if she took the time to walk all the way around to the gate, she would find that the pig was somehow still alive and ready to charge through the opening.

They all stood and watched until the pig's writhing stopped.

"Good thing," Lucia panted, "the next step," and she glanced over at Ward, "involves boiling—"

She had expected him to be laughing with relief over their shared achievement, but no, he was wincing, groaning, bent over his gashed arm. The lower sleeve ran a blurry, muddy brown and red. Olivia and Quinn looked from their father to their mother, wide-eyed.

The three of them helped Ward back to the house, where Lucia washed the pig spit and grit out of the wound. Then she took out her sewing kit, sterilized a needle first with a match and then with rubbing alcohol, and stitched up Ward's torn flesh as his face clenched. The sounds he made trying to stay quiet had an otherworldly quality. Lucia would have preferred hearing him bellow. She was certain he was frightening the children. They continued to watch, two shocked jack-o'-lanterns, preternaturally still. Lucia had no choice but to let them.

When it was over, Ward staggered to the bedroom and sprawled atop the covers. Lucia sent the children to the room they shared, went back outside alone, and started up the tractor. She lowered its hook and tried to fish it down between the rope-tied trotters of the inert body lying in the dusty grass, now no longer pink but grayish, blotchy.

She did not succeed in hooking the rope on her first few attempts, and on the last try she made an accidental slash with the hook's point in the flesh of the lower leg, a mishap that the book had warned against because of the risk of contamination. So instead, she made the proper cuts to bleed the pig, the way the book said, just where it lay, and then sprayed it down with the hose where it lay, and then stared at it lying there in the grass with a pool of blood and mud congealing around it.

Now the pig would somehow have to be maneuvered and hoisted to the ceiling hook, and she did not think she could manage it herself. Even if she managed to lift the flesh on the tractor without damaging it, she did not have enough muscle to switch it over to the hook in the shed all alone.

She turned the machine off, went in, and approached, hesitantly, her own room's door.

"Babe," she said. "I hate to ask. I just can't manage the . . . the body. On my own."

Ward buried his face in the mattress and made a strangled sound. He used the elbow of his good arm to push his body up again. He staggered to the back door, went out, and swung it shut behind him. Then it groaned open again, just a notch.

"Hey? Aren't you going to come help?" he asked.

Raggedly, Lucia stood up and walked after him, leaving the sleeping children inside.

Ward, who had had far more practice with the tractor by now than Lucia, made a much neater job than she had of hooking the rope that tied the trotters. At the door of the shed, Ward placed a low step under the ceiling hook and, growling, hauled the carcass from one hook to the other, where it swung, dripping red on to the pale grey concrete.

"I'm not totally sure what you needed me for," Lucia wondered aloud, but Ward didn't say anything. He was still engaged in checking the angle of the hook and the position of the rope to be sure it would hold.

As soon as he was sure he had the meat secured, Ward doubled over. This time his groan echoed into the woods. He curled down over his damaged arm.

"Let me check it," Lucia said.

"I didn't pop the stitches," he countered, as he felt his clean sleeve carefully and sucked air through his teeth. "There's no blood."

"Let me check it anyway."

He held the arm away from her. "Lucia, I'm fine."

"Yes, that's what it sounded like."

"If you were that worried, you could have gotten under the thing to support some of the weight. Just—if it had occurred to you."

Something in his tone stung her. "Sorry, I've never done this before," she parried.

"Like I have?"

"It's not like it's some kind of competition to prove who's—" She did not know how to finish her thought. *More inexperienced? More innocent?*

Ward glared at her. However his mind filled in the blank, what it supplied was both a mystery to her and clearly not what she had meant to say.

"Right. So don't undermine me."

"I just want you to be okay."

"Then don't *undermine* me." He brushed past her and jogged to the house, leaving her to follow alone.

Again the next morning, again the little round. Ward was already in the field when Lucia woke to the sounds of Quinn screeching over—what? The sound of the squirrels in the trees? The look on Olivia's face? Breakfast clothes yard screeching garden screeching cleanup screeching lunch screeching stories songs nap screeching. Lucia gave up on the ideas she had had of baking. She hauled Olivia and Quinn out to the garden with her, where they anemically helped her weed for about a minute and a half before they got the idea to take turns being Mommy and the pig. While she pulled lamb's-quarter out of the lettuce, they practiced shooting each other, with a stick for a gun.

"I know, but I can't help it," Lucia heard Ward ranting into his cell, as he exited the house and began walking toward and then past and then away from them without acknowledging them. "The apple orchard hires a crop duster, and that's how their chemical shit gets over on to our land. I don't think their pilot can even tell the difference between their trees and ours in the spring. Even if it's not his fault—it could be getting over here in the wind, or in the water—maybe if they were aware they could do something to stop it. So I called them twice, and then I wrote a letter, but they've ignored me every time."

Next came a lull as he listened. Lucia paused with her gloves full of lamb's-quarter.

"Well, because it doesn't serve their profit motive. If they use conventional, it's less work for them to keep pest levels down. They don't care about the long-term—"

His voice faded out.

Everything these days was "the long term" with

Ward. He seemed to Lucia to have forgotten that, in the short term, they still had to live. When one night at dinner Ward asked her why she was no longer baking from scratch and had started buying store bread—"I thought we agreed, it wasn't ideal?"—Lucia strained the muscles in her throat trying to hold down a scream.

He had no more idea of what she did with her days than she had of what he did with his. Every time the children fought while she was collating CSA customers' orders and special requests for the week, or figuring out the intricacies of another government document on organic farm recordkeeping (or grant writing, which Ward had not thought to ask about), she cringed and berated herself for another failure to teach them how to be pleasant human beings. But how could one person continue to handle all this along with gardening, spot weeding, housecleaning, organizing, washing laundry by hand, line-drying, remembering to bring clothes in before it rained, re-washing them when she forgot and they fell off the line into the mud? How, when there was also the scratch-cooking, the floor-scrubbing, the compost-turning, the website, the box packing, the Friday deliveries?

"Hey. Do you think the budget could stand a proper washing machine?" she asked one evening as they were brushing their teeth.

"I thought we agreed not to do that," Ward

mumbled through a mouthful of the activated charcoal toothpaste he special-ordered from a catalogue. "Maintenance costs—sodium laurel sulfate—residues in the wastewater—*waste* of water—"

"Yeah, it's just that the handwashing takes so much time, and I could do a lot more to promote the CSA if—"

Ward spat into the sink. "Hey, speaking of time, let's not waste it by keeping on revisiting decisions we've already made, yeah?"

Everything Lucia was doing was equally vital, and yet she could not treat anything she was doing as though it were too important to be interrupted. Her brain felt like cheese being pushed through a box grater, smears left on handle and plate. The worst of this was that Ward seemed to consider her mind to be of more value in this state than in a condition of wholeness. What prevented her from protesting was her knowledge that Ward could have said the same in reverse. The argument would not be worth starting.

So while Ward, with his slowly healing arm, worked himself dizzy in the fields, Lucia, wanting to meet his energy with an equal intensity, made enemies with herself. She fought off her own ignorance and fatigue, her desires for novelty and rest, just as she fought off aphids, powdery mildew, cucumber beetles.

One morning, after a week spent picking curled gray and white grubs out of the squash vines, she walked out to see a ravaged grid. She must have missed the grubs' eggs whose inhabitants had consumed her zucchini, her greens, her tomatoes.

"'Trust nature,' yeah, uh huh," she muttered under her breath. "Trust nature to ruin your life."

"Mama? The plants died," said Olivia, staring.

Lucia bit down on bad words. "Yep. Come on, let's clear them out so we can start over."

That evening it fell to Lucia to update their website. The next day, she had to call each customer to tell them availability would be suspended until further notice. Each trusting "Hello" drove the pushing pressure of shame deeper into her lungs, the knowledge that her family's success depended on her and that she was failing.

When they first moved, Ward had started attending church in a nondenominational congregation mostly populated by the wealthy—construction tycoons, private accountants, owners of eight-bedroom vacation cabins and country showplaces. Though some of these church members had eagerly taken up some of the farm's first CSA subscriptions, and even now a certain percentage were still loyal return customers after the summer's mischances, Ward had felt socially out of his depth among them.

Now Ward had switched to a church where he said people were "more down-to-earth." Though Lucia saw no visible evidence of change in his actions or temperament, she was willing to accept that he must somehow feel it of help. He did not go every week, but from time to time he would drop a name. Friends would make life better, Lucia thought. For friends, she would have been willing to overlook disagreements, even to make a non-issue of her own nonbelief.

During their third summer on the farm, Ward came to Lucia and asked if they could talk after the children were in bed. From the urgent look on his face, she expected to be told that the bank had denied them any more loans, that they had no choice now but to sell and move back to the city. She anticipated that conversation with a blend of defeated sorrow and grateful relief.

They sat down together at the table. He took both her hands in his, angling his body toward her in a pose that recalled his proposal.

"Lucia, this weekend will you bring the children and come to church with me?"

Her mind blanked. "I guess so. Why?"

"It's best if a family attends together, this new pastor says."

"I didn't know you felt that way."

"I don't want to pressure you, but he's been asking after you for weeks now."

"Me specifically?"

"Well, anyone who attends alone, to invite more people. But yes, also you. He brings it up every time we see each other."

"Huh. Well, if it's important to you, I guess."

"It is. I know you didn't grow up with this stuff any more than I did. But the more I read online about it, and talk to some of the guys about it down at the shop where I have to take the tractor, the more it interests me. Did you know there isn't just one version of church? I always thought they were all more or less the same, but it turns out there are hundreds, and they're all incredibly different from each other."

Lucia didn't ask when he had time for this reading, nor did she point out that an endless reliance on glowing search bars was one of the things they had promised each other to try to give up.

"Do the kids have anything nice to wear anymore?" Ward asked.

"Yeah, I put away a dress for Olivia and a pair of slacks for Quinn."

"Well, could you take them out and wash them?"

She did, but when Sunday breakfast had been cleared away Olivia resisted the dress, screamed that its buttoned lace collar was strangling her, pretended not to be able to breathe in it. Quinn could only make sense of this by believing in some true threat that Olivia could see though he could not. He too began to screech and thrash.

From the hallway bathroom where he was shaving, Ward bellowed: "Lucia, can't you keep them down? I just nicked myself."

Lucia's throat constricted. "I'll get you a band-aid,"

she called, but then forgot to go for the first-aid kit. She walked into the children's room and tried to sing, but no song would come out. She forced the notes, but the children could hear their falsity.

So she stopped singing and began to talk as if to herself, wistfully, about all the nice things she and Daddy would see on their drive by themselves down the highway—flowers, cows, big-big-*big* trucks, the red barn with SEE ROCK CITY painted in white letters on its black roof—which Olivia and Quinn would miss if they had to stay at home all alone without any Mommy or Daddy to keep them company.

As Lucia hoped, they did not realize her bluff, and they wanted to avoid being left out more than they wanted not to put on dress clothes. Quinn predictably resisted the seat harness, but all Lucia had to do was murmur, "See Rock City?" to settle him.

The church was nearly an hour's drive away. Lucia had never challenged Ward on the fuel costs. She looked over at his profile while, out the car window, the green and brown countryside scrolled by behind it.

They pulled up to the church on a white gravel road that twined down a hill in the shape of two tire tracks. On the other side of the hill, the land opened out into a wide clearing beside a small lake. An assortment of cars, most of them gleamingly new, rested on a gravel parking lot. Older bodies—a frayed Cadillac, a rat-colored Oldsmobile, three or four pickups like theirs—disrupted the pattern of sleekness.

Ward stopped the truck at the far edge of the gravel lot and helped his family climb out. Lucia carried Quinn while Ward held Olivia's hand.

The church's smooth white boards were of new construction, its tall, clear doors plate glass. A path wound past it around a small lake, where boats stood moored near a gazebo at a landing. Meeting halls and dormitories clustered together in the leafy distance, like a clique huddled together at a party.

The nave glowed like the inside of a new refrigerator: still, pale, cool, bright. Heads turned to examine the Tarrants as Ward walked them all the way up to the front row and settled them along an empty bench. A quiet unofficial smattering of applause glittered through the rows nearest them. It occurred to Lucia that this was the cleanest place she had been since they had left their Birmingham apartment. When they sat down, Quinn left Lucia and clambered into Ward's lap; Lucia held an arm out to Olivia, who self-consciously slid an inch or two closer.

Behind them she heard a rustle as of skirts shifting on cushions, hair being tossed, arms nudging arms. Lucia wanted to turn her head. She heard a small voice nearby say, "Look, Mommy, new kids," and just as abruptly, saw a mother's hand creeping over the little face to stifle speech.

The preacher, a stringlike man in his sixties without a thread of hair on his shining sunburnt scalp, climbed into the pulpit. His cleanshaven face wore an expression that reminded Lucia of a caged wildcat. Into the wall behind him, there was carved an empty space, closed up with clear glass, in the shape of a cross.

"John, fifteen, two. Be pruned in your minds," the man shouted without preface. "Cut out anything from your lives that does not fit with spirit."

Lucia sat forward. She had known better than to expect gentle star-crowned virgins, but this did not even make sense.

"Store not up that which decays, but instead do without it, and turn your eyes toward everlasting life."

But is there really any such thing, Lucia thought, as *everlasting life*. We cycle and cycle, seasons pass, but all cycles and all seasons end.

"Body decays, but spirit lives," the man continued. "We read it in the book of nature."

A low buzz or hum thrummed through the floor and into Lucia's soles. She inched closer to Olivia on the bench. The bareheaded preacher clapped his hands together. Lucia flinched.

"And what is it that saves? Not the body of our nature. Body is only matter, and matter belongs to spirit. But in the end, it is spirit that saves. Spirit and truth."

"Amen," murmured a man somewhere off to Lucia's right.

"In the end it is only spirit that is truth."

More murmurs of "Amen" rose from farther reaches of the room.

"In the end, only spirit saves!"

The clamor of "*Amens*"—and beneath them, but maybe only in Lucia's imagination, grumblings of dissent—grew immense.

"Matter doesn't matter, because spirit controls matter. Body is for spirit to do with as it wants!"

A wave of noise that was neither a cheer nor an Amen broke out and washed away.

"Body is as a seed that dies. As easily as it grows, so easily does it cease. It grows still and cold. We plant it in the earth and we await the harvest of spirit!"

The microphone sang with reverb.

"Our place, therefore, is the earth and the depths of it. Let us all know our place!"

Lucia clutched Olivia close to her side as though someone were trying to snatch the girl away from her. Olivia felt her mother's fear in her own flesh and wriggled free. Lucia had to restrain herself from grabbing up her daughter and sprinting down the aisle. The only thing that stopped her was the knowledge that running would call attention to them. She wanted no chance, absolutely none, of being forced to interact with anyone or anything here.

Lucia heard and saw nothing else, though there were readings and intercessions; an update from a recently returned missionary; a long list of announcements about picnics and summer camps; a blaring hymn. Finally, the piano fluoresced into baroque cinquefoils of sound. Lucia rose and turned to Ward to ask if he would hand her the truck keys, but now he was absorbed in talk with a greying, wrinkled man wearing a thick blue flannel button-down.

Any day before this one, anywhere else, she would have fished the keys out of Ward's hip pocket, but here she was afraid of what someone might say about the gesture.

"Ward?"

He didn't seem to hear her. She touched his shoulder. He glanced over to see her posture, at which he drew the keys from his pocket and held them out to her, while he kept on talking without looking at her at all.

That night, as soon as the door to the children's room swung shut, Lucia turned to face Ward where they stood within the ring of recently emptied CSA tables.

"I'm sorry," he offered before she said anything.

"Was that preacher saying what I think he was saying?"

"You have to understand how he meant it. It's all just metaphor."

"I don't know how you can stand there and listen to that kind of thing."

"Let's not start this. No one wins this. If we start it, we already lose."

"It started a long time before us. I don't know

how you can justify exposing the children to that."

"We don't really know who God is."

"How you can justify letting Olivia hear that."

"We have to listen if we want to find out."

"But not just listen to anything anyone says."

"I don't know what to think yet. I have to find my way."

"Well, I can't go with you there anymore."

Then she went alone to bed and left Ward standing bewildered among the boxes: staring at, or stared down by, the alphabetized scroll of names rolled out along their walls.

III

Their second and third harvests were sold, the next two summers, at the transitional price, aided by the silent workers who came and received their pay and went.

It was not until September that the certifiers had been able to slot Ward into their schedule. In the autumn morning fog, Ward swore as the screen door swung shut in his face. Lucia watched him watching the USDA agent, suited and tied, stroll back down the packed clay pair of wheel tracks toward the Lexus he'd surely been annoyed to have to drive out all this way, just to tell them—what?

Lucia stepped between Ward and the screen to close the main door.

"We're letting out the cooler air," she said.

"No certification," Ward murmured.

"Yeah. Well, ten miles doesn't mean a lot to a creek, I guess."

"Or to a crop duster."

"You'd think at that distance the residues would be diluted enough not to contaminate our land."

"They must be spraying that place too often."

"We'll have to keep trying."

Lucia had only seen the crop duster overhead four or five times in the last two years, but just her not having seen it didn't mean it hadn't been there. She placed her hand on Ward's chest. He put his thumb in her palm, his fingers along the tarsal bones, and pulled her hand away from his body, though he kept hold of it.

"We're not far enough away?" Ward asked—not Lucia, not the air, not the children: himself, maybe. "We didn't go far out enough. To have a pure life."

Lucia hesitated as to what to say in response. "It's not like it's our fault."

Ward shook his head. "Nature doesn't care what's your fault and what isn't. It only cares how many parts per million of thiabendazole are in the dirt."

"Huh. I thought the farmer was to the earth as the spirit was to the body. In control."

He glared. "Don't make fun."

She shrugged. "What else is there left to make?"

"I thought you forgave me for that day."

"Forgiving and forgetting are two different things."

Up to now, Ward had managed to bring in a little venison each autumn. This year, both because of not getting the certification again and because they really had no budget for ammunition, he told Lucia he didn't plan to hunt.

"We'd be better off just spending that money at the store, if we had it," Ward said. "As it is, we don't have it. We're going to need to apply for state assistance."

A lurch of aversion accompanied Lucia's thought

of what her long-dead father, accustomed to double shifts and lifesaving procedures and, above all, independence, would have said about this. She knew that ought not to bother her, but it did. Before taking time to think, she said what he would have said:

"So we can make up for our own shortfall with the money of people just like the people we used to be. So why not just go back and become those people again? Why keep hitting our heads against this wall?"

"Give up so easily? At least we can resist a little."

"We need strength to resist. I'm just about used up. There isn't any more left of me."

Ward laughed bitterly. "And I'm not used up? I thought that was our whole idea. To make the best possible use of ourselves. To spend ourselves instead of hoarding. To have, I don't know. A little generosity of spirit."

"To be generous, you have to have something to give that's yours. Something that matters."

Ward sighed. "I don't want to argue anymore. Just. Please. Would you figure out how to make the application, so we don't have to go into any more debt to feed the children. And promise me you won't start getting trash. Please no packaged cereal, please no granola bars."

"Okay, got it. None of the things the children would like. Or that would be easy for me."

"Those things cause obesity, if not now then decades from now. In the long term. Do you want that for them, really?"

In the event, the state turned down their application for aid anyway. They did not qualify because the value of their assets was too high. If they could have sold off the western fields, it might have made the difference, but though Ward looked into this—even offering the land to the conventional apple orchard's owners—he couldn't find a buyer, and the idea melted away.

That fall, Lucia started sending the children to school for the free lunches. At the same time, she started gathering the dandelion greens and roots from the garden; she started foraging in the woods, to find a little something for herself. She spent half a morning trying to learn to tell true morels from false but could only find the poisonous variant and gave up. It was hard to be generous when you were dead.

One morning in October, gathering firewood amid a smattering of leaves like yellow paint splotches, she discovered a knot of dead pea shoots under an upturned planter. The white, curled roots' resemblance to bean sprouts made her try cooking and eating them. When she vomited into the composting toilet an hour later, she had no doubt about the cause. The following week, a try at making acorn flour meant more wasted work, resulting in a bitter, brown, inedible dust.

They had a bushel or two of pears left, which Lucia shifted from the CSA stock to their own pantry, anticipating customer complaints but prepared to take the heat. She started making a kind of rice porridge, watery and thin, but useful to deceive their stomachs into thinking they had had enough. She used the ends of cabbages and carrots to make broth, which the children would drink with salt for breakfast. She salvaged halves of softening zucchini, portions of blighted tomatoes, pale portions of brownly bruised pears—whatever had grown too withered or too damaged to sell in the CSA boxes. The bathrooms took on a constant low-grade upset-stomach odor.

She shredded the woody ends of broccoli into something approximating salad. She cut sprouted green ends off potatoes and moldy chunks off squash to make variously tolerable variations on vegetable soup. She continued to set aside the greater part of the good produce for the wives of the tycoons and the accountants.

These evenings, Olivia began bringing books to her mother, wanting to be read aloud to again "like you did when we were little," as though at eight and five they were not still little. Lucia offered her *The Long Winter*—the one where the Ingalls ran out of supplies, survived on cornmeal for months, would have starved to death if the young men had not dug the stuck train out of the snow—but instead Olivia insisted on Hansel and Gretel: *Everything is eaten up once more; we have only half a loaf in the house . . . The children must be got rid of . . . There is no other way of saving ourselves.*

Lucia shuddered. She closed the book and put it aside.

"Finish it, Mama," Quinn pleaded.

Lucia pushed through the candy house, the spun-sugar windows, the icing roof tiles, with her stomach growling. She pushed through Hansel in prison, putting the chicken bone through the bars to make the witch think he was still starving. She pushed through Gretel tricking the witch and shoving her into the oven.

Thoroughly unsettled, she sent the children to bed and then lay awake in the darkness. She reached over to Ward in their chilly room and tried to wake him in the way he used to like, but he slept on, so deeply unconscious that she grew frightened. The clamor of her flesh rang hollow, a bell without a tongue.

Again another day, again the little round.

Lucia sat up to see a chunk of loose hair on her pillow, which would not have bothered her except that this had begun happening to Olivia, too. As Ward had predicted, the children's teeth were decaying.

It did not upset Lucia that her cycles had stopped, as she did not want them. It did not upset her that she had trouble sleeping, as this gave her more time to work. But it upset her to see Quinn lie listless on the floorboards, too tired to care if he had a blanket. It upset her to see Olivia's clever, busy hands crossed limp on the empty table, head draped over an open textbook that she wasn't really studying.

The Monday before Thanksgiving, an early ice storm knocked out their power and ruined the overwintering garden, so that they again failed to make CSA deliveries. Lucia had to spend the day on the phone making abject apologies and processing refunds.

The following day, the children's Thanksgiving break began. Breakfast clothes chores cleanup lunch stories books cleanup whining playtime whining cleanup whining whining whining. She put them in the truck with plans to drive them over to nearby Danton, which she knew would not exactly put a stop to the whining but would thin it out, make it easier to ignore.

"Where're you planning on going?" Ward stepped up to the half-open truck window as Lucia was getting ready to turn the key in the ignition.

She told him.

"No, you're not," Ward said. "Sorry. Can't spare the gas right now."

Thanksgiving made Lucia sad and grateful, sad to be so grateful. They had corn and bean salad with their rice porridge, greens cooked in garlic, pumpkin soup, and brownies made from a mix that Lucia, back in the summer, had lifted from the church donation box and put in her purse without being noticed.

That night Lucia raised the subject they had been avoiding.

"Love, you're not going to like hearing what I'm

going to say, but this experiment isn't working. We need to sell."

"No. Out of the question."

"I'll go to the real estate office on Monday."

"The property is in both our names. You can't sell unless I agree. Which I don't."

"Why not?"

"We're just on the verge of succeeding, here. We just need one good year to get the flywheel spinning. Our certification will come through in the spring, I know it. We'll test and find no pesticide residue. Then we'll be off and running."

"Even if that were true—"

"Lucia, I thought we were together on this. How can you want to give up so easily?" Ward's eyes had grown red and watery. He went on as if what he said next were being cut from him with a heated knife:

"Don't you know what it means to me to have a *place*? I was dragged around my whole childhood like a piece of luggage, from this city to that one, not belonging anywhere. Do you want that for Olivia and Quinn? I don't."

"I only want what you want. I want us to live right," Lucia tried to soothe him.

"Good God," Ward spat, "then help me out here. What in the hell else do you think this is that we're doing, out here, other than trying to teach Olivia and Quinn that it means something to *live right*? That there *is* a right and a wrong way to live and that we have to live the right way?"

The words of Ward's preacher reverberated in her head, a playground taunt. *Body is for spirit to do with as it wants.* She went to the bed, lay down, and curled up, but she did not sleep.

Now the Christmas break from school began. The children had two weeks off; the day fell on a Sunday this year. The thought of a tree, of gifts, landed with Lucia like a cruel-minded joke. She knew that it was going to come and go and that they were going to be disappointed with what little she had managed to scrape together for them, almost all of it out of a parcel the women of Ward's congregation had put together.

Even so, the CSA boxes were packed by Wednesday, so there was all of Thursday to fill before Friday deliveries. Before Ward could see her or say anything to her about it, Lucia packed them up and drove into Danton.

The day hung damp in thick evergreen branches, grey and heavy like laundry forgotten in the rain. Fog haunted the hollows. Lucia turned on the radio to the oldies station and drove, feeling guilty about the cost of the fuel she was using. *Oh honeydew why won't you be true.* The children were playing some game that involved shouting out the names of things they saw and laughing hysterically at each one: *Horse! Brushpile! Old tire!*

They reached the old main street of the town,

where Lucia thought she had seen a Salvation Army, but it turned out to be only a thrift store and they did not need ceramic frog planters or the empty zip pouches from new sheets or half-worn-out shoes. Quinn whined for small plastic trucks and Olivia for a soccer ball; Lucia fished in her pocket and came out with a handful of dimes and pennies. The store manager, a young woman with a skein of slim braids twirled high on her crown, looked pained as she let the children exchange the items for the coins, though Lucia knew they could not possibly have had enough.

As they wandered down the tree-lined walk, Lucia spotted a little storefront labeled in reflective mailbox letters *The Women's Center*. She went in and settled the children in a corner near two chairs. While Quinn immediately turned one chair into a truck bridge, Olivia perched on the other and took a forced, thin interest in the brochures that lined the literature rack. Lucia uneasily watched her thumbing one called *In A Crisis? Know Your Choices*.

No one seemed to be behind the desk. The room's interior walls were painted an insulting pink and plastered with faded motivational posters: *What Got You Here Won't Get You Where You're Going. Your Success Depends On YOU.* Festooned over these and over the desk's front edge were fake pine garlands flocked with imitation snow and glitter, some of which had fallen and left a whisper of sparkle in the tightly woven industrial carpet.

Lucia rang the cup-shaped service bell and waited. Finally, a woman with a short red-dyed perm and an upholstery-patterned floral t-shirt appeared. Lucia walked up and attempted to tell her their situation.

It took some time to make the woman understand that Lucia was not pregnant looking for choices, and also that Ward did not hit her or use drugs or drink too much.

"We're just hungry," Lucia said.

"Does your husband have a job?"

Lucia assured her he did: "If anything, too much of one."

The woman looked faintly annoyed. "Then what is your issue exactly?"

It pained Lucia to have to say it again, and perhaps producing that frisson of shame had been the woman's intention. "We don't have enough food. For the family."

"We don't run a food pantry. You might try one of the churches."

"Yeah, I don't think that's a very good idea."

"Well, maybe we can help your husband find another job."

Lucia thought of Ward, of his feelings on selling and moving. "We farm," she said by way of explanation.

"Yeah, hobby farms don't pay. No one told him that before y'all started?"

"It isn't a hobby farm. It's our livelihood."

"Huh." The woman's face took on a shrewd look. "You'd better ask the Sorensons how they make it work. They're the only farming family around here that's not got another income stream. Investments, you know, or remote work. Or like the folks who run the apple orchard—they do it on some kind of old family money."

"Can you introduce me?" Lucia felt lightheaded. She had not had breakfast, not only this morning but for how many mornings now, she couldn't remember. The thought of explaining her situation to yet another fresh person made her feel nauseated.

"Well, I can't just give out contact information without permission. That would be unprofessional. What I can do is, when I see Margie Sorenson at church on Sunday, I can ask her if she'd be willing to reach out to you. May I give her your number?"

Lucia explained that she didn't have a cell anymore, only Ward did. She gave the house line without adding that they did not have an answering machine.

The tone of the children's quiet play had shifted; Lucia sensed a brewing fight. She tensely took one of their hands in each of hers and walked them to the door.

"Hey!" the woman called after Lucia. "If you come back next week, I might be able to pull together some kind of an opportunity for you. Manning phones, maybe."

Lucia turned her head, knowing from the little pulls they gave that if she let go of either Olivia's or

Quinn's hand one or both children would bolt.

"That's okay. Thanks," Lucia shot out in a tone like a pistol report.

With no small difficulty she again loaded up the children, who did not want to go in, and drove a bit farther east than she had ever explored before. They crossed the Tennessee border and stumbled across a golf course next to a gated neighborhood ringed with stone walls. Behind the wall Lucia could see a playground whose purple and blue plastic tubes and painted metal bars twisted and rose, swooped and curved. She clenched her muscles, steeled herself to deal with the children's inevitable begging, but they had both fallen asleep in the backseat.

Past the neighborhood, the hills sank down and gave way to open meadow. In the center of the meadow rose a new-looking church, surrounded by a sea of cars parked on the grass. From behind the cars smoke was rising. Lucia worried about a fire before she smelled the smoke of a fleet of charcoal grills. She parked the truck near the margin of the lot.

Lucia had grown so accustomed to her stomach growling that she had taken no notice of it until now. The children stayed asleep. Lucia cut the engine, rolled down the truck's windows, and ran toward the cookout line. She filled four plates with pulled pork and rolls, sweet potatoes and mashed potatoes, coleslaw and corn on the cob. Without even a finger left to grab a napkin, and worried that if she upset the plates' balance the food would spill and be wasted, she raced back to the truck. She laid the plates on the passenger seat next to her, chose one, and devoured the meal before the children had the chance to wake up.

Her belly hurt from the sensation of fullness. It had been so long since she had really eaten all she wanted. She sat fighting off little waves of nausea for a few moments. As soon as these passed, she split one of the full plates into two portions, using the plate she had just emptied to serve the second, smaller meal. Then she woke Olivia and Quinn and handed them each a plate.

They also ate quickly—Quinn too quickly: he threw up on the way home and had to be cleaned as best Lucia could manage with a half pack of dried-up baby wipes she found under the seat. When she had finished, she stood still a moment, considering what she held. *Compost*, she thought firmly, and then just as firmly, *No*.

She threw the sour wipes into the face of Mother Appalachia, there on the shoulder of the road.

When they got home near dark and found Ward indoors, combing his hair after a shower, Lucia presented the rest of the untouched food. He looked at her strangely but did not ask where it had come from.

"Welcome back," was all he said, in a voice that contained everything he had felt on waking up and finding her gone.

He ate his meal and thanked her and put the paper plates carefully into the compost bucket and the plastic fork, a bit reproachfully, into the trash.

The night before school break ended, while the children slept, Lucia took a shower and then stood staring into the scarred bathroom mirror at her own wet and snarled and overgrown hair, which had not been cut since Birmingham. The bathroom was not heated and she shivered as she dried herself.

She frowned at her own thighs, which yes were smaller now but still looked to her superfluous, limp and light as tangles of cooked pasta. *Cow*, the thought troubled her, *pig, the branch that is pruned* and she dismissed it but it came back; again, she pushed it away, and back it came.

A gruesome thought drifted across her vision like a floater. *Meat suit.* A bad joke. Or a good solution? She laughed at herself and went to bed.

But it occurred to her again the next morning as she drew water and poured it into the pot to boil. It occurred again over the stove, as the gluey scum burbled to the top of the oatmeal, as she popped a knife through the skin of the last late wrinkled pear from the season, as she sliced the flesh thin and chopped it into sweetening for her children's breakfast.

She would need to work after dark, while her family slept. She would need to be fast and determined and above all secretive. But it could be done.

That night at bedtime the children could feel

Lucia's tension. They bickered more than usual, begged for stories, cups of water, hugs, kisses. Lucia granted it all, buoyed up by her own feeling of cleverness. She would soothe every hunger at no cost to anyone but herself.

When the last eyelid dropped, Lucia stood up, stretched silently, and crept down the hall so as to silence the floorboards. Ward, sleeping soundly, wouldn't notice. It would be done so quickly, and it was not as if he looked at her anymore anyway. She had to stifle a shrill laugh.

Earlier that day Lucia had cleared a workspace in the pig shed. The spot Lucia had chosen had a view of Ward's neatly kept tool bench. She could see her breath. She'd prepared what she would need: a few things from the kitchen, plus a lighter to sterilize her tools beforehand, a bucket of clean water to deposit them in, a cast-iron skillet. A tarp, for underneath. A threaded needle, for after.

The first cut along the outside of her thigh scarcely hurt, so exalted she felt that she would now be able to nourish her family with her body. If they asked questions, she would lie: *The neighbor brought us some bacon, wasn't that lucky?* The blatant transparency of the lie was, to her mind, part of its effectiveness. No one could look her in the face and suggest the truth.

But how often could she manage this? She had thought maybe once a week or so but now maybe not. Maybe every other. The next one misshapen.

Another. Best she could. How much longer. The needle now quickly. She ought to have. Should not have been. More blood than there. Too deep? Should not be so much. There should. She wanted.

Lucia finished sewing and staggered to her feet. She covered the skillet with a clean napkin; she had to hold it with both hands. Steady. Rest first. Meat would keep outdoors overnight.

She levered her work up on to the wire shelf that bounced noisily beneath its load. Lucia tensed to prevent the skillet falling. Most of the weight was still cast iron. She trembled; she felt deflated. Had it been worth all that.

As the skillet slid back again from the shelf toward her crumpling body she wavered, then braced for the blow she never felt landing, so transported was her flesh to have given all it could.

As she lay on the cold concrete floor, as her head seemed to float and split above her, did it fully occur to her what this would look like. As if—but—there on the tool bench lay a strong rope and there, hanging from the ceiling, the pig hook. It would have borne more than her weight. No. That was not what she meant. But what was it—she scraped and strained, a last search for a lost word as her breath began on its own to leave her—what was it she had wanted to say?

Inside the house the children woke on their own, dressed themselves, and went to the pantry for whatever might happen to be there. Olivia found some of the biscuits Lucia had made for dinner the night before. Since there was nothing to put on them, she and Quinn ate them dry and poured themselves water from the spigot of the stainless-steel filtering tank.

Today Ward slept later than he had planned. When his eyes opened on their own it was already light. Lucia was not beside him. He could hear the shuffling of shoes and backpacks.

He pulled on shorts, opened the bedroom door and, barefoot, stood watching his children get ready for the school bus on their own.

"Where's Mom? Already in the garden?"

Olivia shrugged. Her dark gaze measured and weighed and found him wanting, just as he had always felt Lucia's had.

"I thought she was with you."

Ward found work pants and boots and went out expecting to find Lucia where the children told him she was not, because sometimes they did not bother to check that what they presumed was true was really true before they said it. But he did not find her there, nor in the orchard, nor walking along the hedgerow clipping greens for a wreath as he had imagined she might be.

He called her name, turned in circles, and spotted the door of the pig shed, unsecured, creaking in the breeze.

"Stay there," he ordered Olivia.

Ward did not know, as Lucia would have known,

that Olivia would wait until he was halfway to the shed and then follow him slowly without rustling the dry grass under her feet. Ward did not know that Quinn would follow Olivia. Had he known, he would not have let out the sound that he let out when he saw what he saw on the floor of the shed.

He turned around in the doorway and roared at them.

"Children. Back to the house."

Olivia turned and began to walk stiffly, as though having to force her legs to listen to her mind, but Quinn stepped forward.

"Dad? What is it?"

"Quinn. Now."

"Where's Mom?"

"I said now."

Afraid of his father for the first time in his life, Quinn spun and ran after his sister, knowing from the sound that no matter what lay in the shed he did not truly want to see it.

They huddled alone in the house for the hour it took the ambulance to arrive, but Quinn already knew without being told that it was too late, had been too late for a long time before that to expect any rescue from the lazily twirling red light that bathed their father's face and hands, that, from a distance, gave to the bare black branches and to the tangled dark hair around his sister's forehead the look of blood on blackberry thorns.

Solo

Unhappy families, happy families: consider. Who knows the difference; who can tell from a distance? From up close? Look all you like, only tell me: On which side of the divide do the Torinos stand or fall? (Which is it we do—stand or fall?)

After the girls emerged premature, survived sepsis, anemia, croup, they turned three, four, five. Tiny Persephones, back from the underworld. I gloried in their glow. Their sudden health felt miraculous; their brown bodies lithe with muscle, uncanny. They stepped like herons, floated like dragonflies, leapt and hung aloft. *Sign them up for dance*, whispered their grandmother. *I'll pay*, she added.

So I signed my life away. Not that I knew this at the time—do we know, beforehand, ever? Why else do we hedge, backtrack, complain, afterward? *I didn't sign up for this.* Except: I did. When children bring gifts, we accept. When the teacher whispers *Juilliard*, whispers *little potential Copelands*, the mother is sold.

Consider years of servitude, predawn wakings to wash and fold skirts, leotards, tights: theatrical pink, toast, jet. Spangled costume changes in sweaty curtained stalls, green rooms, marquee-bulbed mirrors. Meals blended, iced, drunk on the run. Protein powders, vegetable juices, kefirs, yogurt tubes, nut butters. Banana after banana (my God, the shopping: carts and carts). Hotel rooms. Homeschool, eventually. Secret drive-through chicken sandwiches eaten, *en route*, in the dark. Waffle fries in ranch: uncompetitive, indulgent, irresistible.

Consider little lives fueled, schooled, this way. Consider where their father fit in—or didn't. Where friends. Where knowledge. Where laughter. Where acceptance.

Today, hours spent typing into Excel pay for gas to fill the car to drive, after lessons, two hours to the city (should we move to the city?), to sit in the green room drowsing over a popular novel, never finished. Someone sporting home-bleached highlights and spray tan impertinently asks *But what are you doing for YOU these days?* For whom? Packing, unpacking, scrubbing, taping, icing, wrapping, massaging, painting, powdering, combing, braiding, straightening, lacquering, lining, pinning, unpinning, stitching, ripping, mending. Screaming, sometimes. Driving, always.

Consider the goal to which we are driving, attainable only three minutes at a time in any hushed dark auditorium. In tandem under incandescent heat, under pressure, the girls fly, glow: the girls' solo: poetry, their flow. Consider their glory. Consider the substrate in which it grows. Are they happy? Are we happy? How can I tell you? Would I even know?

Battleground States

after Toni Morrison's "Recitatif"

> *The soul undergoes duress every day . . . [T]he mind should devise a way out but has lost all ability to devise such a thing. It is occupied entirely in violating itself.*
>
> —Simone Weil, "The Iliad, or the Poem of Force"

"Three promises."
"Go."
"One. We never accept exploitation."
"Obvious. Two?"
"We never become oppressors."
"Never. And three I already know."
"No evil men."
"No evil men. Pff. Stupid easy. Why would you."
"Sometimes they're hot."
"Sometimes they are. Well, so what."
"So you got to, you know."
"No, I don't know. What you 'got to'?"
"You know. Lock it down."
"Ain't that breakin' rule two?"

The two women's laughter melted them and fused them.

*

The text from Diane landed in Areta's phone as she was leaving work, waiting tables at a barbeque place not far off the Yellow Line.

I broke rule three, it said.

Areta nearly texted back I broke rule one, but hesitated. Had she? Yes, I have, she decided, and made herself type it out and tap Send.

Now that Diane implicitly challenged her on it, Areta herself couldn't make total sense of how she had gotten where she was, why she had thought it was right to do what she'd done. Make a change, any change, just so long as it got you out of the situation that scared you: she had known better. People couldn't be fixed like that. Ben might not break rule three—nothing he did was intended enough, willed enough, to qualify as truly bad; still, Areta had concluded that Ben couldn't be fixed at all.

But why had she done it, this text from Diane silently asked: why had Areta left school and wound up waiting tables, when this was the exact narrative of decline and stasis she had been born to destroy? It made no sense. This time last year it had looked as though Areta had won the game. Risen above. Had everything she'd worked for, these last five years: spot in the graduate poli sci program at American, apartment in Columbia Heights, friends to meet in Adams

Morgan. True, the job on the Hill hadn't worked out, but she'd made contacts, and she'd had her foot in the door.

Why had she quit, when she'd been so close to winning?

Areta wondered if it was all just a way to avoid Diane—her undergraduate roommate, her former best friend, her unacknowledged rival—a way to stop having to explain everything she did as she did it. Stop having to perform for a mirror of herself, a mirror that always reflected her back as a little less than she'd believed she was. That Diane never openly said anything to make Areta feel this way did not stop Areta from knowing Diane felt it. Diane had stayed in the graduate program; Areta had left it; shouldn't this have ended things between them, the way things always did end if you put enough distance in the middle? But Diane wouldn't leave it alone.

You need to come back, Diane texted Areta. I'll do whatever I can to help you—but how, after five years of knowing each other, could Diane still not understand that Areta would not ask for help and might refuse it even if it were offered? How, after these years of studying together, going to protests together, rising up toward their future together, could Diane not have seen it?

At first Areta hadn't truly meant to quit the graduate program. But at the start of her second year, her Memaw and Mama had died together in a random shooting at the corner market in her childhood neighborhood on a sunny Tuesday in September. Areta knew, because Mama texted her just before it happened, that they had only gone out together to get ginger ale; Memaw had just recovered from stomach flu, and Mama thought the fresh air would be good for her. Areta understood that this was only the last in a long string of unchosen circumstances and incidences that had limited her progenitrixes' lives from start to finish. She felt, only too deeply, the pressure to speak up: a pressure that rose up off the pristine walls and tables of the students' lounge, that shouted out of the glow of her phone screen. She heard all the voices, including the ones from inside herself, saying that she now had a redoubled responsibility to stand forth as a public advocate: all the more so because of the nature of her academic specialty.

Yet Areta could not do it. She could not bear to keep on reviewing the grim details with fellow students and media reps and anyone else who asked. She could no longer face all the ignorant well-meant questioning: How Are You Doing, How Are You Feeling, God I Can't Imagine. She could not read or write any more articles about urban policing or community violence or gun control. The whole topic had begun to make her head feel as though it might go up in spontaneous flames.

So, though her advisor frowned on her decision to step back from school and take a leave of absence, he also signed the paperwork. He grilled her about a timeline for return. He gave her a card for an expensive grief counselor, and he strongly recommended that she make regular appointments. She nodded and agreed and, after one phone call in which she was told the cost of the proposed transaction, threw the card away.

She broke her lease in Columbia Heights and moved to a cheaper place with Ben. She got a temporary office job and lost it because she kept sleeping through her alarm. She got a barista job with insurance, and she lost this one for the same reason. She started working in the restaurant and, this time, maybe because of the evening schedule, she held on to it. Her advisor called her, sounding annoyed, to ask when she was coming back to class. *I can't hold your stipend in limbo forever*, he said. *I need to be able to award these funds to someone who is prepared to face the rigors of this program, someone who is sure they want to be here.*

I'm so grateful for all you've done, but I can't make a commitment to a timeline right now, Areta wrote back, understanding that even with her stipend and her partial tuition coverage she couldn't make rent or cover her expenses unless she also worked, and she was already too exhausted at the end of every shift to keep her eyes open, let alone complete coursework. Her morning body had now shut down entirely; it was as though she could only control her muscles once the sun had cleared the roofline. But it couldn't be grief, she thought, because grief was a luxury item, just another kind of education whose costs no one was going to cover for her.

Areta knew she needed peace and quiet and time to think, and she couldn't get any of these in the restaurant, where the smells of pork and sweet potatoes, coffee and caramelizing rolls worked themselves into her clothes and her skin. She couldn't get them in the clubs where Ben played at night, where she went with him for a change of pace until she realized she hated this pace: blasts of backbeat, guitar riffs, screeching pink neon. She woke up every morning with her head splitting, throbbing, the herbal-bitter smell of Ben's joints smoldering in the bedside ashtray. She needed to leave him, she knew, but she wanted to delay the argument. Looking for a soft landing, she had settled into a holding pattern.

*

I need to make things right, said Diane's next text.

What you do now? Areta added a wink so there could be no confusion, no fear on Diane's part that Areta might mean the judgment seriously.

Diane texted back a photo of a white boy with dark red hair and a pointed nose.

Is he evil? Areta texted.

Three pulsing dots appeared, followed by the cute

cartoon face of a grinning purple demon.

I have to tell you something, Areta texted. Turns out I broke rule three too, tho i didnt think i was doing it at the time

We got to know better

We got to DO better

We GONNA do better

Kiss 'em goodbye and we'll go down to the women's march in a few months and we'll forget any of it ever happened

It'll be like old times

We'll forget everything sad

Areta sent Diane a selfie they had taken when they were both still in school, undergraduates sparkling with hope: two gleaming topaz-toned faces, cheek to cheek; two inky halos of hair arching out of the frame.

*

That night the flimsy barrier between Areta's body and Ben's broke. The next morning, a Saturday, Areta walked down to the pharmacy on 12th and E and had them take a Plan B out of the locked case behind the counter for her, where it nestled between the menthol cigarettes and the pregnancy tests. It was just medicine, she reasoned, and she'd for sure take Vitamin C if she knew she'd been around someone with a cold. Prevention of uterine congestion. Though Areta felt a little uneasy knowing that she wouldn't be alive herself if this had been possible twenty-five years ago, she also knew that she was in no financial position to become a mother and that she could not rely on Ben. It may have been for this reason that she still believed in a secret rule, Rule Zero, a rule she did not share with her best friend—who, after all, had grown up in an airy, tall Tudor with mullioned windows in Cheverly, rather than in a squat red brick building sequestered in the southeastern part of the city. Areta's secret Rule Zero was this: *Don't need anything you can't give to yourself.* And mothers always broke Rule Zero.

*

Areta had heard Mama tell it her way and had heard Memaw tell it *her* way and still didn't know who had told it to her the right way. In default of an authoritative version, she had cobbled together her own understanding—in which, having no other real options, she had to believe.

When Mama came home from her first year of college pregnant with Areta, Memaw was beside herself with fury: *This ain't how I taught you to be.* Memaw had been saving up for the down payment on a house. Now, instead, they rented a cheaper place and put aside the money for the hospital birth. Mama and Memaw fought up until Areta arrived, and after—about meals, chores, work schedules, expenses. But Mama was careful later on to tell her, and Areta believed this part was true: they never fought about the baby. They took it in turns to bottle-feed Areta, to change and gently swaddle her little body and tuck her in her handed-down bassinet. Then they'd go to the kitchen to whisper-scream at each other, keeping it low enough that they didn't raise the crackle of static on the monitor. If they did, that would mean another two hours of swinging and shushing, shushing and swinging. Things got so bad, around the time Areta began to walk, that Mama took Areta to live in a crumbling midtown shelter managed by church folks until Memaw offered to make peace.

As Mama told the story: *that Easter, she sent me a letter, and I agreed to see her. She knew about some egg hunt in a city park, and I thought you'd like it. She talked to me, and for once she made sense. 'If we work together, we can just about get that baby out of this neighborhood. But you are gonna have to listen to me from now on.' And if I have to listen to her, then so do you.*

Memaw's intention had been to raise Areta with a sense of her own power, to nurture her on stories of the great prophets and saints, women and men who cast down tyrants, moved mountains: to bring her up feeling she had only to march around the city and shout to make the walls fall. These were only fairy tales to Areta, but they kept their resonance, even as she came awake to the sadness of how little—besides Areta herself—Mama and Memaw were capable of influencing or controlling in the world outside their apartment.

Areta had been small when they moved back to Memaw's, but she still remembered the shelter: cinderblock walls the color of lime sherbet, iron-barred windows, wild Virginia-creeper vines climbing the brick outside. She remembered its barrack-like dormitory, its narrow single aluminum bedframes holding plastic mattresses meant to be cleaned with Lysol wipes. She remembered, too, a hottish spring day whose morning had been spent walking down a cracked sidewalk sprouting its riot of purslane and shy violet: a day when Mama had carried two full, heavy black plastic bags of clothes and shoes in one hand, while her other hand clutched Areta's arm as tight as possible. Mama scolded her for squirming away again and again to look how the little plants grew: *they just weeds, baby, come on now.*

That afternoon they rode a bus, cleaner and newer than the one they took to go to the store. Areta felt so excited to be out that she kicked and kicked her feet in their buckled white-leather sandals perforated with a daisy pattern, until Mama scolded her for that too, in a hiss-whisper: *Stop. You gonna make everyone think I don't know how to raise you.* Only later did Areta know that Mama had been tacitly saying,

Child, I don't know how to raise you, so I want you to save me embarrassment by making yourself small enough no one notices.

Together the two women had scolded Areta toward excellence. They made Areta fill out and submit college applications; Areta could still see Mama's mingled hope and terror as they stared down the financial aid form together, could still feel the warm skin of their arms at high school graduation as they hugged and screamed, screamed and hugged again. All that last summer together, she had fussed over them as they fussed over her, as they saved up to buy her sheets and wire shelves. Between her work shifts she clambered up ladders to change their flickering lightbulbs, replace the batteries in their smoke alarm because their deadbeat landlord would not do it. *You don't need to do that baby girl*, they'd tell her, but she needed to find ways of working off the pity that lay under her anger. Such a terrible pity for the soft crocheted sweaters they wore at home, the smooth fabric headwraps, the terrycloth slippers, the swells of their breasts, bellies, hips: it made her so sad to see the late light falling on their bodies, falling through the hallway window where the stale smells of the apartment complex quarreled with the cheap lemon cleaners and cinnamon candles the women used to ward them off.

How had she not seen it before? Mama and Memaw were upholstered: they treated themselves as domestic objects, more permanently planted in that apartment than their own thrift-store furniture. She would never be able to extricate them. All that last summer together, Areta choked on the knowledge, scented with fake lemon and cinnamon: the lie of comfort. She could not swallow that lie. It had been to make herself different from Memaw and Mama that Areta had started covering her own slim limbs in the all-black clothes and spiky wristbands people usually expected to see on pallid hobgoblins of high schoolers, before Diane convinced her to sell all that gear at the student-frequented upcycling boutique and start dressing instead in pointy-collared oxfords, slacks, and wingtips. *You got to signal*, Diane had said.

It had been to signal, to defy low expectations, that Areta had studied hard, joined clubs, carried off academic awards. It had always been with a sense of trepidation that she had carried signs in protests, worried that this would interfere with the signal Diane was teaching her to send. Areta had found a kind of freedom in the life of her mind, but she had also found some of the limits around the growth of that freedom, the harshness of its dependence on her own ability to perform it in readily recognizable ways.

Still Areta had performed, had signaled—to test her own strength, yes, but even more so to let Memaw and Mama keep on believing in the power of their own sacrifices. For herself Areta harbored no belief in fairy tales about rising up through hard work. She knew that however hard she labored, it would be no more than everyone expected her to do and no reason why anyone would see fit to reward her beyond what little they already believed she deserved.

When the cobalt-gowned, tassel-mortared valedictorian at her high school commencement spoke of an unfurling of wings, a taking of flight, Areta thought: I'd better find a mirror first, see if I have any wings before I think about stretching them. She found her mirror in Diane, for a while. Now they had drifted apart, but maybe that would sort itself out if they could get back together. Maybe they just needed to find the time.

*

The day she woke up to find the ashtray between their pillows, a lit joint still smoldering in it, was the day Areta told Ben that he needed to leave—*You're gonna die in a fire once I ain't around to babysit you, and it ain't my job to do that anymore, I ain't gonna die here with you*—and posted an announcement on her neighborhood app saying she was looking for a female roommate. Her first thought was to ask Diane, but she felt she couldn't afford to move where Diane was living, and she couldn't ask Diane to live so far from campus. Areta wanted her next life with a roommate to be financial, transactional: someone to whom she would not have to perform nurture as she did with Ben, someone with whom she would not have to explain her every action the way Diane would expect. She already felt like a bubble that any pressure could pop. She knew better than to add more.

*

You gonna get us some of them pink hats? Areta texted Diane.

No girl, aint my color

Mine either. Just bein jocular

Press down this hair? No thank you

Uh uh, let it show

You know I got to

Your one beauty?

I got more beauties than that

Werk

*

That Saturday they met in the wide cool streets down near Fourteenth and Constitution, where in the jangling crowd they linked arms. Not that long ago it had snowed, but now the snow had melted; though the ground was soaked, the day was dry.

They walked, blocks and blocks, in the river of bodies jostling coat sleeve to coat sleeve. That river broke its banks, washed up over the Ellipse and on to the great expanse of the Mall, overwhelming the two dry gravel paths and the soaked oval of grass between them. Fleece rubbed against wool and worked up a spark which stung Areta's cheek.

The warmth of the flooding multitude, the sporadic gleam of the sun through cracks in low clouds made bulwarks against the sharp wind. Areta's lungs began to feel weighty, her sleepless legs twitchy and liquid. Diane's dark halo bobbed above a sea of pink hats. Mingled shouts and chants flooded the open sky between the Monument and the Capitol.

Areta joined her voice to a song being sung up ahead of them that had already begun to doppler, to fade. The notes unlocked something between her shoulders.

"I have to tell you something," Diane said as they passed the red-brick towers of the Smithsonian Castle.

Construction on a cross street vibrated the ground. A distant jackhammer broke up a sidewalk behind a barrier of orange mesh.

"What's that?"

Diane said something long and mumbling, something Areta couldn't decipher.

"What?"

Diane said it again, but the chants and cries knocked the sound away.

Areta pushed air between her lips in frustration.

"Here," Diane said, and held out a small flat object on her palm.

A paper, it fluttered in the wind except where Diane held its corner firm between the finger and thumb of her knit glove.

The paper rippled and the sunlight glared off its gloss so that the greyscale image was obscured by whiteness at first. Then Areta saw it.

"Uh uh," she said.

"Yeah huh."

The bright grainy swirl had a head and a tail. It had four little dots that split, distinctly, into many smaller dots. It had something that might have been a nose and, below that, limned in silver, a chin, a neck.

"That evil ginger do this to you?"

Diane half closed her eyes a moment, her curled lashes speaking either disdain or hidden anger, Areta couldn't be sure which.

"I'll go with you to take care of it," Areta said. "Don't worry, you won't have to go alone."

"That's what I'm trying to tell you," Diane said. "I'm keeping it."

Areta stared hard at the little grey blob, trying to see what Diane saw in it.

"What about him?"

"He isn't evil."

"You said he was."

"I was wrong."

"How do you know? Keep on changin' your mind, soon no one gonna know how to believe a word you say."

Diane didn't respond. Drumbeats and sharp fragments of call-and-response filled the space, seeming to continue their conversation without their voices, without their consent.

Areta decided to press her harder. "Lady, even if he seem good now, you know he got to be *aligned* with evil. You gonna see it before too long and then you gonna wish you saw it sooner."

"He's good. He's good."

"You don't know that. You can't know that."

"He wants us to stay together, raise it together."

"They all go away in the end."

"You don't think they're all evil."

"I'm not sure they're not."

"They're not all—"

"How can you *know*, though."

"Just because a few of them are toxic—"

"They all have that potential."

"You should know how it feels to be judged—"

"They all want to squash anything they can't control."

"—on how you look. On what people see. Before you ever open—"

"They all just want to be at the top. To get whatever—"

"—your mouth—"

"—they want and never have to apologize—"

"—or let anyone think for a second about what you're saying."

"—for anything they've done wrong. To be totally unaccountable to anyone."

"How can you be so hateful?"

"How can you?"

"But if I deny it the chance to live, then I'm just the same—"

Areta wanted to spit but restrained herself. Her voice rose and split. "How the hell can you say such a thing? What makes you think that thing means more than you do? Is worth more than you are?"

"I never said anything like that," Diane said, too gently, too late.

Areta did not realize her hand was rising until it struck the photograph out of Diane's glove. Out of control, Areta's hand continued to fly upward, until the buckle of her coat sleeve carved a curved red streak along Diane's broad brown cheekbone, near her eye. Areta stepped on the glossy paper where it had fallen in a puddle of gritty slush.

Areta tensed and peered into Diane's face, which flinched away from her. She waited for police to notice, waited to be hauled away. But the crushing press and rumble of marchers hid both women from the view of two desultory officers who stood on the gravel across the way, looking bored between the painted benches and the American elms.

Locked into step, held in place against any further movement by the crowd, the women went on marching together.

"Once I thought you understood life, you had so much to teach me," Areta cried, "but you know nothing, nothing. As ignorant as that baby. You don't know how oppressed you are."

At this Diane turned and started to fight her way backward through the crowd to the spot where the photograph had fallen. Areta turned and followed her, forcing a space among fleeces and trenches, peacoats and puffers.

"Hey, watch where you're going," snapped a girl in a North Face jacket with thin blond strands hanging out from under her crocheted salmon cap. She quailed, though, at Areta's scowl.

"No freedom anywhere anymore, not even inside you," Areta kept on, shouting at her friend's back, as Diane struggled upstream. "You're your own oppressor. You don't know it, but you are. Rule two. Rule two!"

Diane reached the puddle with the ruined picture in it and knelt down into the slushy gravel, soaking her leggings and her skirt and coat hems. She pulled off her glove and reached down to retrieve the photograph.

"And if you don't see it?" Areta cried. "You're living in a fairy tale. You've sold yourself for that scrap of bad faith, that's your bill of sale, you don't even own your own self, *he owns you.*"

Diane looked down at the image in her palm, blurred by pale murk and tan mud, and then looked up through the forest of oncoming marchers at Areta. People had started to veer around them, to give the situation space. One, wearing heavy black waterproof boots, stepped on Diane's skirt hem without noticing. Another in burgundy jeans accidentally kneed her in the back and, though she blurted out apologies over her shoulder, she didn't stop walking.

Areta expected Diane to stand up, to lash out, to cry. She expected Diane to chase her down and give her a fine piece of her mind. Areta felt she had surely earned at least that much.

But Diane did not rise and made no sound. She only turned away frowning and traced her other hand in the gravel where the picture had fallen, while the river of marchers parted and flowed on around her.

Areta turned sharply, strode away from Diane, and began to run with all the fire in her bones in the same direction the marchers were walking.

"Hell, stay there all day if you want," she screamed. "I can't wait for you to catch up."

As she ran, Areta flung her hands toward the cloud-streaked firmament, waiting for the walls of the world's strongholds to fall.

Diane, still on the ground, called back something in reply. Yet the noise of the crowd carried her words away before they reached Areta, at the same speed and in the same direction as it had carried away hers from Diane. Each woman then heard echoed back to her, off the chanting wall of human voices, not what the other had really said but only what she herself most feared to hear.

Awards Day

Diamond held down the starched hem of her uniform skirt, swung her backpack down to the floorboard, and crouched into the back seat of the Delacroix girls' Honda Civic. Gripping the door handle, she shut out the pollen-colored, humid murk of the Gulf Coast morning, and, just like every morning, wished she could blink her ears the way she could her eyes. If only she had . . . earlids. She'd shut them all the way to school, every last remaining one of the dwindling days she still had to ride with these white girls. Lord knew they seemed to shut their ears all day long, even though they looked open. *Must be nice*, Diamond thought. *For them.*

Had she locked the front door behind her? Yes, she had. Where was her key? On the chain next to her cross, hooked to the carabiner, where it belonged. *Settle down, baby. Okay. It's gonna be okay.* The car moved forward through tunnels of unpruned neighborhood foliage, reined in by chain-link fences.

Out loud, and especially in front of adults, Diamond was grateful—*so grateful*—that ever since the crash, Helen and Emilia had been driving all the way out here to Pleasant Valley from Springhill, just to pick her up and drop her off every day. Diamond was old enough to drive and had her license, but the Delacroixes could afford the multiple cars her family couldn't, plus the kind of insurance that, if Diamond's family had had it, would have covered a temporary rental. Daddy had to leave for work so early that for him to drop her off wouldn't work—and he hadn't wanted her to have to drop him off, and as for the bus—well, they'd already had that argument.

It started when Martine Delacroix, Helen and Emilia's mother, having heard—who could have managed not to hear?—about the accident, had promised that following Sunday that from now on her girls would pick Diamond up each morning at seven and return her home by six-thirty. Diamond would have to wait for Helen and Emilia's *Our Town* rehearsals to let out, "but it's quiet backstage, she could study there, and maybe they'd even offer her a spot on the crew—"

"Oh no, you don't have to do that, I'm sure it would be out of your—"

"And if Diamond *wanted* to come around and be mother's helper to my little Morgan some Saturdays now and then, we'd be grateful, but we wouldn't expect—"

When Mrs. Delacroix had said all this to Diamond's father after Mass on the pebbled front steps of Little Flower, hedged on both sides by the rose garden that faced the decayed restaurants and new brick bank branches across Government Street, Diamond had known from the angle of his brow and the set of his full lips both that he wanted to refuse and that he did not dare.

On top of it all, Diamond just found the Delacroix girls hard to take. She pulled a short stack of index cards from a small plastic file folder she carried in her backpack's outer pocket. At least, she noted with relief, it was Helen's turn at the wheel today. Whenever Emilia drove, their lives were in God's hands. Even now, Emilia manufactured distraction, applying liquid eyeliner and mascara with the aid of the passenger sunshade's lighted vanity mirror as she complained aloud about some soon-to-be ex-boyfriend:

"It's not like it really matters all that much to me. He just doesn't *get me*, and if it's taken him this long already will he ever—"

"Fire him, drop him, dump him, okay? Do what you want. But can we move on? I'm sure Diamond doesn't feel like hearing you recap this. Again."

"She doesn't mind," Emilia said. "You don't mind, Diamond, do you?"

Diamond said she didn't. She studied her smooth hands in her plaid lap, the curved nails she'd polished herself with such care, curled around the notecards she was studying.

"Look, she's studying," Helen observed. "She's not interested in your life story."

"Helen, *when* will you grow up?" Emilia bent

forward, with a jangle of silver charms, to inspect her sister's increasingly relentless profile. "We need to find *you* a man."

"You think Chase Martin is a *man*?" Helen's thumb jabbed the down arrow on the dual-control A/C past 60, 59, 58, all the way to Low. Emilia made a crude remark about how she could tell Chase Martin was a man. Helen ignored her and changed the subject.

"How's your mom feeling this morning?" she asked Diamond.

"Better," Diamond fibbed. "Thanks for asking."

"That's good. She coming to Awards Day tomorrow?"

"Not sure if she'll be able to. She's still a bit shaky." She was more than shaky; she could barely get up, but Diamond didn't see how Helen had any right to that information.

"Ahh. I'm sorry. I'm sure she wishes she could see you get your scholarship thing."

"That's not for sure yet. But thanks, I appreciate it."

"What do you mean it's not for sure?" Emilia barged in. "We already know you're National Merit. We already know you're on track to be salutatorian. Like, the whole thing is calculated by test scores and GPA, yeah? And who has more points than you? What girl, I mean? The Mercy Weldon scholarship's earmarked for a girl. And you're *it*. You're the girl."

Diamond shrugged. "Nah, I won't pass the service requirement. Don't think they're gonna find two Key Club Saturdays and a peer tutoring shift during study hall very impressive."

"That's a nonsense requirement anyway. What do they expect of us? You know my grades are, like, *no bueno*, but even I still feel sometimes like there's so much homework piled on my head I don't even have time to be a complete *person*—"

Helen spluttered: "Emilia. What the hell."

"What?"

"*Lis*ten to yourself. Do you seriously not—"

"What?"

"'*A complete person*?'"

"What? What did I say wrong?"

"Jesus, nothing. Just it's obvious none of that homework involved reading the original American constitution."

"Oh, *that* again—" Emilia grimaced. In the vanity mirror her darkly painted eyes scuttled crabwise in what felt, to Diamond, like the mockery of performative guilt.

Helen sighed ponderously and apologized for her sister's thoughtlessness. Diamond waved it off—"No worries"—consciously keeping her voice mild. Neither Helen nor Emilia responded. The quiet in the car devolved into torpor. Emilia pulled out a notebook and began to line the top of a page *May 5, 2017*, to begin not an essay but rather a workaround to the school's no-texting-on-campus policy: a note addressed, cryptically, to *Hey Bitch.*

Diamond looked down again and pretended to study (*recession depression inflation*) while she saw and heard inside, again and again, her mother's collapse, her mother's cry, the crunch of metal as the wheel left her grasp. Her mother in the hospital during visitors' hours, banked on all sides by floral arrangements, looking noseless, mouthless under the ventilator mask. Breathless.

Push it aside. *Tariffs embargoes sanctions.* Quiz fifth period: she still had time. They'd be paying off the hospital bills for how long? She could save all of lunch hour to work with, if she hid in the library. *Corrections assets advantages. Profit margins. Wage drift. Equities.*

In the late part of March, halfway through Lent, Mama had suffered a seizure behind the wheel while she was dropping off Diamond at school. Her plan, which they'd agreed on, had been to borrow Diamond's car for the day and then pick her up when classes ended. Instead, the coupe had rolled out of control and crashed into the left-hand side of the pair of metal handrails that ascended the school's front steps. The jolt of impact ambushed Diamond again and again, tightened her joints, split open her thoughts. She had been in the passenger's seat, had clambered free and left the door hanging open, had clung for refuge to the flagpole around which, on another morning, the Students for Life would have been gathered for the rosary. Frozen to the spot as in the worst of bad dreams Diamond watched a flurry of school staff arrive, trailed by curious students rubbernecking from a distance. Next came police cars and an ambulance.

The school bell shrilled, the air settled, and still Diamond stood on the damp grass beneath the flagpole, feeling the dew seep into the grey suede uppers of her uniform shoes, hearing the stars and stripes ripple and snap with the gusts that rolled in over the bay.

Diamond stood there numb to the feel of Mrs. Gautreau's hand on her arm, deaf to the soothing noises the counselor made as she guided Diamond toward the EMT. He settled her in on the padded bench next to her mother's cot; through the open double doors Diamond saw Mrs. Gautreau's plump arms waving away the clusters of concerned faces, of well-intended hands, that stretched toward Diamond's distress in care or in curiosity.

"Go to class," she kept saying, "go to class," as the doors closed.

Afterward the story circulated quickly through the student body, but it took longer to get an accurate diagnosis through folks' heads. Some had thought Mama had cancer. Some speculated she must have been drunk or high—"They *would* say so, these lushes," Helen had tried to console her. Diamond shrugged and didn't respond. She felt that to voice her distress over these lazy misconceptions, to let it be known they upset her, would in some obscure way be to let their casual cruelty win.

Besides, Diamond knew that Mama must have been sick for some time without anyone realizing it. Her hands and feet had been swelling with what they now knew were cysts in her bones, but which Mama had waved aside as *arthuritus.* Her eyes had been red, prone to teariness; her head had ached often, her voice croaked—*pollen*, she'd said, *allergic to this city. Always have been. All those oak trees, all spring long.* She'd had trouble climbing stairs, trouble catching her breath, trouble hearing what they said to her: *just gettin' old, sugar.* At Daddy's prompting she had spoken to doctors, but no doctor had contradicted Mama's tendency to minimize her own symptoms.

It took a catastrophic seizure to make anyone pay attention. Even then, Diamond noticed, some doctors' first impulse had been to lay the blame at Mama's door: *well, how's her diet? Sleep hygiene? Does she exercise?* No one suggested a correlation with excess exposure to ammonia fumes, though Diamond suspected a direct one.

In the seventies, when Mama and Daddy had met at Mass at Little Flower and married, Mama worked as a cleaner in the offices of a shipping company downtown. She couldn't afford to leave work when Diamond was born, but her supervisor didn't see this as his problem, and he fired her for absenteeism within the five days it took her to get back on her feet after the birth. Luckily, Daddy was working then as assistant head of facilities in a caterer's family business, so he was able to help find Mama another cleaning job in one of the buildings a son of the family helped to manage.

Mama took double shifts as often as she could. While she worked, her cousin Ada babysat infant Diamond alongside her own two toddler sons. For both women, long exhausting work hours were normal and affording childcare was out of the question, to the point that Diamond often spent her nights in Ada's boys' outgrown crib. Whenever she could, Mama would pick up Diamond from Ada, going home with her long enough to make dinner and feed her daughter, attend Mass and sleep, before dropping Diamond back off at Ada's place for another round.

In a few years, when Diamond was old enough for kindergarten, Ada became an assistant in a florist's shop. Mama made some changes at this time, too: she was smart and organized and sick of cleaning, and she knew she could do the work, so she applied to the caterers, and they took her on as Daddy's secretary, in the back office. She helped him file paperwork and handle city permits, order supplies and keep inventory. But by then the chemicals' damage to her body had been done.

Though Diamond's family gave her as much as they could, they all also told her—in word and action, as if with one voice—that what she needed in life would *never be handed to you the way it's handed to white folks. You will always have to work twice as hard for half as much.* Diamond was doing her best to disprove that, her best to deny it, fighting all the harder against her own fear that it might be true.

When she wrecked the curve on her Iowa assessments in second grade, Mama and Daddy moved to an older, smaller place so they could afford to send her to Catholic school. Diamond had been eight then. She remembered crying because she missed her cousins, who had been like her brothers. Daddy had comforted her: *It's better this way. You'll be better off in the end. I don't tell you so because I want you to be sad.*

Sometimes it seemed their whole family life had been nothing but saving and saving for Diamond's education. All through her middle-school years they had striven, squeaked by, to keep affording her tuition and to help her stay at the top of her class. They had taken turns after work hours driving her around more expensive neighborhoods than theirs: playing memory games, discussing song lyrics, dissecting news stories with her in the long blue light in the car on the way. They had taken turns waiting and drinking social cups of coffee and feeling the jitters in shiny, freshly renovated kitchens while someone with a degree explained equations and formulae to their brilliant daughter, every step ensuring she would one day leave them behind.

When her entrance test scores turned out to mean that her high school tuition would be covered anyway, they'd thrown her a party. Aunt Ada and the boys, their cousins and their cousins' cousins, had arrived with hands full of flowers and balloons, covered dishes, and music bubbling over out of tape-player speakers.

The moment they had a little leeway in the budget, for the first time in Diamond's memory, Mama and Daddy refused to use it to let themselves live any more softly. Instead, they put it into a college fund—which ought now to be Mama's recovery fund. Which Diamond would continue to fight about. Which meant she needed, they needed, the Mercy Weldon scholarship, four years' university tuition, to come through.

Mama and Daddy always told her they were *happy* to have done all they did for her, *so happy*, but Diamond knew better. Diamond knew that Mama had not been happy for years, that Mama hated her job though she claimed not to mind it. Diamond knew, though they all pitched in at home, Mama felt the brunt of the house's burden and judged herself for its essential smallness and commonness, for not being able to give Diamond the kind of comforts and conveniences her classmates couldn't imagine not having. Diamond knew Daddy's unhappiness sprang from Mama's discontentment, which he saw himself as being to blame for, though he wasn't. And

Diamond could not imagine Mama's illness and all this unhappiness as unrelated to one another, any more than she could imagine that the poisoned air Mama was forced to breathe did not play a role. She had seen the unhappiness embodied in the pale hospital tubes flailing about Mama from all sides, as though some strange squid had suctioned itself to her and was squeezing the life right out.

That squid still seemed to be in the room, though invisible, as Diamond argued with her father about whether she would let the Delacroix girls give her a ride to school.

"It's generous of them," Daddy said to Diamond gruffly, when they got home that Sunday and she began to protest the plan. "They'd like to be kind. You should let them try. Beggars can't be—"

From her earliest childhood, Daddy had incessantly raised this reminder in all kinds of matters—but before he got to *choosers* that time, Mama, from the couch, sighed:

"What's so wrong with a bus ride if she wants one?" Mama paused, working hard to take in air. "She's getting older. Let her decide."

"That's just the trouble. She's getting older," Daddy said, with a worried evaluative gaze at his daughter.

Diamond left the room abruptly, saying she had to study.

When she thought Diamond was out of hearing range, Mama went on:

"I don't believe I'll live to see the fallout," she said, "but you put so much pressure on that child. Don't act surprised if it melts her down one day."

"Then how would you have me speak to her? She needs to know reality. Do I need to pretend with her that it's some other way? Even if I don't tell her how I see the world, she's plenty smart enough to see it for herself."

"To see the world the way it is? Or to see it the way you see it? That the same thing, Charles—you're so sure?"

"She needs to trust me. For that she needs to know I see what's really there. And what's really there is that she cannot ride the bus like some—some waitress. Who could just be accosted any time. She thinks she knows everything, but she doesn't know the world. She needs to be safe."

"She wasn't even safe in the car with me," Mama said quietly.

"That's not what I meant. You know what I meant. After all we have done for her? She cannot take these kinds of risks. And we are not safe out there."

"Nobody is. People aren't."

"Exactly. We are scarcely even people to them."

"Good Lord, Charles, you really want to let her go on thinking that's still true?"

"God knows I wish it weren't. I wish she didn't, but she'll always have to prove herself, prove her worth. We can't allow one thing to go wrong for her, if we can help it. It could sink her. To have worked this hard to raise her up, only for her to—only for—" He couldn't finish the sentence.

The house was small enough, the doors thin enough, that every word carried. Diamond turned up the music in her earbuds and focused on the novel in her hands, *The Scarlet Letter*. She would pretend she hadn't heard. She would wait until Mama was asleep to confront her father on the most important point—though was *confront* what you did when you lashed out in what looked like righteous anger, but only to hide your own confusion, your own fear?

She found Daddy at the kitchen table with his glass of water, his vitamins, his newspaper. She set down her biology textbook on the table and then sat down next to her father without opening the book. His large lucid eyes, usually so kind, now evaded hers.

"So I need to know reality," Diamond said. "So you might as well tell me how we're going to afford this. Mama and the hospital. The car. The damages. I'm no child. I know we can't afford this."

"Dee, I am not gonna sugarcoat this for you. It's gonna be hard. This sarcoidosis she has—with the lungs—it's killed football stars. But you know better than to think your mama's not tougher than some old football star."

"Uh huh. But football stars have money. And us—?"

"We're gonna get your mama the best care. Best we can afford."

How much care was that? Diamond knew better than to ask.

"She can have my college fund," Diamond finally said, slick-cheeked but calm.

"No no no no no. Baby. We are not gonna do that."

"If we have to we will. If she dies I am not going to school on that money knowing I could have saved her with it. I will not keep on going to class if she dies and we didn't use it for her. If we didn't at least try. I'll drop out, give it to somebody else. Give it to Ada so she can get her real estate license, get herself out of that flower shop that's doing her and her kids no good at all. Help someone who needs it more than I do. Work my own way through, for once in my life. Let one thing about all this be even halfway fair."

"Child, you are already working your own way through. And anyway, you've got the wrong idea. Even if we could give your mother the money, which we can't, you would not have to give up your education. There are loans, programs—"

"There are sharks. Isn't that what you always taught me?"

Daddy had to pause, clear his throat. "You'll get a scholarship."

"That's no foregone conclusion."

"Either way. No matter what happens. That money is—"

"That money is the family's. I know that."

He punched the table then, twice, three times, hissing *child, child–*, until it woke Mama. "Charles?" she said brokenly. He had to go to her then.

Diamond followed him at a slight distance, stood at the door of their room, watched him carry the heavy green oxygen tank to Mama's bedside, lever the valve, adjust the pressure, thread the cannula on to the tender half inch of skin just under her nostrils, and wait. He waited there a long time. Finally, he spoke:

"You good, Leah? Okay then. I'm gonna just put this to one side. It's here on the bed next to you. You need it adjusted, you just call for me."

Diamond slipped away.

*

The night before the ceremony, as Diamond went to wash her face before bed, Mama called her name. Diamond changed course, holding her breath as though by sparing herself the air in the room she could save it for her mother.

"Your daddy told me what you said about the account. You have to know we can't do that the way you want. The type it is, they won't let you take out the money for any other reason than your schooling. If you get the scholarship, well, fine. Then you can put the account toward medical school. But it is not for me. It's for you."

"There must be something we can do. Some kind of paperwork I can sign . . . ?"

"It does not work like that, Dee. I see how you might wish it did. For me, I don't wish things any different. I'm glad we did what we did. I'm glad to watch you rise."

"You say that, but," Diamond started, and then couldn't go on.

"I do say that. You don't know by now I mean what I say?"

Diamond couldn't reply. She knew.

"Sweet, the only Awards Day you need concern yourself with is the last one. Judgment. That's God's Awards Day, and it's the only one that matters."

*

The next morning Diamond took a city bus to school. Scarcely anyone ever rode in the clean new coaches, so that they cost the city more to operate than they made in revenue. Still they ran, lit up even in the daytime with long fluorescent tubes tucked between false and true ceilings. One picked her up at Cottage Hill and Azalea and dropped her near a stately red brick Baptist church off Dauphin.

The three neighborhood blocks she had to walk along North Catherine lay quiet as every street in this part of town lay quiet, dampened by dew and, even at seven-thirty in the morning, the pressure of the day's unfurling heat. Morning glories crawled through the grass along the sidewalk. Diamond's shoulders tightened every time a car whizzed past. With a sense of transgression, she left the sidewalk as soon as she could and scurried up across the school's lawn, disregardful of the telltale clippings that clung to the ankles of her white knee socks. She passed through the glass door, heart stuttering.

Homeroom, interminable; first period, unbearable; then down the hall, across the walkway, up North Lafayette and through the other building in a flood of uniformed bodies, until she came to a large, cold, crowded room filled with chairs arranged in curved rows, sloping down toward a raised platform framed by a curtain. The platform's polished boards glared where they were struck by the theater lights. The cushioned blood-colored seats of the chairs hinged on springs. Chattering, gossiping parents filled the front rows—mostly mothers, mostly blonde mothers, most of the blondeness obviously dye, most of their dresses crisp linen draped on thin tan bodies and decked with a jingling excess of silver beadwork. Daddy had to work today; Diamond knew that. This was the busy season—weddings, graduations, engagements. And Mama should stay home. Mama should rest.

Diamond sought out a lonely row in the back. She wanted to go unnoticed. The spring of the first seat she tried squealed like an annoyed cat; the second, the same: third time the charm, she settled herself deliberately into obscurity, equally afraid that she would be left there and that she would not.

The vice-principal took the microphone, soporific: . . . *a privilege to carry forward . . . two hundred and fifty years of . . . called by our gifts which are also . . .* The man's voice growled along through strings of abstractions like the wordless satisfaction of a cat's purr. The man's bare bald head, decked with wire spectacles, gleamed up from behind a tall, lightweight wooden lectionary stand with a microphone clamped to it. From time to time the whole rig tipped forward worrisomely as his swollen belly brushed it.

The stage was banked on either side by mounds of cold white lilies and green curling ferns heaped up on wire tripods, blooms pulled straight from gargantuan vases in a glass-doored refrigerator just hours ago. It was Aunt Ada's shop's delivery van that Diamond had seen parked on North Lafayette between the two Spanish-tiled school buildings. It must have been Ada and her sons who had set this up. Maybe she would get to see them when they came later, to sweep the stage clean of dropped petals and leaves.

A thought now hit so heavily that it sank down Diamond's spinal cord, cold like a jolt of unwanted anesthetic: What if you could win at everything—scholarships, accomplishments, all of it—and still, because you did not look the way someone else wanted you to look, *still* end up sweeping the floor for the next generation's Awards Day?

She wondered how long she would have to ask this question. She wondered if she would ask it again during her residency, as she sluiced blood toward a drain in the floor tiles after a procedure near the end of a twelve-hour shift. Would she ask it again as a senior surgeon assisting a colleague at the removal of a lung tumor? Would her patient die on the table? Diamond, imagining, thought she could see her colleague's mistake about to happen, the imperfection in the line of the attending expert's cut. She might speak a word of caution only to hear that word ignored, put to the side. Diamond might have to know that if she had been in charge, she could have done otherwise. She felt sure she would not be put in charge. She feared she would be left to ask why, that there would be no answer, or none worth hearing.

Diamond decided then that even if her griefs would multiply exponentially and press down ever heavier, growing as the length of days grew, still she would do what she could. She would go in to patient after patient; she would thread cannulas tenderly across faces even when she knew those faces might have hours of breath left, or minutes, no matter what she did.

And it would be into this sorrow that Mama's lost voice, again and again, would break.

In the auditorium, Diamond snapped back to the moment. She heard not the name *Mercy Weldon* paired with her name, not the clatter of polite applause, not the slide of her saddle Oxfords' soft soles traversing the carpeted stairs toward the stage's polished floorboards. Instead, there came the *screek* of the oxygen tank's wheels. Silence gathered at the back of the room and spread outward, upward, to the stage.

Mama stood framed in the doorway, upright, tubed to the tank, grasping its handle with one hand and Daddy's elbow with the other. Diamond heard the smiles in their eyes so loudly that Mama hardly needed to do what she did next, but she did. She stood up straighter and took the deepest breath she could; then, as if she already spoke from the end of time, she filled the auditorium with the echo of her praise: "That's my *girl*!"

ACKNOWLEDGMENTS

My grateful acknowledgments go to the editors of the online and print publications in which the following stories first appeared, sometimes in an earlier version:

"The Convert", *Dappled Things*, Advent/Christmas 2008; "Allie", *Belle Ombre*, January 2021; "Jack", *Across the Margin*, Best of the Web (Fiction), February 2021; "Fragile Objects", *Vita Poetica*, Spring 2021, and *Mid/South Anthology*, Fall 2022; "Solo", Exposition 405 Flash Contest (Honorable Mention) in February 2022; "Omnes Habitantes in Hoc Habitaculo", *Windhover*, February 2023.

None of this work would have come to fruition without the extraordinary Joshua Hren and James Matthew Wilson and the MFA program they founded at the University of St. Thomas in Houston. My gratitude to each of them is beyond anything I can easily express.

As well as to each of them, I am unceasingly, unstintingly grateful to my marvelous thesis reader, Brigid Pasulka, and to my colleagues from the UST fiction workshops and critique groups: Nick Bowen, Eric Cyr, Valoree Dowell, Madelynn Felix, Patrick Gavin, Bridget Lawler, Kelly Anne Leahy, John Nagy, Angie Robb, Lindsay Schlegel, Br. Chrysostom Searles, Dorian Speed, Janille Stephens, Mary Patterson Wallace, Erik Warbrouck, Adriana Watkins, and

Seth Wieck. In addition, Janille Stephens went above and beyond with her extraordinary developmental edits through the Wiseblood fellowship. Christopher Beha's words of expert guidance and encouragement were indispensable.

Special thanks, too, to Bernardo Aparicio, Timothy Bartel, Megan Boler, Cheryl Castillo, Theresa Chano, Sarah Cortez, Elizabeth Evans, Mary Finnegan, Bill Gonch, Cate Harmon, Jennifer Hartenburg, Olivia Kirwin, T.C. Merrill, Natalie Morrill, Josh Nadeau, Paige Parker, Arthur Powers, Ann Thomas, and Heather Wood.

The Carl children have put up very patiently with yet another of Mommy's books. I love them a thousand stars and more.

Joan—so much love, so many thanks. Mom and Dad—much love. thank you for seeing me across the finish line.

Brian—quite simply, everything.

ABOUT THE AUTHOR

KATY CARL is editor in chief of *Dappled Things* magazine and author of *As Earth Without Water*, a novel (Wiseblood Books, 2021). Her fiction and essays have appeared in *Fare Forward, Windhover, Vita Poetica, Belle Ombre, Across the Margin, Exposition Review, Psaltery & Lyre, Sostenuto, Mom Egg Review, Genealogies of Modernity, St. Louis Magazine, Mere Orthodoxy, Church Life Journal*, and the *Mid/South Anthology*, among others.

Made in the USA
Columbia, SC
11 October 2023

24288304R00174